ORION

ORION

The Story of a Rape

A novel
by
Ralph Graves

Barricade Books Inc. • Fort Lee, New Jersey

c.1

Published by Barricade Books Inc.
1530 Palisade Avenue
Fort Lee, NJ 07024
Distributed by Publishers Group West
4065 Hollis
Emeryville, CA 94608

Printed in the United States of America.

Library of Congress Cataloging-in-Publication Data

Graves, Ralph.
    Orion : the story of a rape / Ralph Graves.
    p.   cm.
    ISBN 0-942637-81-X : $21.95
    I. Title.
    PS3557.R2887074   1993
    813'.54—dc20   92-35527
                                                              CIP

0 9 8 7 6 5 4 3 2 1

For Sara

Previous Novels
by Ralph Graves

Share of Honor (1989)
August People (1985)
The Lost Eagles (1955)
Thanks for the Ride (1949)

Acknowledgments

Many New York City professionals generously contributed their time and expert knowledge to this book.

I am especially grateful to Linda Fairstein, chief prosecutor of sex crimes for the Manhattan District Attorney's office; Sergeant Robert Fiston, Manhattan Sex Crimes Squad, N.Y. Police Department; Thomas Reppetto, President of the Citizens Crime Commission of New York City.

I also thank:

In the N.Y. Police Department, Lieutenant Henry Beattie, Crime Scene Unit; Detective Robert Consilio, Manhattan Sex Crimes Squad; Lieutenant Eddie Huggins, Serology; Detective John Whimple, Latent Prints; and Richard Condon, Acting Police Commissioner, who opened all the doors for my interviews.

At Bellevue Hospital, Harold Treiber and John Megaw, administrators of the rape survivor program; Tracy Robin, rape counselor; Dr. Mary Zachary, physician.

At radio station WINS, Eileen Douglas, anchor.

Any mistakes are, of course, mine, not theirs.

Every novel I have known intimately has, at

8   *Acknowledgments*

advice and encouragement. On this novel, I
thank my agent Julian Bach, my friends Jennifer
Allen, William Brinkley and especially Paula
Blasband.

Contents

Foreword   11

Outrage   13

Blow Out the Candles   40

My Poor Nancy   53

A Legitimate   70

The GYN Room   76

Morning After   101

The Tainted Scene   117

A Lot of Maybes   132

How Was Your Weekend?   149

Was It Exciting?   168

Get Back on the Bicycle   173

Not This Year   195

We're Working On It   198

What's Best for Nancy   211

Go Ahead and Cry   217

C.A.T.C.H.   241

Lineup   256

In the Amphitheater   280

Back Home Again   293

Totting Up   306

Heavy Baggage   324

Time to Play Poker   341

A Calculated Risk   358

I Remember   371

The Real Me   386

Foreword

This is a novel. All characters, their names and physical descriptions are imaginary.

But all the procedures—police investigation, medical treatment, prosecution—are real. This is what happens after a rape.

After a New York City radio reporter is raped and robbed, she struggles to find and prosecute her two assailants, her well-meaning parents often bungle their attempts to help her, and her relationships with her boyfriend and best friend deteriorate - but she is able to forge ahead with her career and form new friendships.

Outrage

When Saks opened its doors to the morning crowd, Nancy Whittredge was the second customer into the store. Striding briskly down the aisle past the interminable perfume counter, she was the first one into the elevator and the first one to reach the third floor. She had one hour to find a party dress.

There was nothing wrong with her old party dress except familiarity. Ordinarily, formal parties were a tiny part of her life, but suddenly there had been three of them over the Christmas holidays, and then she had had to wear her old dress again last week for her twenty-fifth birthday. A number of people at her birthday party, including Tommy, were seeing it for the second or third time in a month, but that was less important than the fact that Nancy herself was wearing it for the fourth time. When tonight's charity ball popped up out of nowhere, she knew she had to find something new.

She skipped past the expensive boutiques—Armani and Bill Blass and Valentino and St. Laurent—because she could not possibly afford any dress she might find there. Those were her mother's territory, not hers. She went racing through the racks in the cheaper boutiques, her radio equipment bag and her purse slung over one shoulder, her right arm free to push dresses aside for a better look. As usual, she had no idea what she was looking for, but she trusted herself to know it when she saw it. Saks was a difficult place to shop because the dresses were all mixed in together, different styles and different sizes. Very artistic but not very organized. Her dress might be anywhere. An hour was not really long enough to shop at Saks.

It took half an hour to find it, but there it was. As soon as she came to it, she lifted it off the rack and held it up. All lacy white and gold. Long sleeves with gauzy gold cuffs. A low, pretty neckline with the same gauzy gold fringe. Absolutely beautiful, and it looked about right for size. She checked the tag. Size 8 was right, but the price was wrong—much more than she had hoped to pay. She had never spent that much on a dress.

Well, Nancy Whittredge thought, some problems just have to be lived with. She could take a couple of months to pay for it. The big question was whether it would fit. Not all size 8s were the same, and there was not enough time for alterations.

"I'd like to try this on," she told the saleswoman.

"Oh yes, that's very lovely," the woman said. She probably said it twenty times a day to twenty different customers, but this time she was right.

When Nancy saw herself in the dressing-room mirror, she thought, *That's the real me.* Even with white socks and loafers, it looked wonderful. This was a dress not just for the charity ball tonight but for many parties yet to come. She was suddenly sorry she could not wear it the first time for Tommy, who loved to see her in pretty new clothes. But Tommy was off in Bermuda for his cable sales conference, so he would have to settle for seconds. With this dress there would be plenty of those.

She hung the new dress on its hanger. As she got back into her slacks and sweater, she kept admiring it. *The real me.*

By the time the dress was folded and packed in the black-and-red Saks box and she had signed the credit card receipt and waited for credit card clearance, she was close to being late for work. She hurried across town to

Broadway, encumbered by the light but awkward box and by her heavy equipment bag. She rode the creaky old elevator up to the modernized ninth floor offices of WZEY, the all-news radio station.

When she pushed through the swinging glass doors, it was only three minutes after eleven—not really what anyone could call late. Well, no one except Mike Barnes, the news editor who had given her the charity ball freebie ticket. Mike would have checked his watch and said, "Shop on your own time, Nancy." But Mike had the afternoon-evening shift, so this time she did not have to worry about his disapproval.

She picked up an assignment sheet. As far as she could tell, nothing interesting was going on in New York City today, at least not for her. She quickly scanned down to see what stories Ted Meadows had, but they were no better than hers. Ted, a black reporter who had gone through training with her, was not only a good friend but a very determined rival. She saw him across the newsroom and waved. He came over to say good morning, a trim figure in sports jacket and tie, dapper except for the athlete's shoulders.

"Hi, Nancy. I got to say I don't envy you that delicatessen survey." This was his competitive way of pointing out that she had drawn a poor assignment.

But so had Ted. "Not too good," she admitted, "but more interesting then your housing development, don't you think?"

He smiled, bright white teeth under a pencil-thin mustache. "No winners today."

"Hey, Ted, I just bought a terrific new dress for my charity ball tonight. You know, the one Mike gave me the ticket for."

"You already told me twice. Mike's just trying to make you feel better because I got a raise."

Nancy knew he was kidding. They made exactly the same salary.

All through what turned out to be a routine workday, she thought about the dress and how she was going to look in it. Usually a routine day without breaking news depressed her. And what depressed her most of all was a day when some other reporter got a good assignment and she didn't. She loved radio news reporting, and everybody told her she was good at it, even though she was still new enough to be nervous on any important story. Today she was not depressed because she had the party to look forward to.

At the end of her shift, she left her equipment bag at the station. She wouldn't need it for tonight. She thanked Mike Barnes again for giving her the freebie, although she kept her thanks brief because he never permitted chitchat when he was on duty. His only response was a quick nod. She was as pleased that he had chosen to give the ticket to her as she was pleased to be going.

It was already dark—February dark—when she climbed out of the Canal Street subway station. Dark but not cold. She left her gloves and scarf in her coat pocket as she walked the three blocks to her branch bank. Her purse was slung over her shoulder, the black-and-red Saks box was tucked under her arm.

Although technically on assignment tonight, she would not have to do any real work. Just keep her eyes and ears open, and if anything did happen, phone it in. Charity balls often handed out press tickets to radio and TV and the newspapers in hopes that some publicity might result, although not really expecting any. Her job tonight was strictly protective coverage, so there would be no pressure. Mike Barnes said nothing *ever* happened at charity balls, so tonight would be just for fun. A free press ticket, free drinks and dinner, free dancing, surely some attractive men, and the taxis would go on her expense account. A perfect freebie all around.

At the brightly lighted cash machine cubicle, she put her dress box on the sidewalk to fish through her wallet for her plastic bank card. She slipped her card in the slot to unlock the door, pulled it open, and went inside. She put her card in the machine slot and punched out her code on the telephonelike buttons, marked from 1 and ABC-2 through WXY-9 and then the solitary 0 for zero.

Her code was O-R-I-O-N, the first constellation her father had taught her to identify as a little girl. Orion was still her favorite cluster of stars, the giant hunter with the immense shoulders, the slanting belt, and the bright sword. It was much easier to remember a favorite word than to remember numbers. Tommy, who was supposed to be so good at numbers, once spent half an hour at his cash machine, punching variations on the five-digit numerical code he had forgotten. He never did get it right and had to visit the bank the next day to get it straightened out.

How much cash for the weekend? Her roommate Jenny was away on a long skiing weekend in Vermont, so with both Tommy and Jenny gone, it promised to be a quiet one. It was her turn to buy groceries, beer and white wine. Probably she would see a movie. Then there would be tonight's taxis to and from the Waldorf. Maybe Sunday brunch somewhere with friends. A hundred dollars would do it. She punched the number. The machine thought it over, whirred and disgorged three crisp new twenties and four tens.

A marvelous gadget. She tucked the bills in her wallet and put the wallet back in her shoulder purse.

Outside, with the dress box under her arm, she waited for the light, then crossed to the dark, shortcut side street leading to her apartment. With Jenny away she would have the small bathroom to herself. She would take a long hot shower and then have the thrill of putting on the dress again, this time with the right shoes.

A third of the way down the side street, she heard the quick steps running up behind her. Before she could turn, something hard jammed into her back.

An angry voice said, "Don't make me use this."

She stopped dead on the dark sidewalk. *No, not me.*

"Give me that money you just took out."

The voice was low but very angry. She knew by the timbre that it was a black voice. She could feel the hard barrel of the gun in her back.

"Hurry up, bitch. Don't make me use this."

Shaking, she felt in her purse with her free hand and brought out her wallet.

"Throw it in here."

A paper shopping bag was thrust in front of her. She hesitated, then dropped her wallet into it. *Maybe somebody will come along. Maybe somebody will come right now.* But the side street stayed dark and empty.

"Turn around."

There were two of them. A tall one with the gun and the angry voice. A shorter one holding the shopping bag. She could not see their faces clearly but both were black.

"Jewelry. Right in here."

When she made no move, the tall one yanked up her coat sleeve, still pointing the gun at her, and with one hand stripped off her two gold bracelets and tossed them in the shopping bag. Her parents' Christmas present.

"The ring, too."

She found her voice. "That's my mother's sweetheart ring. It's not worth anything."

"Don't give me that fucking mother shit, or I'll blow your face off. Hurry up."

She dropped her dress box on the sidewalk and took off the tiny amethyst ring that had been given to her mother on her sixteenth birthday, and in turn given to her on her own sixteenth birthday.

"Your watch."

She unbuckled the Mickey Mouse watch she wore as a joke and dropped it in the bag.

"Necklace? Pin?"

She could not answer.

The rough hand opened her coat and felt all

around her neck and chest. She shrank at the hard touch.

"You hold out on us, bitch, I'll kill you."

The hand tore away the linked gold chain she had bought in Paris during her junior year abroad.

"What's in that box?"

"Nothing. Just a dress."

"Take it out."

She stopped to pick up the box. *This is all there is. Then it will be over.*

"Hurry up. You think we got all night?"

She fumbled at the packing string, but in her terror, she could not untie it. *If I don't do it fast, he'll kill me.* Finally she slipped the string off the end of the box, got the lid off, unwrapped the white tissue paper, and lifted out the neatly folded lacy dress. She was glad it was too dark for her to see it clearly. She folded it once more—carefully, so as not to muss it— and fitted it into the shopping bag. It was over.

The shorter one, who had not spoken, whispered something she could not hear.

"Yeah, that's right," the tall one said. He turned to her. "Now we go back to that bank. You're going to take out the rest of your money."

Anything. Just so it's over. Maybe somebody will see us and stop them.

As they walked back to the main street, the

gun in her back again, she did not dare look at them. She kept her eyes down, not looking to either side.

At the corner they had to wait for the light to change. They stood on the curb. She sensed both of them looking at her, one on each side, one with the gun, the other with the shopping bag.

When the green light changed to amber, a car slowed to a stop right in front of them. Through the windshield, she saw that the driver was a young white man, and he was staring at her. She looked right into his eyes.

His glance flicked at her two companions who were holding her arms. Then his glance came quickly back to her face. He *knew* something was wrong. Maybe he would help her. Maybe she could jump in the front door beside him.

Staring straight at him, she mouthed the silent word *Help!*

When the white "WALK" light showed, the two men stepped off the curb and led her across the street. She had just time to look through the windshield again as they passed in front of the car. The driver, hands on the steering wheel, was still watching her, but he did not move.

I should have jumped.

Across the street she assumed they would

turn left to her cash machine, but instead they walked her down another dark side street.

"The bank's the other way," she said. Her voice sounded tiny.

"We going to have some fun first," the short one said.

It was the first time she had heard his voice out loud. It was lighter, younger, less angry than the other one. The meaning of his words did not register.

And then it did.

She did not know this part of the neighborhood, but the two men obviously did. They hustled her past a vacant lot. Low business buildings of some kind, deserted and totally dark, lined the street. They came to a row of what looked like abandoned garages, with closed, corrugated metal doors pulled flush to the pavement.

"Where are you taking me?"

"We just going to fuck you a little bit," the shorter one said. He giggled.

"Shut up, Bernie."

One of the corrugated doors was only partway down. Its lower edge rested on a large trash dumpster that filled almost the entire width of the garage. Between the dumpster and the side wall of the garage was a small black opening, the size and shape of a child's coffin.

"In here, bitch."

The shorter one, still carrying the shopping bag, bent down and squeezed through the opening.

The gun prodded her forward into the black hole.

I'm going to come out of here alive. That's all that matters. Come out alive. Nothing else matters. Whatever they do, whatever I have to do, I'm going to come out alive.

Inside, total darkness. Then, far back in the garage, a dim light went on. Not enough to see anything except the dark shapes of the two men.

They made her take off her coat and spread it on the concrete floor.

They made her take off her slacks. She had to slip out of her loafers to get the trouser legs off.

One of them ripped off her bikini pants. She heard the flimsy cloth tear. Naked from the waist down except for her socks, her body shook all over, but she was too frightened to be cold.

They made her get down on her hands and knees.

Then they raped her from behind, one after the other, in one place after the other. The violent pain made her gasp and cry, but she knew that if she screamed, they would kill her.

She tried to hold back her crying. Angry hands clutched her breasts as though they were handles, squeezing and twisting them through her sweater.

All the time they kept talking to her, saying terrible things, but her mind shut out any sound except her own silent words: *Just come out alive.*

When at last it was over, when the driving weight went away for the last time, she collapsed onto her coat. Finished. She was dazed and destroyed and she hurt all over, but it was finished.

"Get up, bitch."

This time his words came through to her. *I don't want to get up. Ever.*

"You hear me? Get up."

A shoe kicked her bare buttocks.

She pushed herself off the floor and managed to stand. She stared dully at the floor, seeing nothing.

"Now we get that money. Where's your bank card?"

"What?"

"Your fucking bank card. Don't stall me, bitch. Where is it?"

She had to think where it was. "In my wallet." She could not raise her eyes.

"It's in our bag," the lighter voice said.

"Get it."

She heard steps go to the back of the garage where the dim light was.

After a long silence, "Yeah, here it is."

"I'm cold. Can I have my coat?"

"You tell me the code. Don't lie, or I'll kill you."

"It's ORION."

"What?"

"ORION. O-R-I-O-N."

"ORION. It better be."

"Can I please have my coat?"

The shorter one picked up her coat and gave it to her. She shrugged into it and pulled it tight around her. She felt warmer and less naked, but it did not stop her shaking.

"Here, you take the gun, Bernie. She tries anything—anything at all—you just blow her away. I'll get the money. Watch her."

When she heard him leaving the garage, she felt an overpowering sense of relief. She did not think the one called Bernie would kill her, not if she behaved. But the other one, the angry one . . . Maybe if she tried to make friends with Bernie, get him on her side . . .

"Come on back here where I can watch you. Besides"—he giggled again—"I'm tired."

"Can I put on my slacks?"

"Bring 'em with you."

She found them crumpled on the dark floor. He led her to the rear of the garage where the dim light bulb hung on a wire from the ceiling. There was a platform underneath the bulb, some kind of rough wooden bench. She turned her back to him, modestly, and put on her slacks under her coat.

"You sit there. Don't try anything."

She could see the gun in his hand. He sat down on the bench beside her.

"That better be the right code."

"It is."

They waited.

While they waited, she began to steal little glances at him, sideways so that he would not notice what she was doing.

She had been taking pictures ever since she got a camera for her twelfth birthday, and now she began to take a picture of him, one frame at a time, to memorize him. In this dim light, it would be a wide open f-stop.

Very dark black skin. A full black straggly mustache and a little black goatee, just a one-inch tuft at the end of his chin. Round cheeks, almost chubby. Tiny ears set close to his head, with almost no earlobes. Thick, kinky hair, cut in flattop style, steep up the sides and then sheared straight across. Broad, flaring nose. Chunky shoulders, chunky chest. His eyes were small, bright and deep-set in the sockets.

Click.

After ten or fifteen minutes, there was a scrabbling sound at the garage entrance. The other one was back. She hung her head and hunched her shoulders in fear.

"The bitch is lying! Shoot her!"

"You didn't get the money?"

"It's the wrong code, goddamn her. She lied."

His voice was so furious that she did not dare raise her head. She tried to make herself small, invisible. He was coming toward them. He was going to kill her.

"Give me the gun."

She forced herself to speak. "No," she said. "It's the right code. I swear. I swear. You must have done it wrong."

She could feel him standing right in front of her.

"I give you one chance. One more chance. What is it?"

"I told you. It's ORION. I swear to God."

"Write it down."

An oblong piece of paper was thrust into her hand.

"Bernie, give her your pencil."

"I got no pencil."

"There's one in my purse," she said.

Bernie brought her purse from somewhere and found the pencil. She wrote the word in capital letters. *Please make it work this time.*

"Last chance, bitch."

He went away.

"Whew!" Bernie said. "That boy is sure angry. Hope you wrote it down right."

"I did. Jesus, I'm too scared to lie. Don't let him do anything to me."

"Well, we see. You be nice to me, maybe I help you." He slid his hand under her coat and between her legs, squeezing her thigh. "How about a nice blow job?"

She was stunned. Surely all that part was over. "Oh, I can't. I *can't*. Don't make me."

"What you mean, can't?" He thrust the barrel of the gun right under her nose. "You want this instead? He just loves to use this gun."

"Who?" *Tell me his name.*

"My buddy. He'll kill you if you don't do what I say." He lowered the gun. "Come on now." He unzipped his pants.

She closed her eyes. *Nothing matters. Just come out alive.*

The rank stench was the worst thing she had smelled in her whole life.

"That's it, baby . . . First time you ever eat black meat, I bet . . . Tastes good, right? . . . Tastes real good, right? . . . You love it, don't you . . . Come on . . . Come on, don't stop . . . That's it, baby . . . That's it, baby . . . *That's it! That's it!*"

She tried to pull her mouth away, but he held her head.

Then his hand relaxed, he let her go, and she spat on the floor.

What else is left?

When the other one came back, he was enraged.

"You're still lying. I warned you. I gave you your chance. That's all. That's all. Bernie, give me the gun."

"Wait. Wait! I told you the truth."

A hand held a piece of paper under her eyes. "You still saying this is right?"

She took the paper and saw the word she had written. "Yes." Then she had a desperate idea. "Listen, let me do it for you. I'll get the money for you."

A fierce, scornful laugh. "You think we're going to let you go? After you lied?"

"You come with me. I won't try anything, I promise. I'll get you the money."

They talked it over in low voices that she could not hear.

She gave it one more try. "There's four hundred dollars in there. I can get it all for you."

Bernie's voice said, "Worth a shot."

A pause.

"All right. You try anything, you know what happens."

She got off the bench. "I need my shoes."

They went to the front of the garage, away from the light, where she found her loafers and slipped her feet into them.

"Go ahead of her. Hang onto her. I'll get the light."

Bernie's hand gripped her wrist hard. She stooped to follow him through the narrow opening. Then she was outside in the street.

Alive.

They walked back the way they had come. Bernie carried the shopping bag and held her left arm. He was only a few inches taller than she was. The other one had the gun in her back again. They passed the vacant lot, came to the corner and turned up the street toward the bank.

There were cars with headlights. There were even a few pedestrians. The real world.

Up ahead was a streetlight. They would pass right under it. She had not once looked at him. She took a deep breath. It might be her only chance.

As they came under the light, she turned her head slightly so that she could see him out of the corner of her eye.

Profile shot. Taller and slimmer than Bernie, almost as tall as her father. Lighter skin than Bernie. Long black hair pulled back and tied. Straight, vertical forehead. Thin, ski-jump nose.

High, prominent cheekbones, almost like an Indian. Hollow cheeks. No beard or mustache. A long, straight wolf jaw ending in an odd knob of a chin.

Click. She did not dare look again.

The brightly lighted cash machine cubicle was deserted. She hoped the mechanism wasn't broken. She did not see how he could have failed to make her code work.

He used her card to open the door. All three went inside. It was so bright after all the darkness.

"You watch me do it," he said. He put her card in the slot and pushed the last button, the "O" for zero.

Before he could push the second button, she said, "That's wrong. That's the wrong 'O.' "

She took the paper away from him. She took her card from the slot, reinserted it and punched the proper buttons: MNO, PRS, GHI, MNO, MNO—ORION. Her account came up on the screen. *Thank God.*

All he said was "Huh," a grunt of surprise.

Bernie giggled and said, "You blew it."

She drew out the four hundred dollars, all the rest of her money. As the bills came out, Bernie grabbed them and tucked them deep in the shopping bag.

"Let's get out of this fucking light," he said.

They took her out on the street, still holding

her arms, the gun in her back again. They began to walk.

"Where are you taking me? Can't I go now?"

"Shut up."

She could not believe it. After all this, *after all this*, now they were taking her some place to kill her. That's what they do afterward so you can't identify them, they kill you. She began to cry.

"Shut up, bitch."

They turned another corner and walked a few yards to a dark narrow alleyway between two buildings. This was the place where they would do it. They led her into the alley and stopped.

"All right," the angry one said, "you stay right here for an hour. You understand, bitch? An hour. Don't *move*. We'll be watching. And don't tell anybody, or we'll find you and kill you."

They were *not* going to shoot her. They were letting her go. She felt a great surge of relief.

"I promise," she said. And then, with her life unexpectedly handed back to her, she said, "Listen, let me have my dress. It's no good to you."

No answer. The alley was so dark, she could not even tell if they were looking at her. She wanted to save something, anything, *something* from this night.

"Look, I did everything you said. You got my jewelry. I got you all my money. I did everything you asked. Please let me have the dress."

Silence.

Then Bernie's voice. "Ah, shit, who wants it?"

She heard the rustle of the shopping bag, and then the dress was pushed against her chest. She clutched it to her.

"One hour," the angry voice said.

And they were gone. She was left alone in the alley.

She did not know how long she waited. Five minutes? Ten minutes? She knew they were not watching. She knew they would be gone.

Taking only the broadest, best-lighted streets—streets with people on the sidewalks—she walked home to her apartment. For the first time she realized how painful it was to walk. Her breasts were sore, too. And her mouth was horrible. At the thought she realized she was going to be sick. Sick right on the street, just like somebody coming out of a bar late at night. She managed to wait until she reached a wire city trash basket, then threw up in it. She held her dress out of the way.

She knew she could never wear this dress, not after tonight. She could not even pay for it, with all her money gone. Probably Saks would take it back if it wasn't damaged. But that was not the point. She had saved something. She would keep it, even though she would never wear it.

Her keys were still in her purse. *How did I get my purse back? When did that happen?* She let herself in the street door, then slowly climbed the stairs to her third-floor apartment. Each step hurt. She wished Jenny had not chosen this weekend to go off skiing.

She unlocked the double-locked door, stepped inside, found the light switch, shut the door behind her and leaned back against it. For a moment she was too shattered and dazed to move. Her eyes wandered around the small, familiar living room filled with the sparse furniture contributed by her parents and Jenny's parents. She was home. She was safe—at least for this moment. She wondered if she would ever feel really safe again.

But she could not just stand here. She went to her small bedroom and hung the beautiful dress in her closet, smoothing out the wrinkles. She emptied her coat pockets and pants pockets on top of the bureau, just dumping everything in a pile. She dropped her coat on the bed. Now to brush her teeth.

She and Jenny shared the bathroom cubicle

that held only a toilet, shower and washstand. She turned on the fluorescent light switch. It flickered but, as sometimes happened, would not go on. She tried it on and off several more times: no light. She burst into tears. Still crying, she brushed her teeth in the dark.

She longed to shower, but she knew from what she had heard and read about rape evidence that she must not do that. Or go to the bathroom either, for the same reason. She probably should not even have brushed her teeth, but that had been essential. And anyway, after the vomiting, there would not be any mouth evidence.

She must notify her radio station that she could not carry out her assignment. She returned to the living room, sank into the cracked-leather easy chair that had once been her father's and dialed Weezie's private news desk number. The station call letters were WZEY, but the entire news staff, right up to the executive director, called it Weezie.

The answer came after one ring. "Barnes."

His crisp, no-nonsense, let's-get-on-with-it voice helped pull her together a little. He had been a wonderful teacher when she was new on the job, and she still considered him her mentor. She was honored to be one of his favorite reporters.

"Mike, it's Nancy Whittredge. I can't do that charity ball tonight."

"Oh? Well, that's okay. Nothing's going to happen anyway." The crisp voice changed in tone. "Nancy, you sound funny. Are you all right?"

"No. No, I'm not. As a matter of fact, I've just been raped." There was such a long pause that she said, "Mike? Hello?"

"Yes. Jesus, I'm sorry. Where are you? Are you hurt?"

"I'm home. I'm all right—sort of. No, I'm not. But anyway, I'm not dead."

"Was it somebody you know?"

"Unh-unh. Two black guys on the street."

"Jesus. Have you called your parents? The cops?"

"No, I had to let you know. In case you wanted to send somebody else."

"For Christ's sake, Nancy, it's only a charity ball."

"I know, but I didn't want—"

"Forget it. Don't you think you better call your parents?"

"Yes, I guess so." She wondered what it would do to them. Especially to her mother.

"I know so. Anything I can do, you call. I'm really, really sorry. Now call your parents. And the cops. And you better see a doctor."

"Listen, Mike. Don't tell anybody, okay?"

"I won't. Now make those calls. And take care of yourself."

How can I take care of myself? I don't even know who I am anymore.

And yet until tonight, she had felt quite sure.

Blow Out the Candles

Like all parents, her parents could be impossible, but they did know how to throw a birthday party.

Her mother Carol loved giving parties, especially large ones, but there had to be some legitimate excuse, preferably a family occasion. She was not one to celebrate Bastille Day with quiche and tricolor paper napkins. Nancy's twenty-fifth birthday, in the last week of January, definitely qualified.

Nancy and her father started off thinking small. George Whittredge always thought large in business matters and small in social ones. Perhaps, he said, they could have a small dinner party with Nancy's favorite dish, roast beef and Yorkshire pudding? Nancy could invite Tommy, and her roommate Jenny and

Jenny's lawyer boyfriend. And Basil could come down from college.

"Or we could all go out for Chinese," Nancy suggested. "Peking duck. Everybody likes that, and Mom wouldn't have to do all the dinner work."

"Terrific," her father said.

"Nonsense," Carol said. "Twenty-five is an important birthday. I mean a *real* party."

"But we just got through the holidays," Whit complained, without much hope.

Nancy wrote out her guest list, but Carol made most of the other decisions. As usual, Whit counseled restraint on each proposed implementation—cloth napkins, real glass-ware, number of flower vases, number of hot hors d'oeuvres—but he did so out of habit, knowing that his vote on these elements car-ried no weight. But when it came to drinks, he imposed leadership. He overruled Carol's and Nancy's argument that, for this young crowd, it was all right to serve Codorniú Spanish champagne, Fontana Candida Frascati and the liquor store's house vodka.

And so here they were on her birthday, with two rented coatracks in the lobby, along with a rented off-duty doorman to check fifty win-ter coats, not counting the coats of the caterers. And, in the high-ceilinged, twelfth-floor apart-ment, her friends were drinking glasses of

Veuve Clicquot and Sancerre and Absolut. The hors d'ouevres were the best Nancy could remember, and enough, as Carol had instructed the caterer, so that no one would have to go out to dinner. Baby potato skins stuffed with sour cream and red caviar. Giant shrimp with curry dip. Teriyaki beef skewers. Spicy Thai chicken nuggets. Luscious little lobster rolls. Chicken livers wrapped in bacon. Carol said chicken livers were passé but gave in to Nancy.

"Yikes," Jenny said, an expletive carefully preserved from their school days, "your folks really went all out." She snatched two more lobster rolls from the passing tray. "Here, sweetie." She popped one into Sid's mouth.

Nancy did not favor the public feeding of boyfriends, but her roommate could get away with anything. Jenny was not pretty—her face and chin were too long—and her figure was nothing special, but Nancy had watched her attract boys since their first year together in high school. Nancy was still shy then, but Jenny just took it for granted that boys would like her—and indeed most of them did. Right now Sid Carson, an otherwise promising young lawyer, wore a foolishly fond expression as he chewed his lobster roll. Sid was pressing Jenny to move in with him, but Jenny wasn't ready for that much commitment.

"Listen," Nancy told her, "help look after the Weezies, will you? I don't want them to bunch up and talk shop."

"Sure. Who's the gorgeous black girl by the fireplace? Is she a Weezie?"

"No, that's Marissa Something, a model. She's Ted's new girl."

Ted Meadows stood at the fireplace beside Marissa. He was a good three inches shorter but didn't seem bothered by it. He didn't bother easily.

"Good for old Ted," Jenny said. "Where's Tommy?"

"He had another office crisis." Tommy, a programmer for cable television, averaged three or four crises a week. Nancy saw more people coming in the front door, but none of them was Tommy. "*Scusi*, I better go say hello."

Practically everyone was here now—old schoolmates, her younger brother Basil, half a dozen Weezies, some neighbors from this building, where she had grown up, and some new ones she and Jenny had met in Tribeca. Many had brought spouses or lovers or dates. It was a full house.

Her parents were playing host and hostess with cheerful charm. Her father enjoyed parties, once the dither of preparation was past, and Nancy could tell by her mother's smile, now relaxed, that she was pleased with the way the evening was turning out: plenty of bustle and talk and laughter and movement.

Nancy was pleased, too. The only thing missing was her two most important guests.

She and Tommy Horgan had been fairly serious about each other for almost a year. "Fairly serious" meant they were not sleeping with anybody else or even seeing anybody else. It also meant serious enough for her mother to ask if she and Tommy were going to get married, but not serious enough for Nancy to say yes, or even maybe. Carol was disappointed. She liked Tommy almost as much as she liked the idea of Nancy getting married. Nancy's own feeling was that she probably wouldn't marry before she was thirty, another five years, and by that time, it might or might not be Tommy. But regardless of what happened in that distant future, right now it was high time for him to walk in the door. She looked hopefully at the front door, but nobody was there. Not Tommy and not Mike Barnes.

Of course Tommy would arrive eventually, no matter how serious his office crisis, but Mike Barnes might not. The other Weezies knew she had invited him, but they didn't know she had chosen this night for the party because she knew Mike was off duty and free to come. He had said he would try to make it.

He had even asked if he could bring some-body, and she said of course. Everybody knew Mike Barnes was divorced under what were said to have been unpleasant circumstances, but since he never said anything about it, no one else dared to.

All the younger staff members hoped Mike would become the next news director, even though they were slightly afraid of him. He was only in his mid-thirties but seemed older and more experienced and certainly more authoritative than his age. When Nancy and Ted Meadows were going through the train-ing program together, Ted used to do imita-tions of Mike. "Objectivity is a myth," Ted would say, adopting Mike's low, gruff voice. "There's no such thing as 'objective' reporting, Meadows, so don't let me catch you even talking about it. But there is *fair* reporting. If you're not fair, you won't last long." Or again, on the subject of their technical equipment, which Mike taught them to respect as though their jobs depended on it: "Only two kinds of reporters ever have equipment problems, Meadows. Young squirts who don't take the trouble to learn, and old farts who get careless. I have no use for either one."

Ted never did his imitations when Mike Barnes was known to be anywhere in the building.

Drinking her glass of champagne, which really was better than Codorniú, Nancy moved through the apartment—the living room and library and dining room—to make sure everybody was all right and having a good time. She gave her mother a sincere thank-you kiss. It really was a good party, with everybody acting friendly and affectionate.

She found Ted and Marissa in the library with Jenny and Sid. Sid was arguing with Ted about the New York Giants. "They need a top wide-receiver," Sid was proclaiming, a bit too loudly. "And they'll have to trade a good linebacker to get one. I mean a *good* linebacker."

Ted, who had had a football scholarship as a wide receiver, seemed glad to drop the subject when Nancy joined them. "Guess old Barnes isn't coming," he said. He was looking very trim and snappy in his blue blazer and flowered Liberty tie and his neat, pencil-thin mustache. Except for the wide shoulders, Ted didn't fit Nancy's picture of a football player.

"It's only eight-thirty," she said. "He can still make it."

Ted shook his head. "No," he said, "see, you're not really a favorite. Now if I'd asked him to *my* birthday party . . ." Big smile.

In spite of the smile and the teasing, Nancy

knew Ted had been impressed when she invited Mike Barnes and was even a little worried that Mike might actually come. She and Ted were constantly exchanging evidence to prove who was the best and most-favored new reporter.

Before she could get off an answer, she felt a small bite on her right ear, and Tommy's husky voice said, "Happy birthday. Guess who."

Well, at last. Without turning around, she said, "Gee, who could it be? Is it Clarence? Or Mortimer? Or maybe—?"

He put his arms around her and squeezed her back against him. His arms came up under her breasts. She liked his strength and the frank way he used it.

"Sorry I'm so late," he said. "Hi, Jenny. Ted. Hello, Sidney."

They all said hello, and then Ted said, "This here is my Aunt Jemima."

Marissa, who had apparently endured that introduction before, said, "I'm Marissa."

She and Tommy shook hands. Nancy could see Tommy was a bit awed, as though he had just been introduced to an admired celebrity. His square, blocky face with the bright eyes, usually full of mocking merriment, was oddly respectful as he looked up at Marissa. Nancy wondered what it was like to be beautiful *and*

over six feet tall. Pretty damn good, she supposed, although one might get tired of the
shock effect.

"So what's your excuse?" she asked Tommy.

"Oh, Jesus, the usual. The rights to a made-
for-TV movie fell through, and we suddenly
had a two-hour hole in the Friday night schedule. I had to find something to fill it. Don't ask
what I came up with."

Cable television programming, Nancy had
learned, operated on the uncertainty principle.
Well, it didn't matter now. Tommy was finally
here. He gave her only a light birthday kiss
because others were present. More and better
later.

Her mother came hurrying into the library.
"Oh, there you are, darling. Your Mr. Barnes
is here."

Nancy shot a gleam of triumph at Ted. He
shrugged and held up his palms in an exag-
gerated *What can I say?* gesture.

"'Not really a favorite,' huh?" Nancy said.
"Excuse me."

She weaved her way back through the
crowded living room to find Mike Barnes
getting a drink at the foyer bar.

"Hi. You made it."

He turned from the bar. He had a way of
looking you over, sizing you up before speaking. His light blue eyes, sharp and narrowed

in his thin face, studied you as though expecting to discover proof of guilt. It used to make Nancy nervous until she realized he did it with everybody.

It was a surprise to hear the low, gruff voice emerge from the tall, thin body. "Of course I made it. Happy birthday."

Nancy held out her own glass for more champagne. "You didn't bring anybody?"

"No, just me."

"Come on," she said. "I'll introduce you around."

Mike Barnes stared at the noisy living room full of people. "It looks kind of late in the party for introductions." He smiled at her, a smile that warmed his stern face.

"Quite a few Weezies are here." And she wanted to make sure that all of them knew that Mike Barnes was here, too.

"Don't worry, Nancy, I won't be lonely."

As they started into the living room, they heard a long piercing whistle. The level of noise dropped.

"What's that?" Mike said.

"Oh God, it's my father. And he *promised.*"

The whistle came again, this time achieving silence. Nancy could see people crowding in from the other rooms to find out what was going on. Had her father forgotten his promise? Or just decided to ignore it?

Her parents were standing in front of the fireplace with Jenny and Tommy beside them.

Her father said, "Nancy made her mother and me promise not to give a speech or a toast. So, of course, we won't."

A ripple of laughter.

"However, we made no such promise about anyone outside the family. Jenny?"

How sneaky, Nancy thought. But at least she would not have to stand here and be eulogized in front of her friends by her own parents. At least Jenny would behave.

"Where's Nancy?" Jenny asked.

In the doorway beside Mike Barnes, Nancy held up her hand and waved.

"Oh, okay. I just wanted to make sure you didn't run away the second your father whistled."

More laughter.

"Nancy hates speeches, so I won't make one, even though as her high school classmate and current roommate, I'd have *plenty* to say." Jenny raised her champagne glass to Nancy across the room. "All I want to say, and what we all want to say, is happy birthday, kiddo."

Applause and scattered cries of "Hear-hear." Nancy always wondered how people managed to clap with glasses in their hands.

And then Tommy. Standing there at the fireplace beside Jenny and her parents, he waited cheerfully for the attention to shift to him. He was taller than Jenny but much more solid—almost blocky. He was always trying to lose weight, but not very hard and not very successfully. Nancy thought he was a delightful looking man, with short, straight black hair and eyebrows and a marvelous smile that now encompassed the whole room. Her mother was beaming at him with approval as a potential son-in-law.

"I don't have the honor to be Nancy's classmate," Tommy said. Pause. "Or her roommate." Another pause, and then he raised his eyebrows in a way that made everyone laugh, especially Nancy. "But I've known her well for some time, so I'm qualified to offer a toast." He looked at her for a long moment and smiled. "To Nancy, the very nicest girl in town."

More applause.

"I take it," Mike said, "that's a special friend."

"Yes. That's Tommy Horgan. Do you like him?"

Mike gave her a look that made her realize how silly her question was. Then he said drily, "It's a little early to tell."

There was not enough space in the dining room for everyone to witness the ceremony of the Black Forest birthday cakes. But her mother made sure all the principals were on hand and that the overhead lights were dimmed before the cakes were borne in from the kitchen, candles blazing. Her parents and Tommy and Jenny and Basil and Mike Barnes and most of the other Weezies.

"Now remember," Carol said, as she had been saying every birthday since Nancy was an infant, "be sure to make a wish."

Nancy looked down at the neat circle of candles. What should she wish? There was really nothing to wish for. Her parents, her close friends, her job, her colleagues, her apartment—they were all she could ask. And tonight, a very successful party, and at the end of it she and Tommy would go home and make love, which would also be successful.

I have nothing to wish for. I like everything just the way it is.

She blew out the candles.

Only last week.

My Poor Nancy

Carol Whittredge was wearing her bright red velours jumpsuit, her favorite winter at-home costume when there were just the two of them. Whit, who had had to work late, had just got out of his jacket and tie and into his beige cashmere sweater, her most successful present to him in several Christmases. He wore it practically every night.

Whit mixed her daiquiri, a drink he did not approve of in winter and considered barely acceptable even in mid-summer. He poured his own "flagon of vodka" on the rocks, and they settled down in the library. Dinner was safely on hold.

Whit began what was clearly going to be a long, funny, involved story about his problems with a city building inspector on his latest real estate development project. Carol was going to have to wait to tell him about her day's adventures as a docent, featuring an obstreperous fourth-grade class in the Egyptian wing of the Metropolitan Museum. One of the many good things about their marriage was that, after twenty-six years, they never ran out of things to tell each other.

The telephone rang.

Whit, annoyed to be interrupted, said, "You get it. If it's for me, tell them I'm not home. Tell them I ran away to join the Foreign Legion."

Carol smiled at the familiar line and picked up the receiver. "Hello."

"Mom?"

"Hello, darling. How nice to hear from you." And to Whit, "It's Nancy."

She heard Nancy begin to say something and then start to cry.

"Nancy! What is it?"

Between gasps Nancy said, "Oh, Mom. I've been raped. And robbed."

"My God. Oh, darling. Oh, darling. When? Where are you?" And to Whit, "Nancy's been *raped*!"

He was across the room in three quick steps and took the phone from her before Nancy could answer. He spoke in his take-charge voice: "Nancy, where are you? . . . Are you all right? Are you hurt? . . . How bad? . . . Is Jenny there with you? . . . That's too bad, but you stay right there. Yeah, I know, but we'll be right down, as fast as we can . . . Don't do anything. Except double-lock the door. Don't let anybody in until we get there . . . No, not even any neighbors. And don't call anybody else . . . No, not even the police. Wait till we get there."

"Let me talk to her."

But Whit had already hung up. "Get your coat," he said. "And better bring your drink. By God, I'm going to bring mine."

All the long way down in the taxi, from the upper East Side to Canal, they held hands tightly, saying almost nothing to each other. There was nothing to say. Every few minutes Whit asked the driver to go faster until finally the driver said, "Listen, buddy, you want me to run lights and get us stopped for a ticket? Or you want me to get you there the best I can?"

Whit subsided. They sat there forever, holding hands in the back seat of the taxi, sipping their drinks from the Waterford crystal glasses, Carol in her mink jacket, the nearest handy garment she had grabbed out of the closet. She was too stunned to think. Her mind kept repeating to itself over and over again, *My poor Nancy, my poor Nancy*, with nothing to add to it.

When they reached the four-story building, dark except for the ground-floor apartment and Nancy's two lighted windows on the third floor, Whit gave the driver a ten-dollar bill. Uncharacteristically he did not ask for change. He helped Carol out, both of them still carrying their now-empty glasses. Carol was glad Whit had thought to bring their drinks, which had furnished the only tiny touch of comfort during the interminable ride.

They pushed Nancy's 3-A button. She must have been standing right beside the door waiting for it, because instantly her distorted voice crackled over the intercom: "Who is it?"

"It's us. Mom and Dad."

The door release buzzed. They pushed in and began the climb to the third floor. Suddenly Carol felt afraid to see her daughter. Would she be changed in some terrible way? Maybe even disfigured?

Usually when they visited, Nancy would be out in the hallway, leaning over the bannister and calling a greeting. Now there was no sound except their footsteps on the stairs. The 3-A door was closed.

Whit knocked and said again, "It's us."

Carol heard the bolts turn in the Segal double locks that Whit had had installed for safety. Safety! The door opened.

"Oh, Mommy, I'm so glad to see you."

She hadn't called Carol "Mommy" in years. Carol shot a quick glance at her daughter's face before taking her in her arms. She was shaken by the way Nancy looked.

Muffled in Carol's arms, Nancy said, "Mommy, they got my jewelry. Your Christmas bracelets, and—and your sweetheart ring."

"That doesn't matter," Carol said, although it did.

Now that they were here, Whit called the local police precinct, reported a rape and robbery and gave the address. He was convinced it was quicker to deal directly with the precinct than to go through the 911 middleman.

"Those goddamn cash machines," Whit said when Nancy told how the robbery happened. "They're a menace. Anybody can see you take out money at night. They ought to be outlawed." He was very angry, but at the same time Carol thought he was relieved to have something impersonal, mechanical and non-sexual to berate.

The police were quick. They heard a car pull up with a screech, and by the time Whit got to the window and saw the sky-blue-and-white patrol car, the front door buzzer was already sounding. He pressed the release button and then opened the apartment door. Carol and Nancy came to the door, too, and stood behind him.

"I'm nervous," Nancy said in a small voice. "I'm scared."

Carol put an arm around her shoulder.

"They're on our side," Whit said.

"I know. But I'll have to talk about it."

There was a tramp of boots on the stairway, one set actually running up the stairs, the other coming more slowly. Around the bannister appeared a small figure in a black leather jacket with a silver-colored shield, black cap, and black trousers. The holstered revolver at her belt looked almost as big as she was. She carried a long thin leather notebook.

"I'm Officer Cruz," she told Whit as she reached the door. "And that's Officer Brine way back there protecting my rear."

"I'm George Whittredge. This is my wife and my daughter Nancy. Come in."

Officer Cruz came in, quick and jaunty. She was not much older than Nancy. Her black cap didn't quite come up to Whit's shoulder. She studied Carol, who still had her mink jacket draped over her red jumpsuit.

With a start, Carol realized how ridiculous she must look. "I didn't have time to change."

Officer Brine arrived, white and enormous, looming like one of those pro football linemen Whit watched on television. On him the holstered revolver seemed like a little toy. He said hello politely, and Whit shook hands with him.

"Let's get your statement," Officer Cruz said to Nancy. She took off her cap and jacket and dropped them on the table by the entrance. She had a thin, intense face and short, fluffy black hair.

Carol realized that she did not want to hear the terrible things her daughter would have to tell Officer Cruz. "I'd rather not listen," she said.

"I'd rather you didn't either," Cruz agreed. "She'll tell me more without you. You all stay here. We'll use the bedroom. Come on, Miss Whittredge."

During the next twenty minutes, Carol fidgeted, while Whit and Officer Brine discussed sports in an irritatingly serious manner. She tried to imagine what Nancy was saying. Then she tried not to imagine it.

When at last they emerged from the bedroom, Carol saw that Officer Cruz was furious. She was slapping her long leather notebook against her leg as she strode over to Whit.

"You *look* like an intelligent man," she said. "How come you told her not to call us?"

Whit was slightly taken aback. "I thought we should be here with her first."

"Yeah? Well, *we* should have been with her first. How much time'd you cost us? Half hour? An hour?"

"What difference does it make?"

Carol could see Officer Cruz forcing herself to be patient. "Sometimes they hang around afterward. Talking about how great and smart they were. Or they might have staked out that cash machine again. They might even have gone back to the garage.''

''What garage?''

''The garage where it happened. Where we're going right now. Come on, Brine.'' She picked up her leather jacket. ''Get your coat, Nancy.''

Carol noted that her daughter had gone into the bedroom as Miss Whittredge and had come out as Nancy. ''Can we come, too?'' Carol asked.

''Sure, we got room. In fact, you better. Right after we check that place out, we'll be taking her straight to Bellevue.''

''Bellevue Hospital?'' Whit said, as he held Carol's jacket for her. ''Is she badly hurt?''

''For medical checkup. And to collect evidence. Let's go.''

As they started downstairs with Cruz leading the way, Whit said, ''Our hospital is New York Hospital. That's where our doctor is, too. I think we'd rather go there.''

''That's nice,'' Cruz said over her shoulder, ''but we're going to Bellevue. They have the best rape program.''

Carol had never before been in a police car. She, Whit and Nancy got in the back seat, Carol in the middle where she could comfort her daughter, although she had no idea how to do it. Cruz had ordered Nancy to sit next to the window where she could see out. Brine drove, with Cruz in the front seat beside him.

"Go slow," Cruz said. "Nancy, keep your eyes open. If you see anybody that looks like them, sing out. We'll check the bank first."

The car crept through the streets, largely deserted now because many of the buildings in this area were daytime businesses, stores and warehouses now closed for the night. Nancy looked out the window. No one spoke.

There was no one in or near the bright bank cubicle.

"Which street did they grab you?"

"Right over there, just down the block a little."

"They must have been watching the cubicle from that corner."

Whit cleared his throat. "Are there a lot of robberies from those cash machines?"

"Yeah, quite a few. But usually they just take your money and beat it. Okay, Nancy, where's the garage?"

"Next block on the left. Past that vacant lot."

It was a one-way street in the other direction, but Brine took it anyway. Cruz turned the car's searchlight beam on the fronts of the buildings as they drove past.

"There," Nancy said in a shaky voice. "The third one."

Brine stopped the car. The searchlight focused on a garage door held partway open by some huge object. Carol saw a small dark hole at one end. What a horrible place. And Nancy had had to go in there with those men. Carol felt sick at the sight.

Cruz jumped out of the car. She had a flashlight in one hand and her service revolver in the other. She had put on gloves and had tucked a paper bag under one arm.

"Brine, you stay with Mr. and Mrs. Whittredge. You couldn't squeeze in through there, anyway. And you better report in. Come on, Nancy."

Nancy got out. Carol watched the two figures approach the garage door. Nancy's walk was peculiar—almost a limp. She ought to see a doctor right away. Then, one after the other, the two women vanished into the dark hole.

Brine was using the car radio to tell his precinct that they were investigating the scene of the rape and would then be taking the victim to Bellevue Emergency.

"Mr. Brine," Carol asked, "will she see a good doctor at Bellevue?"

Brine shifted his bulk to turn halfway around. He rested one arm over the back of the seat. "More likely a nurse practitioner," he said.

"They're specialists. And also a rape counselor."

"Could we call our own doctor and get him to meet us there? Could you use your car radio to reach him?"

"I wouldn't advise it, ma'am. He'd just get in everybody's way. They know what they're doing at Bellevue. Lots of cops take rape victims there."

They were gone a long time. At last the flashlight beam shone out of the dark hole. Cruz and Nancy came back to the car. Cruz had holstered her revolver and was now carefully holding the paper bag away from her body. Suddenly Nancy stopped and bent over, retching. Carol's heart went out. Cruz should not have made her go back inside that terrible place. After a minute Nancy stood up, wiped her mouth with the back of her hand and came on toward the car. She still had that funny pained walk.

"You find anything, Cruzzie?"

"Shit, what a picnic!" Officer Cruz said happily as she hopped into the car. Nancy got in more slowly to sit beside Carol. "Like some detective movie. We found her wallet with everything in it except the money. They just threw it in the dumpster on top of the trash. *And* her ripped panties. *And* the company pencil she used to write out her bank code. There's probably no prints on that, but more corroboration. *And* she said one of them wiped his prick off afterward, and I bet I got the handkerchief, and I bet it's loaded with goodies. *And* I scooped up a sample where she spit out the semen. Bonanza!" She turned to Carol and Whit. "Sorry, excuse me," she said.

Carol was too shocked by what she had just learned to say anything, but Whit turned to Nancy and said, "Jesus, you did *that*?"

Nancy did not answer. She just nodded. Then she said in a whisper, "I had to."

"Well, but for God's sake—" Whit began.

Carol hit him hard in the ribs with her elbow. He stopped.

"Okay," Cruz said, "we'll lock this up in the trunk, and then next stop is Bellevue."

Brine drove all the way across town to the beginning of First Avenue, where he turned left. He used the siren a couple of times to clear traffic ahead of them.

Carol had never been inside Bellevue, but she had seen it countless times. The vast, dingy, red-brick complex stretched from Twenty-sixth Street through Thirtieth Street between First Avenue and the East River. It was seven or eight stories high, with squat central towers rising even higher than that. Row after row of blank, faceless windows. She knew it was the oldest public hospital in the country, and it sure looked it. In appearance it was more like a prison than a hospital.

At Twenty-ninth Street Brine turned into a drive that wound behind the old brick buildings and then along the river's edge to the lofty tower of New Bellevue. The car pulled up at a wide entrance marked EMERGENCY in foot-high neon letters. Smaller letters underneath announced BELLEVUE HOSPITAL CENTER. Half a dozen white ambulances were parked outside.

"Here we are," Cruz said.

Everybody got out, Nancy gripping Carol's hand.

"It's kind of a zoo," Cruz said, "but the triage nurse will take her right away."

"What's a triage nurse?" Whit wanted to know.

"She's the boss. She decides which cases are urgent and which can wait a while. But rape cases are always urgent here."

Right inside the entrance was a dim, lobby-like area with white-sheeted, wheeled stretchers lined up in compact rows. To Carol they looked as though they were waiting for some mass disaster to happen—an airplane crash or a hotel fire. She kept a firm grip on Nancy's hand.

They threaded between the stretchers. Brine and Cruz led the way through a wide glass door, and the Whittredges followed. After the dim stretcher-lobby, the light here was shockingly bright. A glare reflected off the cream-colored linoleum floor.

Against one wall was a formidable structure labeled "Disposition Desk." It reminded Carol of the bridge of a warship. A curved, waist-high wooden barrier was topped by Plexiglas panels with round openings, like bank tellers' cages.

Several people stood at this barrier, badgering the nurses through the holes in the Plexiglas. A middle-aged woman with a yellow scarf over her head was screaming at the nurses in some Scandinavian language. Carol had never thought of Scandinavians as screamers, but this woman was protesting at the very top of her voice. A black man with a blood-stained towel wrapped around his left arm was waving it at the nurses and demanding instant attention. Two new patients were lined up to check in. A white-coated doctor with a stethoscope dangling from his neck argued with one of the nurses behind the barrier.

"Zoo is right," Whit whispered to Carol.

In front of the Disposition Desk, seated in armless plastic chairs, at least two dozen people waited for treatment. Constant traffic moved in and out of the room—doctors, nurses, hospital attendants hurrying to the desk to report something or ask some question and then hurrying back to wherever they came from. The room was bustling and noisy.

"We should have gone to New York Hospital," Whit said.

Carol looked at her daughter. She seemed dazed by the sight and the turmoil.

"Come on," Cruz told Nancy, "we'll get you checked in. They have to fill out a registration form on you."

"Can't my husband do that for her?" Carol asked. She did not want to let go of Nancy's hand.

"No, the triage nurse has to talk to her personally."

"Suppose she was unconscious," Whit said.

"Well, she isn't," Cruz said cheerfully. "Come on, Nancy. You folks better wait here."

Carol gave a last squeeze before releasing Nancy's hand. She watched the two police officers march Nancy to the desk. Without seeming to use any force, Brine shouldered his way to the center and cleared space for them. First Cruz and then Nancy talked through the Plexiglas grill.

The procedure took only a few minutes. Then a nurse appeared from somewhere and led Nancy away.

Carol was reminded of that terrible day, years ago, when she watched Nancy being wheeled away to the operating room for an emergency appendectomy. Peritonitis. Carol had wondered then if she would ever see her daughter alive. This felt just the same.

Nancy did not look back as the nurse led her down a corridor.

Cruz and Brine returned to where Carol and Whit were standing.

"Where are they taking her?" Carol asked. "Where are they taking her?"

"The GYN room. Listen, we'll be getting back to the precinct now. Can we drop you somewhere for a drink or some supper? This will take a couple of hours."

"No, we'll wait here," Carol said.

"We'll wait," Whit said.

"Pretty crummy place to wait. You sure?"

"Thank you," Carol said, "but we'll stay right here."

Cruz shrugged. "Suit yourself. We'll be off then. Good luck."

"Don't worry, she'll be all right," Brine said.

Carol felt like asking what makes you so damn sure, but she didn't.

When the police officers left, Carol looked at Whit. He seemed as shaken and bewildered as she felt. What were they going to do to Nancy in the GYN room?

"Whit, I don't think I can stand it in here."

"Me neither."

They went out into the dim, narrow lobby through which they had entered. Whit lifted her up onto one of the wheeled stretchers and then sat beside her, their legs dangling over the edge.

To wait for Nancy.

A Legitimate

When the phone rang at the Manhattan Sex Crimes Squad, Billy Cooney picked it up.

"Sex Crimes, Detective Cooney."

"Yeah, this is Cruz. First Precinct. I have a Rape One for you, plus armed robbery. Two perps."

Her voice sounded young and excited, as though this might be her first rape case. In New York law, Rape One was top of the line: forcible rape with or without a weapon, with violence either threatened or expressed, penetration achieved, with or without ejaculation. Cooney jotted down the basic information: name, address, phone number of the victim, circumstances and location of the crime. It was an ugly one, although luckily the victim had not been severely injured. Often they were battered. Sometimes they were dead.

"Any arrest made?"

"No."

"Did you put a description of the perps on the radio?"

"Of course."

"Where's the victim now?"

"We left her at Bellevue for treatment."

"Have you called the Detective Borough?"

A slight hesitation. "I thought I was supposed to call you."

Yes, this was probably her first rape case. "You are. But call Manhattan Detective Borough, too, and get them to assign the case a log number."

"Okay. I have a lot of physical evidence, too. Collected at the scene."

"What evidence?"

Officer Cruz described what she had gathered at the garage.

Oh yes, very definitely her first rape case. "Who's in charge down there tonight?"

"Sergeant Evans."

"Let me speak to him."

After a pause a heavy voice said, "Sergeant Evans."

"Cooney at MSCS. Can Cruz hear you?"

"No."

"Well, what the hell is she doing picking up evidence at a crime scene? Doesn't she know enough to leave that for the forensics in the Crime Scene Unit?"

A pause. Then the heavy voice said, "I guess not. She's brand new, and she didn't want to risk it getting lost."

"Well, chew her ass out. You know they want an untainted scene."

"Like hell I will. She's the best young cop I got. I wish all of them were that eager."

"You going to let her keep on doing things like that?"

After another and longer pause, the voice said, "Suppose you worry about catching the perps. I'll worry about this precinct. She won't do it again."

"Can you put a car on the scene overnight so nothing else gets fucked up?"

"I already did that."

"Well, tell her to voucher her evidence and get it to the lab."

"Already told her."

"And get her paper work up here in the morning. First thing."

They both hung up.

Billy Cooney checked the rotation sheet. Every case that came in to the Manhattan Sex Crimes Squad was assigned to the next detective in line. No favoritism, no discrimination, no juggling in any way. This didn't mean that the right detective, man or woman, always got the right case, but it was the fairest way, strictly by rotation. The name at the top of the list was Carl Vincent. Cooney wished his own name headed the list, but he and Vincent worked together a lot, so he would probably have a piece of this one.

This case was what they called a "legitimate" rape. Not just a boyfriend or a prostitute or a drug addict, but a real stranger-to-stranger rape. Maybe a quarter of the cases MSCS handled each year were "legitimates." They were usually the most interesting and the most difficult— and the most satisfying if you caught the perpetrators. This time, the right man was getting the right case.

He looked across the room at the heavyset detective with curly gray hair and rolled-up shirt sleeves.

"Hey, Carlo," he said. "This is yours. A legitimate."

At Bellevue Emergency, Cooney followed Vincent through the entrance corridor, past a well-dressed middle-aged couple sitting on one of the stretchers. They looked like they did not belong at Bellevue. Cooney wondered what they were doing sitting out here in near darkness.

The frantic triage nurse told Vincent and Cooney that the victim, Nancy Whittredge, was in the GYN room for examination and treatment. "But her parents are around somewhere."

"Those folks on the stretcher," Cooney said. "The ones we passed on the way in. I bet it's them."

Vincent nodded.

One of the things Billy Cooney liked about working with Carlo was that he didn't talk too much. This gave Cooney, who loved to talk, much more air time.

When the couple admitted they were the Whittredges, Vincent introduced himself and Cooney, and they showed their IDs, although there was not enough light for the parents to see them.

"We'd like to talk to your daughter as soon as possible," Vincent said. "Right after they've finished with her."

The man stood up. He was taller than Carlo but at least fifty pounds lighter. "She's already talked to the police," he said, in a firm, definite voice.

"That was the precinct officer," Vincent explained. "I'm in charge of the investigation."

"She's in no shape to do any more talking tonight."

"Yes, sir, but—"

"It will have to wait."

"It's important to—"

"Tomorrow." The man took out his wallet and gave Vincent a card. "She's coming home with us. You can call her at this number tomorrow. But not before noon."

Vincent put the card in his pocket.

"Don't lose that," the man said. "It's an unlisted number."

Billy Cooney smiled to himself. The thought of Carlo losing anything having to do with a case was really very funny.

"If you don't mind, I'd like to start a little earlier than noon."

"I'm sorry, but we do mind. You may not have heard the circumstances, Mister—I didn't catch your name."

"Vincent. Detective Vincent."

"Well, Mr. Vincent, she's been through a terrible ordeal."

If it had been Cooney's case, he would have been tempted to give it to the father right there. *Don't tell us about the ordeal of rape. We know more about that than you'll ever know.*

But after a moment, all Carlo said was, "Yes. I know."

The GYN Room

Pat Ford, a twenty-four-year-old graduate student in social work, ran from her taxi to the Emergency Room, dodging people in the corridor. When she reported in to the nursing supervisor, she checked her watch. Only eight minutes and fifty seconds from the moment her home phone had rung. The maximum time for a rape counselor to get to the hospital was supposed to be fifteen minutes, but she always tried to beat that.

"Very good," the supervisor congratulated her, looking at the wall clock above her head. "Nine minutes."

"I make it eight minutes and fifty seconds."

"I count to the nearest minute."

Pat Ford did not know this supervisor. In fact, a volunteer counselor on standby call two nights a month, she knew none of the hospital personnel except those directly associated with the program. "Well," she said, "if you don't mind, please write me down for eight minutes fifty. Where is she?"

"In the GYN room. Her name is Nancy Whittredge. We just put her there a few minutes ago."

But Pat Ford knew how long a few minutes could feel to a rape survivor, especially sitting alone in an obstetrics-gynecology room in a strange hospital. She pushed through the door and walked the few yards down the corridor to the GYN room. She tried to remember everything she had been taught in the hospital training course and everything she had learned from her four previous experiences as a counselor. Each case was different. You had to play it by ear and react to the patient's needs.

She knocked on the door's glass panel which, for privacy, was draped on the inside with a hospital sheet. It had been drilled into the counselors that knocking on this door was the first vital step in restoring authority to a woman who had just been stripped of every shred of authority by the rapist. She had lost control over her own body, her own life. Pat Ford would be the first to start trying to give it back to her.

She knocked again and waited. When the program started at Bellevue, it took a month to teach the doctors and nurses to knock on this door, but it took another year to teach them to wait for an answer. They were always in such a hurry and so used to being in charge that they just knocked and opened the door in the same motion.

A voice said, "Come in."

Pat walked in and closed the door behind her.

She was sitting, fully dressed in sweater and slacks and loafers, hunched over in the yellow-green swivel chair. It was the only seat in the cramped cubicle, unless you wanted to count the brown leather examination table with shiny stirrups that dominated the eight-by-ten space. Pat had yet to see a rape survivor sitting on that table. Directly above the table hung a large color diagram outlining the stages of "Pregnancy and Birth." It was a singularly inappropriate exhibit for a rape victim to have to look at. Of course, most patients in the GYN room were not rape victims, but Pat had often thought that the poster should be removed before a rape survivor was brought in here.

"Hello, Miss Whittredge. I'm Pat Ford. I'm a rape counselor. I'm here to help you in any way I can."

The woman sat up in her chair. A pretty young woman with sunny, short brown hair and enormous brown eyes, clouded by anxiety and fear. In Pat's experience, a show of emotion—almost any emotion—was better than the tight closed-in expression that some women had after a rape. Emotion was preferable to withdrawal, and talk was preferable to silence.

"Hello," she answered. "I'm Nancy Whittredge."

"Do you mind if we talk?" Pat leaned back against the exam table. "I don't know what would be most helpful to you. Perhaps you can tell me?"

No answer.

"Is there anyone you would like to call? Your parents? Your boyfriend? The police?" As always when she was on standby, Pat's purse was filled with quarters for possible phone calls.

The woman shook her head. "No, thanks. My parents came with me—they're out there in the waiting room. My boyfriend's away this weekend. The police brought me here."

That's good, Pat thought. The parents were on hand for support, and the rape had been reported to the police. The estimate was that perhaps only about one in ten rapes was ever reported, although, of course, no one really knew. Whatever the right number, it was the most underreported crime in the country.

"What's going to happen to me here?"

"That's entirely up to you, Miss Whittredge. It's your choice. By the way, would you rather I called you 'Miss Whittredge' or 'Nancy'?" That, too, gave the woman another choice.

"Oh, Nancy's fine."

"All right, and I'm Pat."

"How do you mean, it's my choice?"

"Just that. Nothing will happen without your permission. It's all up to you."

"Oh. Well, all right. But what happens? What do they do?"

"If you agree—and only if you agree—a nurse practitioner or a doctor will give you a general physical to make sure you're all right. That you aren't hurt. Sometimes you could be hurt and not know it. And then—but again only if you agree, it's up to you—you get a pelvic exam, and they collect evidence for possible prosecution. You can always decide later whether or not you want to prosecute, but if you do want to, this is the right time to collect the medical evidence."

"I can't prosecute," she said in a forlorn voice. "I don't even know who they were."

"They?"

Nancy Whittredge nodded. "There were two of them."

"I'm so sorry. That must have made it even worse. Do you want to talk about it?"

Sometimes they wanted to talk about the rape, sometimes they wanted to talk about something entirely different—job, family, boyfriend—anything but the rape itself. On very rare occasions, Pat knew, they did not want to talk at all and asked to be left alone. So far, she had not run into one of those. But even if that happened, the counselor was supposed to stay at the hospital for at least an hour, in case the woman changed her mind.

"I think I'd like to talk about it, but—I don't know—it's very hard."

"Yes, of course it is."

"The thing is, I could have avoided it. I've been thinking about it. I had two different chances. I took a dark short-cut street to my apartment. If I'd stuck to the main, well-lighted streets, the way you're supposed to, it would never have happened."

"You can't be sure of that, Nancy. Believe me, it can happen anywhere. It could have happened in your own apartment. Half the rapes happen in the woman's own home. Don't blame yourself. Blame them."

Nancy smiled for the first time, a tiny smile. "Oh, don't worry, I blame them all right. Just the same . . . But no, I suppose you're right, I can't be sure. They had a gun, so they could have stopped me anywhere."

"A gun? That must have been terribly frightening."

Nancy nodded. "It sure was. I was scared to death the whole time. I thought they were going to kill me. Even after all the rapes, and even after I got them the rest of my money from the bank, I still thought they were going to kill me."

"I'm not surprised, strangers with a gun on you." So it had been multiple rape *and* robbery. "You said you could have avoided it twice. What was the other time?"

Nancy told an emotional story about a car at a stoplight with a driver who noticed something strange: two black men herding a frightened white girl across the street.

So they were black, Pat thought. That would probably make it even more difficult and complicated for Nancy.

"I *know* he would have helped me. If I'd just jumped for his car door, it would never have happened. I had my chance, and I blew it."

This was tricky territory because Nancy obviously believed she could have saved herself. Women almost always blamed themselves, one way or another, for a rape. They thought it must somehow be their fault. Pat thought carefully about what to say.

"Yes, but he might *not* have helped you. Or suppose his car door was locked? And worst of all, they might have shot you right there. You never know what's going to happen with crazy people and a gun. Nancy, if you'd jumped, you could be dead. The important thing is that you're alive. You survived. And now you're safe."

"No, I should have jumped. I'll never forgive myself."

"You don't have to forgive yourself. They're the ones who did everything."

"I know, but it's just that—"

There was a knock on the shrouded glass panel of the door.

Nancy looked at Pat Ford, silently asking what to do.

Pat silently looked back at her: *It's up to you. It's your decision.*

"Come in," Nancy said.

The door opened and a nurse practitioner entered. In one hand she carried an oblong cardboard box, the Vitullo Kit. She was dressed entirely in white, not just white but sparkling white—her uniform, shoes, stockings. Most nurses at Bellevue did not look so formal.

It was Dorothy Jenks. Although they had never worked together, Pat knew her from the monthly support meetings of counselors and nurse practitioners and doctors to discuss problems or possible improvements in the rape program. She was a tall, handsome woman of forty-five with great personal dignity—an imposing presence. Her speech, though as formal and proper as her dress, had a musical sweetness that came from somewhere in the Caribbean. She was black.

Given what had happened tonight, Pat Ford wondered if a black nurse would cause Nancy any special problem. She must be alert for that.

"Good evening, Miss Whittredge. I am Mrs. Jenks. I am here to take care of you, if you so wish. Good evening, Miss Ford. Have you had time to explain our procedures to Miss Whittredge?"

In a hospital atmosphere that thrived on the use of first names, Pat never would have dreamed of calling this grave, imperial woman "Dorothy." "Hello, Mrs. Jenks. Yes, but just in general terms."

"I shall explain it as we go along. Miss Whittredge, I want you to understand that I shall do nothing without your permission and approval."

"Nancy, would you like me to wait outside?" Pat asked.

"No, please stay." She glanced at Mrs. Jenks. "If that's all right."

They usually wanted the counselor to stay because, if she was doing her job right, she was already a familiar, friendly presence.

"I hope you will want to tell me about what

happened to you," Mrs. Jenks began, "but the first thing we wish to do is a blood test. The reason for this . . ."

Pat had heard the doctors and nurses speculate about how quickly the entire rape examination and treatment procedure could be completed if they did not have to explain each step and then ask permission to do it and then answer questions about it. Most thought it could be finished in an hour, perhaps a little longer depending on complications, but the speculation was purely academic. Since it took two to three hours to get the blood test results for preexisting pregnancy before medication could be given, there was no special hurry. A blood test for venereal disease would also be made, but those results would take a week.

"You mean," Nancy asked, "you can tell right now whether or not they made me pregnant?"

"No, no," Mrs. Jenks said. "We can only tell if you were already pregnant before the attack. If you were, we would give you different medication."

"Well," Nancy said, "I've been on the pill since I was sixteen, so it isn't likely."

"Even the pill is not infallible, Miss Whittredge."

After she drew the vials of blood from Nancy's arm and sent them to the lab, Mrs.

Jenks took a hospital gown from the cabinet drawer and handed it to her. "If it is all right with you, please take off everything but your socks. Miss Ford and I will wait outside while you change." This was another little courtesy to a woman who had just been robbed of all privacy.

While Nancy was changing into the hospital gown, Pat swiped another chair from a nearby office so that Dorothy Jenks could sit down while she interviewed Nancy. Part of the counselor's job was to make things as easy as possible for the nurse or doctor, but you had to have been through it a few times before you could anticipate what was needed.

Pat Ford had been in the program for two years. In the early days, it was called the Sexual Assault Victims Assistance Program, or SAVA for short, which had the nice connotation that they were "saving" something, as indeed they were. Now, alas, it had become the Victims of Violent Assault Assistance Program, with the silly acronym of VOVAAP. *What do you do, Pat, on those two nights a month when you wait at home for a possible phone call? Oh, I'm working for VOVAAP.* Maybe at the next monthly support meeting she would suggest changing back to SAVA.

Pat leaned against the wall of the GYN room, with its drawn, bright blue Venetian blinds, while they listened to Nancy's story. Nancy recounted a succession of horrors in a surprisingly orderly way, with no confusion and no hysteria. It was as though when Mrs. Jenks asked her to tell what had happened, Nancy shifted into a completely different gear.

This was remarkable. Most rape survivors, whether silent or articulate, went through a period of confusion that only gradually subsided, sometimes after a few hours, sometimes not for days or weeks. For Nancy to be able to tell a coherent story at this time was quite something. She would make an excellent witness. Pat decided to tell her so, just to encourage her.

"You'd be a good witness."

Nancy's chin came up with a first touch of pride. "That's my job." she said. "I'm a reporter."

"Oh really? For a newspaper?"

"No, radio news. WZEY."

"I listen to that. Maybe I've heard you."

"Maybe you have. Someday I hope to get into television news—if my nose isn't too short."

"Your nose doesn't look too short to me," Pat said, although indeed it seemed a bit dainty compared to the huge brown eyes.

"It all depends on what the camera sees."

Mrs. Jenks continued to draw out the details. As she listened, Pat thought about how terrible it must have been for Nancy, isolated in that dark garage, enduring one outrage after another while hoping not to be murdered. Pat was constantly amazed, even after all her time in this program, at the extent of violence and craziness that lurked out in the New York streets, waiting for opportunity.

At the end Mrs. Jenks said, "So they had vaginal, anal and oral intercourse with you."

Nancy nodded. "Yes," she said, her voice turning shaky, "and some places several times."

"Animals," Mrs. Jenks said, almost to herself.

She then conducted the general physical, explaining each step and writing her notes on the Emergency Medical Services form. For the patient, this was the least traumatic part of the examination because much of it was familiar to anyone who had ever had a physical. Blood pressure. Ears, nose and throat. Neck. A careful check for any head trauma. Listening to heart and lungs. Checking the abdomen for tenderness.

While prodding Nancy's stomach, Mrs. Jenks said, "You have contusions on your breasts. Did that happen tonight?"

"It sure did," Nancy said. "They hurt."

Then the neurological exam: eye pupils, cranial nerves, reflexes, skin sensation.

When she finished this, Mrs. Jenks picked up the oblong cardboard box she had brought with her into the GYN room. "Now, if you are agreeable, Miss Whittredge, we should do a pelvic and rectal examination and collect evidence. This is called a Vitullo Kit or, more properly, a Vitullo Evidence Collection Kit. There are a number of steps . . ."

All the rape counselors had been lectured on the use and importance of the Vitullo Kit. Vitullo was a cop in Chicago's sex crime division. He got disgusted by the number of rape cases that were lost or thrown out of court because vital evidence was missing, or botched, or incomplete, or mislabeled, or mishandled, or even just mislaid, either by the police or by the hospital or by the police lab.

Since Vitullo knew from experience which rape evidence was important and how it should be collected, recorded and preserved, he designed an inexpensive kit that any trained doctor or nurse could learn to use. It contained slides and slide holders, cotton swabs, swab boxes, two separate combs for collecting samples of head hair and pubic hair, envelopes, heavy-duty paper bags, labels, an orange stick to collect skin scrapings from under the woman's fingernails, and finally a six-inch strip of bright red tape to seal the kit when all evidence had been gathered. The tape had space for the date and the medical officer's initials, and it read "EVIDENCE DO NOT OPEN." Once sealed, every time the kit changed hands—from hospital to police precinct to police lab—it had to be logged in and out so that the chain of evidence remained unbroken.

By now the Vitullo Kit was in widespread use. Bellevue alone used about a hundred and fifty every year at a cost of fourteen dollars each. Pat thought the best part of the story was that the manufacture, marketing and distribution of the kit had been underwritten by a generous grant from Hugh Hefner's Playboy Foundation.

The thorough pelvic exam, with speculum and black rubber tube with a light source at the end and swabs and smears and rubber hospital gloves, was a particular ordeal for a woman who had just been raped. Not painful but invasive, intrusive.

"I hope you have not showered or douched?" Mrs. Jenks asked.

"No. I knew enough not to do that. But I *had* to brush my teeth. I threw up on the way home, so I guess any mouth evidence was lost then."

"Perhaps not."

From one of the cabinet drawers Mrs. Jenks took out the hand-held ultraviolet lamp and ran it all over Nancy's skin. Wherever there were semen traces, they lighted up under this lamp so that Mrs. Jenks was able to collect specimen samples for the kit.

While Pat helped Mrs. Jenks by writing identifying labels on the various evidence envelopes, she kept talking to Nancy—or, more often, just listening. Listening was the main thing a counselor did.

Nancy kept talking about the two men and trying to analyze their different behavior. Even while Mrs. Jenks was examining and then cleaning and treating her rectal lacerations, Nancy was talking.

"The shorter one, Bernie, he was—I mean when he wasn't doing things to me or making me do things to him—he was—I know this is going to sound funny—he was almost friendly. As though he wanted me to *like* him. I think he even wanted me to like the sex parts. And then at the end, when they were letting me go—*ouch!*"

"I am so sorry."

"That's all right. It's just very—"

"I shall put some topical antibiotic ointment on this, and then it will not be so painful."

"Bernie was the one who gave me back my new dress. But the other one, the one who kept calling me 'bitch,' I had the feeling all through it that he was just looking for some excuse to kill me. I don't think I'm making that up.

Anyway, I know I'm not making up how I felt.
When he came back from the bank and
couldn't make the cash machine work, he was
so angry—I mean it was more than just anger.
It was real rage. Fury. I could feel it. I was so
scared I couldn't even look at him. And when
he was—during the sex, I knew he wanted to
hurt me. Not just screw me but really *hurt* me.
As though he wanted to wreck me as a person,
one way or another."

Listening, Pat thought the trouble with being a counselor was that you became so sympathetic, trying to give so much support and
encouragement, that you got emotionally
caught up in the woman's experience and
started to live it yourself. It was exhausting,
draining, but at the same time she probably
would not be able to sleep tonight after this
was over.

From her training manual and lectures, she
thought she could recognize in Nancy's story
the two main types of rapists, although the
teacher said there was usually an overlap
between them. There was the compulsive rapist, who tried to resolve his own sexual problems, whatever they might be, by acting out a
sexual fantasy, pretending that his victim was
a willing partner. And then there was the
predator, whose primary motive was destruc-
tion.

"Now, Miss Whittredge," Mrs. Jenks said, "I am going to suggest something that may seem strange to you, and I shall do it only if you wish me to. If you decide to prosecute— which you do not have to decide tonight—the law enforcement agencies might find it helpful to have pictures of the injuries you sustained. Your breast contusions and your rectal lacerations. I can take Polaroids, if you wish."

Nancy shook her head. "No."

"Very well."

"That's up to you, Nancy, like everything else," Pat put in, "but you might want to think it over for a minute. It's just another form of evidence."

Again Nancy shook her head. "To me that's too personal. I don't want pictures of my breasts and ass lying around in some police file."

Pat thought it was the wrong decision, but at least Nancy was able to be decisive.

"Very well," Mrs. Jenks said again.

The Vitullo Kit was much too small to contain Nancy's clothing, which might have semen traces as well as other evidence, so Pat got out a heavy-duty hospital bag. Mrs. Jenks put Nancy's slacks and sweater in the bag and sealed it with cellophane tape.

"I'll get you some clothes to go home in," Pat told Nancy.

When the results of the blood tests came
back, Mrs. Jenks told Nancy that they were
negative—no prior pregnancy or anemia—so
they could proceed with the normal medication. There would be ceftriaxone, an antibiotic
shot to prevent gonorrhea, and doxycycline
pills, two a day for ten days, to prevent
chlamydia, a more and more common venereal disease. There would also be a strong dose
of Ovral to prevent pregnancy. As for AIDS,
nothing could be done here tonight, but if
Nancy wished, she could see Bellevue's AIDS
program doctor tomorrow, and she *might* be
offered "a somewhat controversial and exper-
imental medication called AZT." Nancy should
come back to the hospital in a week, when
Mrs. Jenks would have the results of the
venereal disease test, which required time to
grow in culture. She should also come back in
four to six weeks for a syphilis test, and she
should have an AIDS test six months from
now and again a year from now. It took that
long for the AIDS virus to manifest itself.

Nancy listened, but Pat saw that, like most
rape survivors, she was more interested in
emotional issues than in medical ones. The
only point that really seized Nancy's attention
was when Mrs. Jenks said she should not have
any alcohol while she was taking the medication.

"No *drinks*?" Nancy said. "For ten days after a rape, no drinks? That's *medieval*."

Mrs. Jenks smiled for the first time in more than two hours. She had a wonderful smile. "Oh yes, Miss Whittredge, I am very afraid that is true."

Then Nancy had another thought. "Pat, I forgot my parents! They've been waiting forever. Would you mind telling them I'm okay?"

"Of course. I should have thought of it myself. What do they look like?"

"You can't miss my mother. She's wearing a red jumpsuit."

While Mrs. Jenks was giving Nancy her medication, Pat went out to the Emergency Room. It was still as busy and crowded as when she first walked in. Nobody in a red jumpsuit, though. She wondered if Nancy's parents had tired of waiting and gone home. God, she hoped not. What Nancy most needed now was family support and safe transportation to a safe place to spend the night. It was vital for her to feel safe.

Pat asked the triage nurse if anybody knew where the Whittredge parents were.

"Last time I saw, they were headed outside. Maybe they left."

Damn them, Pat thought. But maybe they just went for a walk.

She found them sitting on a stretcher in the
dim outer lobby. "Are you Nancy's parents?"

They both hopped off the stretcher.

"Is she all right?" the woman asked.

"She seems fine. I'm Pat Ford, your daughter's rape counselor, and I've been with her
the last couple of hours. You should feel
proud of her. She's taken this amazingly
well."

"Thank God she's all right. We've been
talking. How much danger is there of pregnancy or disease?"

Pat explained what was being done about
both. With the proper medication, in itself a
good reason to report a rape, the chances of
pregnancy or disease were minute. Then she
said, "What your daughter mostly needs is
comfort. She says you're taking her home with
you?"

"Yes," the father said. "For as long as she
likes."

"Good. If you don't mind, let me give you a
little advice. No matter how she sounds, she is
going to be extremely fragile, maybe for quite
some time. Don't be surprised at things she
does and says."

"Like what?" the mother said.

"I don't know. But you don't get over
something like this right away. For instance,
she may not want to be left alone. Or she may

not want to see anybody except family. She
may not be able to go to work. She could be
nervous just about going outdoors. Does she
have a regular boyfriend?"

"Yes," the mother said, "a very fine young
man. But he's away this weekend. Is that bad?
That he isn't here?"

"Not necessarily. At least it's one less com-
plication for her to deal with. Another thing.
She may want to talk about the rape, or maybe
she won't. On the whole, it's better if she does.
And if she does, I hope you will be there to
listen."

She could see them both nodding in the dim
light.

"And one more thing, terribly important. It
wasn't her fault."

"Of course not."

"Well, Mrs. Whittredge, you'd be surprised.
Most women blame themselves, somehow, for
a rape. And a lot of parents and friends also
blame her. They think it must have been her
fault. That can be very damaging. Now I must
get back and finish up with Nancy. She won't
be long. She just wanted me to let you know
she's all right."

"Thank you very much, Miss Ford. I don't
know if Nancy will want to discuss details
with us, and I'm not sure I want to hear them,
but just for our own background, how bad
was it?"

The mother's question almost made Pat angry. What did she mean: Was it a *nice* rape? "Just awful. Terrible. But she's alive."

Pat stopped at the VOVAAP office to get the package of handout materials for Nancy to take home. At the social work office, she picked up a set of white cotton underpants and bra and, from the clothes contributed by the Bellevue Auxiliary, a pair of brown corduroy trousers and a shaggy green sweater that looked about Nancy's size.

When she returned to the GYN room, Mrs. Jenks was sealing the Vitullo Kit with the strip of bright red tape. She would take it personally to the hospital security room where it would be logged in and locked up for the night until the police came to collect it tomorrow.

Mrs. Jenks then turned to Nancy, who was sitting up on the exam table, still in her hospital gown.

"I shall say good night now, Miss Whittredge." She shook hands formally. "May I say that you have been a splendid patient, and that I wish you a speedy recovery from your ordeal. Please do not fail to take your medication." She turned to Pat, with a slight bow of her head. "Good night, Miss Ford. Thank you for all your help."

When she had gone, Pat gave Nancy the

clothes. "Not very elegant, I'm afraid, but they'll get you home."

Nancy accepted them with appropriate distaste. "Mom and I are the same size, so I won't have to wear these for long."

Pat waited in the corridor until Nancy was dressed. Then she explained the envelope of handout material: the printed flyer about coping with rape; the map showing how to get to the VOVAAP office; the information sheet about AIDS; the list and explanation of the medication she had received; the sheet entitled Emotional First Aid, with its description of the various emotional reactions Nancy could expect to have and its encouragement to talk about the experience—and, if she felt like it, to cry about it.

"And this," Pat said, "is our number to call if you have any questions or just want to talk about it with somebody. Or you can make an appointment to come in and talk. You'll get a staff social worker who will know exactly what to do and how to help."

Nancy looked at the card, then looked up at Pat. "I won't get you?"

This was one of the hardest things about being a volunteer counselor. You spent these hours giving everything you could think of to give, you became emotionally intimate with a total stranger, you came to care so much about

what would happen to her, how she would
survive—and then you were required to step
aside.

"I'm afraid not," she said. "You'll be much
better off dealing with the trained professional
staff. I was just here to help you tonight."

Nancy was slightly tearful. "But I *know* you.
I can *talk* to you."

"Well—thank you, Nancy. But it's the hospital system, and it's really for the best."

"But—"

"Listen, I do care about you, and I'll ask the
social workers how you're doing. I'll find out
how you're getting along. And besides, now
that I know you, I'll be listening for you on the
radio."

"Will you? Will you really?"

Her eagerness made Pat feel tearful, too.
"Sure. I promise. Come on, let's go find your
parents."

Morning After

The fight started while Nancy was still asleep in her old bedroom.

Right after breakfast Whit took his coffee mug to the library telephone and, armed with Nancy's bank account number, went to work. Carol thought there were far more important things to be doing, really vital matters to discuss, but Whit was determined.

He dialed, listened for a moment and then hung up. "The executive offices have a tape recording," he said.

"What did you expect on a weekend?"

"A tape recording." Whit said this almost with satisfaction, as though it was just the challenge he had been hoping for. A distinct look of pleasure lighted his long, thin face with its strong nose and jaw. A very attractive face for a man. Fortunately, it was a face that their son Basil had inherited and, equally fortunately, that Nancy had not. "However," Whit announced, in a tone of insider expertise, "there are other ways."

He dialed his own banker at home and told him about the cash machine robbery. "Richard, listen, I need to reach at least a vice-president this morning . . . No, I don't want to wait till the workweek. Who do you know over there? . . . Yeah, I got it, Walter Bissinger . . . But you don't know where he lives? Hell, they all live in Greenwich, don't they? . . . Well, see if you can find out and call me right back. I don't want to miss him because he's gone off to play golf, or whatever you bankers do on Saturday morning . . . Yeah, I know it's February, but those Greenwich executives probably have a heated indoor course . . . Okay, I appreciate it. I'll wait."

He hung up.

"I think we should call Basil," Carol said. Basil was one of those names that had sounded good at the time of birth, rather romantic to a young mother, but then you were stuck with it forever.

"Richard's going to call me right back. Besides, we'll never catch Basil on a weekend."

"We could leave a message at his dorm."

"After I finish this."

Richard called back within five minutes, and Whit wrote down the number. "Thanks, you're a prince. Talk to you next week." He told Carol, "It's not Greenwich, but almost. It's Byram."

He dialed again.

"Mr. Walter Bissinger, please . . . He doesn't know me . . . Just tell him it's a bank emergency . . .

"Mr. Bissinger? This is George Whittredge in New York. Richard Lyman gave me your number. I want to report a serious crime last night at your Branch 104."

Carol listened as Whit took him through the robbery story. He left out the rape altogether.

"You have a computer record of every transaction, right? So you'll find a number of insertions of my daughter's card, with nothing happening, the guy couldn't work the code. And then finally a withdrawal of four hundred dollars . . . Right . . . Oh, that's bank policy, huh? It sounds like you must have been having a lot of trouble with those machines . . . Yes . . . Yes . . . Okay, good . . . And, Mr. Bissinger, what about the first hundred dollars? . . . Good. Sorry to have to bother you on a weekend."

Whit banged down the phone in triumph.

"They're going to pay it all back—bank policy. The whole thing, the one hundred and

the four hundred both. They'll put it in her
account just as soon as they check their computer tape. How's *that*?"

He was so pleased with himself that Carol
could not hold back. "Great!" she said. "Terrific! Your daughter's been horribly raped,
and all you care about is money."

Whit stared at her. He pressed his lips
together into a thin strip. She could almost
hear the sword slide out of the scabbard. Then
he said, in his iciest voice, "That is a preposterous thing to say."

"It's not preposterous. Here you are fussing
about the money, when we have a lot of *serious*
things to talk about and really important calls
to make."

"I considered that 'a really important call.'
At least it accomplished something. Just what
did you have in mind?"

"Basil, of course. And Rex. And—"

"What's Basil going to contribute? Even if
we found him, which we won't. And why
Rex? Nancy's already been examined and
treated by a specialist."

"It's not the same as seeing our own family
doctor."

"No, you're right about that. It's much
better. How many rape cases do you think Rex
treats in a year? Or in the last decade? One,
maybe?"

"That's not the point, and you know it. She ought to have a total physical, with x-rays and everything, and I'd like to be sure Rex approves of all that medication they gave her. She ought to see her own gynecologist, too."

"Here, you want to use the phone? Want to see what doctors you can line up for a Saturday morning appointment?"

"Don't you dare be sarcastic with me. Not today. I'm just trying to help Nancy."

"I'm trying to help her, too. And furthermore I just did. She cares about that money, even if you don't. It was her whole account."

"Oh, Whit! We could just give her a check."

" 'Oh, Whit!' I know we could, but this way the bank pays her back. They're saying to her it's not her fault."

"We already know it's not her fault."

"Listen, what do you want me to do? Go down there and walk around Tribeca and try to find those two shits?"

"No, I want you to think about Nancy."

Carol began to cry, and that made her even angrier, because she hated to lose her self-control in an argument. It made Whit angrier, too. He always said crying was a woman's last refuge in a losing proposition.

"Goddamn it, I *am* thinking about her. That's all I'm thinking about."

"Well, if you'd thought about her earlier,

you wouldn't have let her live down there in the first place." This was such an unfair charge that Carol knew it would take all her skill to defend it.

Whit had no difficulty seeing the opening. "As I recall," he said, in his most infuriatingly reasonable voice, "we both thought it was a great idea for her to be off on her own. In a nice apartment, with a roommate she's known since high school. With new locks on the doors and new grills on the windows. Am I mistaken? Have I forgotten something?"

"Yes, but not in that neighborhood."

"Did you say something against that neighborhood at the time? I thought you said it was romantic. In fact, 'picturesque' is a word I seem to remember hearing."

True, *picturesque* had been Carol's precise word. "You're the one who's supposed to know all about New York real estate. You should have stopped her. You should have said—"

Whit jumped to his feet, pointing his finger at her the way he did when he was convinced he was right beyond any conceivable riposte. "Now let's get something straight, Carol. Tribeca is not Harlem. It's not even the Lower East Side. *Thousands* of people live there, and believe it or not, most of them don't get raped and robbed. I will even venture to say that a very, very high percentage of them do not get raped and robbed."

"Well, my daughter did." She could hear the unpleasant shrillness in her own voice.

"Oh, it's *your* daughter this morning? What an amazing coincidence. Because *my* daughter got raped and robbed, too. Maybe we should compare notes. Maybe together we can come up with a clue."

"That is not the least bit funny."

Whit jabbed his finger at her again, preparatory to another assault. Then he stopped in mid-gesture, arm frozen, staring sheepishly at the doorway.

Carol turned. Nancy was standing there, hollow-eyed and hair tousled, hugging herself with her arms across her chest. She was wrapped in Carol's flowered robe.

"Oh, darling, you're awake."

"How could I be anything else? I heard you two shouting all the way down the hall."

"Well . . . I'm sorry. I guess we're both upset about you."

"Jesus, just what I need this morning. My parents fighting over me. Oh, Dad, put your finger down."

Whit lowered his arm.

"I'm sorry," Carol said again.

"There's some good news," Whit said. He glared at Carol, then smiled at Nancy. "I talked to the bank. They're going to give you back all your money. All of it, the whole five hundred."

"That's good," said Nancy, not sounding all that thrilled. "I was wondering how I was going to pay bills."

"Come, sit down," Carol said, patting the place beside her on the couch. "Want some coffee?"

"Yes, I guess so."

"Sit down. I'll get it for you."

"I can get it, Mom. I'm not crippled."

While Nancy was in the kitchen, Carol said in a low voice, "Now you stop this. We have to help her."

Whit did not answer.

When Nancy came back with her coffee and sat beside Carol, she said, "You know, when I was little and heard you two arguing, I was afraid you were going to get divorced. I really thought that."

"Sometimes we even thought that," Carol said.

"It used to worry me a lot. Basil, too."

"How did you sleep, darling? Do you feel any better?"

"No. Awful. I kept waking myself up with nightmares. Crazy ones. I don't even remember what they were." She shook her head. "I didn't really get to sleep until a little while ago. And then you two started in."

"I'm sorry. How do you feel?"

Nancy thought that over. "Weird. As though I wasn't me. As though I was somebody else."

Carol squeezed her arm. "Well, you are you. You always will be."

Without warning Nancy began to cry, and Carol took her in her arms, holding her tight. Whit plainly did not know what to do. Then he came over and awkwardly patted Nancy's shoulder.

"I wonder," Nancy said between gasps. "I wonder who I am. I wonder if I'll ever be me again."

"Yes," Carol said fiercely, "you will be. You must be."

When the tears stopped, Nancy rubbed her eyes and sat up straight. "Sorry," she said. "That just came over me. Does Basil know? Have you told Basil?"

Carol raised her eyebrows at Whit: you want to explain why you haven't done that?

"We were just going to call him," Whit said, "but he's probably not there."

"Well, let's try anyway. I think I'd like to tell him myself."

"Wouldn't you rather Dad did it? It might be easier."

"No, Pat Ford said it's better if I talk about it. I might as well get in practice."

Nancy picked up the phone and, without

having to look up the number, dialed Basil's room at Trinity College. The three of them sat in silence while the phone rang and rang.

"I guess he's—" Nancy started to say. Then she interrupted herself, a quick warmth coming into her voice. "Pesto? It's me. Did I wake you up?"

"Pesto" had been Nancy's pet name for her younger brother ever since she learned that the main ingredient of his favorite pasta sauce, *pesto genovese*, was fresh basil.

"Too much party, huh? Listen, I called because a real bad thing has happened . . . No, not the folks. To me."

Carol and Whit heard Nancy's end of a very long conversation with her brother—the bank, the street, the gun, the jewelry, the garage, the police, the hospital. They picked up some ugly details they had not heard before.

"Every single orifice," Nancy said. "I just thank God I wasn't a virgin, you know? I don't know what that would have done to me."

When Nancy told Basil about her new dress and how she managed to get it back, Carol felt a jolt of alarm. Nancy had taken a terrible chance to plead and argue with those men. They could just as easily have shot her, right there at the end when it was finally all over. It was obviously a source of pride for Nancy, one small triumph out of the wreckage, but surely the risk had not been worth it.

Near the end of the talk Carol heard the warmth go out of Nancy's voice.

At last Nancy said, "Okay, I have to try to reach Jenny. I'm going to be staying with the folks a few days, I think, so call me here. You want to talk to Mom or Dad?"

She held out the receiver to Whit. "He wants to talk to you, Dad."

Whit said, "Hello, Basil," and then did not say anything for a few minutes, listening. To Carol, his expression seemed to grow blank and cold. Then he said, "No, I don't think so at all. Not at all . . . No, Nancy is all right, the best you could expect . . . They gave her shots and pills for all that . . . Okay, Mom sends love. Keep in touch."

"Why didn't you let me talk to him?" Carol asked. "What was that about?"

"Nothing. He just wanted to make sure she's all right."

"Now Whit—"

"He's upset, naturally."

"But what did he—?"

"I bet I know," Nancy said. Her voice was suddenly so bleak that it hurt Carol to hear her. "Pesto thinks I could have stopped it. Somehow. If I'd really tried. He sort of almost said that to me."

When Whit did not comment, Carol asked him, "Was that it? Did Basil actually say that?"

Whit was annoyed at having to answer. "He's a kid, and he's her brother. He's all worked up. He doesn't know what he's saying."

"Want to bet?" Nancy said. She sighed. "Maybe I'll have better luck with Jenny. If I can find her."

"I thought she was off skiing," Carol said.

"She is, but I think maybe I can find her."

Nancy was certainly her father's daughter when it came to working a telephone. Or perhaps it was her news training in tracking down people. All she had to go on this time was the names of two men who had a season rental for a ski house somewhere in the Stowe, Vermont area.

Using the atlas and the 802 all-points area code for Vermont, Nancy tried 555–1212 information for the two men's names, starting with Stowe itself and then spreading out.

"If it's just a winter rental," Carol said, "they may not be listed."

"One of them's in advertising," Nancy explained. "And Jenny's friend Sid is a lawyer. They're bound to have a listing for weekend crisis stuff."

When nothing turned up in Stowe, Nancy tried Burlington and Montpelier and then Wolcott and Hardwick and Woodbury. She finally found Sid's listing in Morrisville and jotted down the number.

"But they'll all be out skiing, won't they?"

"Mom," Nancy said as she dialed, "you and Dad never did skiing. When you have five couples, there's always somebody who doesn't feel like skiing today. Somebody sprained an ankle, or has the curse, or wants to stay home and make love while the others are on the slopes. There's bound to be—Hello? Hi, this is Nancy Whittredge in New York. I'm trying to reach my roommate Jenny Pines. It's an emergency . . . Okay, good. You don't happen to know the number . . . do you? . . . That's all right, I'll find it. Many thanks."

Nancy looked at her parents, a kind of wild triumph in her eyes. "There! I found out where they're skiing today!"

When this search for Jenny had begun, Carol felt relieved that Nancy had something active to do. Now she was less certain. As she listened to Nancy's next call, she felt sure she could hear something very close to hysteria.

"Good morning. This is Nancy Whittredge in New York City. I have to reach a Miss Jenny Pines, who is skiing there today . . . Just a minute! Just a minute, please. I don't care how many people you have there, this is a police emergency . . . That's right, police emergency. I want you to put up a sign there at the check-in, and another sign at the chair lift . . . All right, both chair lifts. She is to call this number immediately . . .

"Thank you. Now switch me to the cafeteria, please . . .

"Hello, this is Nancy Whittredge in New York City, calling on a police emergency. I want you to put up two signs, right away, one at the head of the food line and one at the beer-and-wine line . . . Right. It should say, 'Jenny Pines, call this number at once . . .'"

When she finished, Whit said, "Nancy, I'm impressed. Do you always use that 'police emergency' stuff?"

"No, I just thought of it."

"Very impressive."

But Nancy seemed to slump after her telephone effort. Carol was alarmed by the abruptness of the change. The life seemed to go out of her daughter all at once, like turning off a light switch.

Carol thought Nancy might feel better if she got dressed. She helped Nancy pick out some clothes—pretty underwear and slacks and a sweater—to replace the hospital garments. It was hard to arouse Nancy's interest, so Carol wound up making the choices. Then she persuaded Nancy to drink some juice and eat part of an English muffin. They talked about going down to Nancy's apartment to get her own clothes, but Nancy said she couldn't visit that neighborhood just now, at least not today. Maybe tomorrow. Maybe never.

When Whit announced that Jenny Pines was calling collect from the ski slope cafeteria, Nancy took it in the bedroom. She was gone a long time. Carol and Whit ignored each other. She was still angry, and she could tell he was, too. Tragedy does not always bring people together.

When Nancy finally emerged from the bedroom, she was crying. "Jenny offered to come right home," she said, "but I told her not to bother. She said she'd come see me the minute she gets back." She sniffled. "I wish she'd come."

"Then why did you tell her not to bother?" Whit asked.

"I don't know."

"Call her back."

Nancy simply shook her head. She wiped her face with her hands.

"Darling," Carol said, "do you know where to reach Tommy? Shouldn't you tell him?"

Nancy shook her head again. "I'm scared to. I don't know how he'd take it."

"Oh, but surely—"

"Mom, I don't *want* to talk to him. I feel so—I feel so *dirty*." She began to cry again.

Carol put her arms around her and held her tight. She cold feel Nancy shaking. Remembering Pat Ford's advice, she said, "Whatever you want, darling."

Whit chose this moment to say, "We forgot to tell you, Nancy. Last night at the hospital, a detective said he needed to talk to you. A Mr. Vincent."

Nancy stepped out of Carol's arms. She looked jolted. "But I already talked to the police. I already told them everything."

"That's what I said. But he still says he has to talk to you. I told him not before noon."

"Jesus, I don't want to go through that again."

"You don't have to, darling. As that nice Pat Ford said, it's up to you to decide. About everything."

"How can I decide, Mom? I don't even feel like me."

The Tainted Scene

In the cool, sunny February dawn, Carl Vincent parked outside the abandoned garage. A blue-and-white police car was on guard across the street. A uniformed female cop, Officer Cruz, summoned back this morning in spite of having worked the evening shift, was standing at the garage entrance—a diminutive figure.

This case was off to a bad start. Although the rape had been reported fifteen hours ago, Vincent still had not talked to the victim. And thanks to her protective father, he would not talk to her for several more hours. Crime Scene Unit, notified last night, had been too busy to get here then, thanks to a homicide in Staten Island, of all places. Rape was a priority crime, but not as high priority as homicide.

Vincent hated delay. Witnesses forgot, evidence deteriorated. He should have talked to the victim last night, and Crime Scene should have been down here last night. Of course, thanks to that small female cop standing right there, the scene was badly tainted.

Unlike a lot of white old timers, Vincent didn't care one way or the other about black cops or Puerto Rican cops or female cops, or, in this case, Puerto Rican female cops. All he cared about was cops who did it right. This one did it wrong.

To add to his general annoyance, his wife Martha, in spite of sixteen years' practice, pretended not to understand why he had to go to work early Saturday morning after working Friday night. "It's my case," he said. Then, as an extra dig, Martha asked if Billy Cooney was working, too. "It's not his case."

Carl Vincent stayed in his car, glaring occasionally at Officer Cruz, until the Crime Scene Unit station wagon arrived. Then he got out to watch them unload their gear. Cruz, he noted grudgingly, stayed at her post by the garage entrance.

Both CSU detectives were younger and slimmer than Vincent. They lifted out their heavy suitcase crammed with cameras, lenses and lights, and then their black forensic kits filled with swabs, vials, tweezers and all the other tools of their trade.

Vincent explained the setup to them: the

garage itself, the narrow entrance, the details of the crime, the fact that some critical evidence had already been removed.

"So it's tainted," one of them said, as though the removal of evidence was Vincent's fault.

The whole reason for the Crime Scene Unit was to insure that evidence was collected expertly and completely. If others picked up evidence, they might contaminate it or lose it. And if an arrest was ever made and if the case ever came to trial, the prosecution would be forced to concede that the evidence had not been collected according to strict police procedure. It was just the kind of admission that could trouble a jury.

"Talk to her," he said, indicating Cruz. "She took it, so she can show you where she found it."

The CSU men got out their cameras. First, the exterior photographs to define the location: up the street, down the street, across the street and then a wide-angle view of the garage door showing the buildings on either side. Then a close-up of the garage entrance. One detective took the pictures while the other wrote down the captions, frame by frame.

While they were shooting, Officer Cruz came up to Vincent. Thin, eager young face. Black eyes, bushy black hair sticking out from

under her cap. She must be close to the
minimum height. Minimum age, too.

"Good morning. I'm Cruz."

Vincent went into what cops called the
hairbag act: the old experienced hand lets the
rookie know that the rookie doesn't know
anything. "Oh, yeah, you're the kid who stole
all my evidence."

She was tough. She didn't flush or cringe.
"It was a mistake," she said. "I didn't want
anything to get lost."

"Don't they teach about that anymore at the
Police Academy?"

"Yes. But I was excited. I forgot."

Her frankness, her refusal to dodge, almost
won him over. "Cops work better when
they're not excited," he said in a milder voice.

When CSU finished the exterior shots, and
before shooting interiors, they opened their
toolboxes and began going over the narrow
garage entrance, inch by inch. With all that
traffic squeezing in and out last night, there
were likely to be clothing fibers caught in the
wooden frame or on the end of the dumpster.
And maybe bloodstains, and maybe human
hairs, and maybe God knows what else.

This was not Carl Vincent's kind of work.
He liked dealing with people. He liked to ask
questions, pore over the answers to figure out
what he still needed to know, then ask more

questions. And then, if things worked out, he would make an arrest. If things continued to work out, the guy would be put away for a good long time. The longer the better. That was Vincent's idea of police work.

He could never do this Crime Scene work. Crime Scene detectives never interviewed or questioned anybody. Their job was to identify and collect everything that might turn out to be evidence, and then to label, catalogue and preserve it.

Not for me, Vincent thought. He was a street cop.

When they finished with the doorway, they took their tripods and floodlights and squeezed inside the garage. Cruz followed behind to show them how and where it had happened. Vincent, too, could now go in for a look, as long as he did not trample over their territory.

But as he studied the opening, gauging its width against his own width, he doubted that he could fit through, even if he took off his coat. He had a vision of his thick chest and shoulders wedged halfway through the opening with the rest of him struggling outside. He even imagined having to call on Cruz and those slim CSU men to extricate him.

He would settle for a look from outside. He always wanted to see where a rape happened, to get the feel of the place, maybe to gain some little insight into the victim's experience, or into the mind of the perp.

He got down on one knee on the sidewalk and looked in past the edge of the dumpster.

The Crime Scene men had set up battery-powered flood-lights to illuminate their work. It was a typical abandoned garage. Bits of trash and rubble lay scattered over the cracked and broken concrete floor. At the back stood a long wooden bench, and above it a single lightbulb dangled from a ceiling cord. The bench held random scraps of paper, odd chunks of wood, a couple of rusty tin cans. Under the relentless floodlights, the garage was bleak, ugly, forlorn—deadly. Vincent tried to imagine how it must have seemed in the dark last night to Nancy Whittredge.

He hated rape more than any other crime. More than homicide. With all the drug killings these days, chances were a homicide victim had as bad a criminal record as his killer. In drug murders, it didn't much matter who killed who.

But Vincent thought of rape in terms of his own wife, his own mother, his own daughters. His mother was now sixty-seven and his daughters were only fourteen and twelve, but age was no protection against a rapist. He had worked on cases where little girls were raped and old ladies in their eighties.

Kneeling in the doorway, he watched the detectives soak up the contents of the garage.

The rough surfaces were not promising for fingerprints. Vincent had hopes for the plastic switch that turned the dangling lightbulb on and off, but the Crime Scene men, after dusting it, said it looked like a useless mess of overprints, one print on top of another. They collected them anyway, lifting them off the switch with wide strips of cellophane tape. Cruz, standing out of their way in the front of the garage, pointed out the spots where she had collected her evidence.

When CSU finished with it, the garage was no longer of technical interest, although Vincent intended to find out who owned it and why that door was held open by that dumpster and why the electricity was still on. No point asking the CSU men what they had found. They would not speculate until after their film had been developed and their evidence analyzed by the lab. Then he would get a full report and a full set of prints.

He said a gruff goodby to Cruz and the CSU detectives and drove back uptown. He parked his car in the lot beside the Twentieth Precinct building on West Eighty-second. A three-story building, dark gray brick for the first floor and then two floors of pebbled concrete. He rode the elevator to the third floor offices of the Manhattan Sex Crimes Squad.

Vincent had no intention of waiting till noon, as requested, to call the Whittredge apartment. He would start right now. Maybe he would get the victim herself and could begin asking questions. If he got her father, Vincent would say he was just calling to set up the meeting. Maybe the father had calmed down this morning and would say come on over now.

The number was busy. He waited a couple of minutes and dialed again. Still busy. He poured a mug of coffee and stirred in two sugars and two spoonfuls of Coffee Mate powdered cream. He knew he should use Sweet 'n Low and skip the cream, but if a cop couldn't enjoy coffee the way he liked it, what was the point of coming to work?

The goddamn Whittredge phone was still busy. Vincent didn't know how he was expected to work on a case if he couldn't even talk to the victim. As he had often done, he could order the telephone operator to break in on the call, but that might infuriate Mr. Whittredge.

Or he could just go over to the Whittredge apartment and break in the door. He had not broken in a door since his days on the narcotics squad, but he hadn't forgotten how, and he certainly had the weight for it. It would be a pleasure to break in the door of a luxury apartment.

The phone stayed busy. He imagined this Whittredge household totally preoccupied with interminable telephone gossip. Obstructing justice.

Well after twelve, the Whittredge phone finally rang, and a woman's voice actually said, "Hello."

Now righteously indignant, Vincent managed to suppress everything he felt like saying. Instead, he said, "This is Detective Vincent. Is Miss Nancy Whittredge there?"

He heard the woman's voice say, "Nancy? It's that detective."

After a moment, a younger woman's voice said, "Hello."

Vincent took a deep breath. Now he could get started. "Detective Vincent, Manhattan Sex Crimes. I've been trying to reach you."

"Oh. Yes, sorry, I guess the phone's been pretty busy." She sounded very nervous. They usually did.

"Yes, pretty busy. I'd like to talk to you."

"What about?"

"I've been assigned to your case. I'd like to go over it with you."

There was a pause. Then she said, "Again?"

She had given her statement to Officer Cruz last night and then had had to repeat her story at Bellevue. But as far as Vincent was concerned, those versions did not count. "Yes. I can come over there."

"Oh." Another pause. "When were you thinking of?"

"Right now."

"Well . . ."

He would not let her delay. "Miss Whittredge, we've already wasted a whole day. You want to catch those guys, don't you?"

Now her voice firmed up. "Yes. Yes, I do."

That was a good sign. "Be there in about ten minutes."

He straightened his tie, rolled down his shirt sleeves, put on his tweed jacket, and combed his curly gray hair. He still looked like a cop.

Vincent had to wait in the spacious marble lobby while a uniformed doorman buzzed the Whittredge apartment and spoke on the intercom. Then the doorman said, "The elevator to your right, sir. Twelve-B."

He walked down a wide carpeted hallway. An expanse of mirrored glass, set in foot-square panels, covered the entire right-hand wall. His reflection was not only large but decidedly hulking. The dark polished wood of the automatic elevator looked as though it had been waxed this very morning.

There were only two apartment doors on the twelfth floor. Neither was marked with a name or a letter. Which was B? He chose the one on the right with an ornate brass knocker.

It made a deep chunky sound. Good thick brass. Instantly the door was opened by a pretty young woman. Her face was unmarked, but she must be the victim.

He had his wallet open to show his ID, but she did not even glance at it. "Please come in," she said.

As he walked past her into a foyer the size of his bedroom, he said, "Always look at a cop's ID, Miss Whittredge. You never know."

He had to reassure her mother and father who, like most well-off people, were unaccustomed to having a police officer in their home. He had to answer a handful of questions from the father, meanwhile taking quick glances around the living room so that he could report to his wife Martha. Martha always wanted to hear details whenever he was in an especially nice apartment. In the sex crimes field, this did not happen often.

At last he and the girl were left alone behind the closed door of "the library." There were more stereo and television components and CDs and cassette tapes than there were books. He took out his notebook and ballpoint pen.

"Okay, Miss Whittredge," he said, "I know you've already done this, and I know it's real hard for you to talk about it. But I want you to take me through it. Right from the start. Don't leave out anything. I don't know, and you

don't know, what might turn out to be important."

After fifteen minutes he knew he had a good
one. In spite of her obvious distress—the pale
face, the twisting hands—she remembered a
lot of details, and when she couldn't remember, she said so. Her fear and desperation had
not kept her from paying attention to her
captors and to her surroundings.

When he pushed her about the garage,
suggesting that the two men might have just
picked the first handy spot, she shook her
head. "No, they knew exactly where they
were going. They knew the neighborhood,
and they knew that garage."

"How do you know?"

"Because as soon as we crossed the street,
they headed right there. They didn't wander
around. Also they knew where the light
switch was. One of them went straight to it in
the dark."

"Which one?" He did not care which one,
but he did care about her memory.

She had to think. She sat there in the chair
opposite him, her body hunched against the
remembered horror, and put her hand over
her face, as though to blot out the present so
that she could recall last night. At last she said,
"It was Bernie. Because the light came on
while the other one was still holding the gun
in my back."

"You sure?"

"Yes."

Her face might be unmarked—no bruises, no cuts, no swellings—but her eyes were tired, and there were lines of strain at the corners of her mouth. While she talked, she kept on twisting her hands. He wished he could let her go. He knew how hard this was.

He had read the description of the perps in the precinct report, but now he wanted to find out how solid it was. "Tell me what they looked like."

She described them, first Bernie and then the other one. Good, thorough detail.

"How sure are you about their height?"

"I'm five-four-and-a-half, and walking beside me, Bernie was just a couple of inches taller. No more than three inches."

"Counting that flattop hairdo?"

She nodded. "And the other one. My father's six feet. When I looked up at him, he wasn't quite as tall as my father. Five-ten, maybe five-eleven—right in there."

"And you never saw him full face?" Vincent was already thinking about the sex crimes picture file.

"No, just profile. And just that once."

"But you think you would recognize him?"

She shivered. "Yes. I think so."

He pretended to consult his notes. "Now I believe you said he was very light-skinned?"

"No. Lighter than Bernie, who was very dark. But not light-skinned. Just lighter than Bernie."

Good. She was sticking to it. "And a little goatee?"

"No, Bernie's the one with the goatee. Very small, just a tuft."

He pretended to catch himself. "Oh, yeah, that's right. Now what finally happened to your bank card? After all that back and forth about the code?"

"I don't remember. I guess they kept it. Or threw it away. Anyway, my father talked to the bank, so the account is canceled. The card's no good anymore."

"Right." He closed his notebook and put his pen in his jacket pocket. "Listen, Miss Whittredge, I have to ask you a favor. I want you to come down there with me tonight. See if we can find them."

He expected her to resist, and she did.

"I don't want to go there. I'd be scared to."

"You'll be safe. We'll go in an unmarked car and take another detective. We'll both be armed. You won't have to get out of the car."

He thought she might be going to cry.

"I'm really tired," she said. The catch in her voice was almost a sob.

"I know, but let me tell you something." He stood up, stiff from sitting so long. He looked down at her. "Let me tell you how they think. They had a great success last night." When she winced, he said, "Not just the rape. They pulled off a successful robbery—five hundred bucks and some nice jewelry. And it was *easy*. They didn't come close to getting caught. And on top of that, they had a long sex party with a pretty girl. You know what they think, Miss Whittredge? They think they are *smart*. They think they are two really smart dudes. So they think, *Hey, man!—Let's do it again*! That's how perps are. That's how they think. If it worked once, it'll work again. And they like to go back to the same place—familiar territory."

He bent down to stare into her sad face, the big eyes, the trembling lips. He was willing her to work with him.

"If they come back tonight, we don't want to miss them."

A Lot of Maybes

The doorman said, "That car is here for you, Miss Whittredge."

Nancy got up from the lobby sofa. In spite of a nap, she still felt tired. Her parents had tried to persuade Detective Vincent to postpone this excursion until tomorrow night, but he was stubborn about it. She was dressed in sweater and slacks and, because it had turned colder, a down jacket—all borrowed from her mother.

Opposite the canopy stood an old black Chevrolet with Detective Vincent at the wheel. As soon as Nancy appeared, the back door opened and a man jumped out. Under his open leather jacket, a gun butt stuck out of a belt holster.

"Hi," he said. "I'm Detective Cooney. Billy Cooney. Okay if I call you Nancy?"

She liked him at once. He was about thirty,

much younger than Detective Vincent. Friendlier, too.

She started to climb in the back seat, but Cooney said, "You better sit up front with Carlo. You'll see better."

They walked around the car, and he held the front door open for her. She got in beside the big dark shape of Vincent.

All the way down to Tribeca, Billy Cooney kept up a steady stream of chatter about cases he was working on, other detectives in the Sex Crimes Squad, the damage that police hours did to his social life. Nancy wondered if he was trying to make her feel at ease or if he was just naturally loquacious. She found it hard to pay attention. She hated having to go back there, especially at night. Exactly the same time of evening as last night, just as Detective Vincent had recommended. Hard to believe it was only last night.

When they crossed Canal Street, Vincent said, "Knock it off, Billy, we got to work." At a stoplight he turned to Nancy. "Keep your eyes open. I'll drive real slow, we'll go back and forth around the area. You see anybody looks anything like them, anything at all like them, sing out. Don't wait to make sure, just tell me."

The light changed.

"We'll start at the bank."

And suddenly there was the brightly lighted cubicle where it began. Nancy could see herself there last night, her dress box under her arm, happy about the party she was going to, drawing out her cash for the week-end ahead.

A different person. A different world.

She must not think about that. She must look for them, Bernie and The Other One. They had caught her. She wanted to catch them.

They cruised the neighborhood, up one street, down the next. No one said anything. Detective Cooney was leaning forward from the back seat, his head between Nancy's and Vincent's as they scanned the streets and sidewalks. With most businesses closed for the weekend, this part of Tribeca was quiet on Saturday night.

Here was the street where they grabbed her. That was the dark corner area where they must have been hiding so they could watch the bank. She could pinpoint within a yard or two the spot where she had heard the foot-steps and then the voice and felt the gun in her back.

The first time they drove past the garage, Nancy felt sick at her stomach. The car slowed to a crawl. There was the awful black opening. Nancy turned her head away.

"No light inside," Vincent said.

They drove on. Back and forth, around and around.

Then Vincent widened the circle. They drove past bars and restaurants where there were more lights and more people. She studied every face and figure. They drove past the bus and subway stops. She looked at each person. They drove past Nancy's apartment, now totally dark with Jenny away skiing. Looking up at the black windows, she did not know how she could live there again. Not for a while, anyway.

Vincent kept returning to the bank and to the garage so that she had to see them over and over again.

After almost two hours he finally called it off. "I guess not tonight," he said. He headed back uptown.

Nancy slumped in her seat. She was exhausted. She realized she had been tense the entire time.

"Now," Vincent said, "I know you're tired, so get a good night's sleep. Sleep late. Then in the afternoon, I want you to come over to the station and look at some pictures."

"But it's Sunday."

"Ha!" Cooney said. "What's Sunday to Carlo?"

"Yeah, I know, Sunday, but I want you to do it while your memory's still fresh."

"What kind of pictures?"

"Pictures of people who might be your two guys."

"Mug shots," Cooney explained. "Sex offenders."

Steering with one hand, Vincent fished in his pocket and handed her a card. "This is the address, Eighty-second between Columbus and Amsterdam. And that's my phone number, in case you remember something you forgot to tell me."

He paused. "Since we're going to be working together, I'm going to call you Nancy and you better call me Carl."

But Nancy had heard Cooney call him Carlo. "Carl or Carlo?"

"Either one."

"We had this woman detective a couple of years ago," Cooney jumped in with the story. "Italian. Nina. Nina Carbaccio. Everybody liked her, a damn good detective, too. She changed all our names to Italian. I was Guillermo. I ask you, do I look like Guillermo? And we had Roberto and Maria and Rafael and Lucia and everything, all Italian, everybody in the squad. Even Big Zeke—he's black and about eight feet tall—she named him Zecco Grosso. We all thought it was pretty funny. But then Nina left, and we all went back to our old names. Except somehow Carlo stuck. Hey Carlo, whatever happened to Nina?"

"Down at headquarters, some desk job. Too bad, she was good on the street. Now listen, Nancy, you be there tomorrow. Don't forget. You're not there by two o'clock, I'm coming after you."

She told the taxi to let her off at the corner on Columbus, and she walked down the block through the falling snow. She dreaded spending the afternoon in this police station. She had dealt with the police many times on news stories, but it was completely different when she was the focus of their attention. She was afraid of their questions and of things they might ask her to do. All she wanted was to stay home with her parents in that safe, safe apartment and try not to think about it.

It was cold enough for the snow to stick to the sidewalk. The gray three-story building was labeled "Twentieth Precinct." Two blue-and-white police cars were double-parked on the street, and a three-wheeled police scooter stood on the sidewalk near the front door.

She walked through the door into a large lobby with a bare linoleum floor. A sign ordered her to check in at the front desk, a thick glass window behind which a uniformed cop was sitting. He was on the phone.

Nancy waited and listened. The cop was asking what was the date of the robbery, as he

leafed backward through a tattered notebook
filled with handwritten entries. Behind him
Nancy could see other cops at other desks.
"Wanted" posters were plastered all over the
walls.

She thought of turning around and going
home. She could just walk out and grab a taxi
and never talk to the police again and never
look at any pictures. But then she thought of
what the two men had done to her.

Finally the cop hung up the phone, and
Nancy told him she had an appointment with
Detective Vincent in Sex Crimes.

"Third floor. Either the elevator or the
stairs."

Did he guess she was a rape victim? Of
course. And of course, everybody on the third
floor would know. She better get used to it. As
Pat Ford told her at Bellevue, it's nothing to be
ashamed of, it wasn't your fault. But she still
felt ashamed, as though she had been caught
doing something wrong. She did not want
people to look at her and know she had been
raped.

She walked up the painted gray stairs to the
offices of the Manhattan Sex Crimes Squad.
Mike Barnes had taught her that whenever an
assignment took her into a new place, she
should immediately think about how to de-
scribe it in a sentence or two, in case the

station asked for atmosphere. She was in the habit of doing this even when not on assignment, just for practice.

Her instant impression of the Sex Crimes office was one of crowded disorder. Formica desks and swivel chairs were crammed into a square bullpen. Phones and typewriters everywhere. The pale yellow cement-block walls were covered with posters and phone lists.

Only two of the desks were occupied. A pretty black-haired woman sat at one, typing furiously at high speed. But since she was using hunt-and-peck rather than the touch system, she had to be a detective, not a secretary. A huge black man with a shaved head sat at another desk, taking down notes on a telephone conversation. She remembered Billy Cooney speaking of a black detective called Big Zeke.

An open door on Nancy's right revealed a more spacious office. An older man wearing glasses sat at a large desk in the center, reading through a sheaf of reports. Nancy said, "Excuse me, I'm supposed to see Detective Vincent."

He looked up. Then to Nancy's surprise, he stood up to greet her. He was tall and thin. "You must be Nancy Whittredge. I heard you were coming over. I'm Sergeant Blaine." He held out his hand and they shook hands. "I expect Carlo's watching the game. Come on."

She followed him across the bullpen and into another crowded office, this one ringed by dark green files and lockers. Down the middle of the room ran two gray tables, with a color TV set at the far end. Detective Vincent was eating what looked like sweet-and-sour pork out of a paper carton while he watched the Sunday afternoon basketball game.

"Visitor for you, Carlo."

Vincent stood up. He wiped his hands on a paper napkin, then wiped his mouth. "Good for you," he told Nancy. He looked at his watch. "You're even early." He folded up the debris of his lunch and stuffed it in a wastebasket.

"I'll leave you," Sergeant Blaine said. And then to Nancy, "Good luck."

"Well," Vincent said. With a final look at the basketball game he turned off the set. "Take your coat off. Get comfortable. You want some coffee?"

One of the iron rules of the news business was that you always took coffee whenever you got a chance. "Yes thanks."

He lifted a coffeepot from a hot plate and poured two mugs. "Cream? Sugar?"

"Just black, please."

He handed her one mug, stirred sugar and milk into the other. "Let's talk for a minute first," he said.

They took chairs at the table. Today Carl Vincent seemed even more determined. His small brown eyes, sharp and tough, stared at her several long seconds before he spoke.

"The pictures you're going to see are men who've committed sex crimes in Manhattan. Most perps do the same crime over and over. Rape or robbery or burglary—whatever—they keep on doing it. Now your two guys, we don't know any pattern, but chances are they maybe committed rape before. Maybe they even got caught. If so, maybe we have a picture of them, or at least one of them. If so, maybe you can pick it out."

"That's a lot of 'maybes.'"

Vincent rubbed his hand over his hair and then down the back of his neck. "Yeah, well that's pretty much what I do for a living. You start with all the 'maybes,' and you get rid of a lot of them, one by one, and then what's left is some 'probablys.' No so many of those. Then you work those over, get rid of the ones that don't fit. If you're lucky, you wind up with just one. Then you got a hit."

"Suppose," Nancy said, "there's no picture?"

Vincent shrugged. "So it gets rid of one set of 'maybes,' and we have to try something else. But you gave me good descriptions, so that's where we'll start."

He stood up, walked over to one of the dark green filing cabinets and pulled out a drawer. It was a long shallow drawer. When Vincent put in on the table, Nancy saw it contained two dense, endless rows of paper cards.

"Now this is hard work," he said. "Really hard, because you have to concentrate. All the pictures in this drawer are male blacks, and after a while you can start thinking they all look alike. But they don't. They really don't." He almost dared her to disagree.

"There's another hard thing. Some of these pictures are pretty old, sometimes three or four years. Take Bernie. Maybe he's a couple of years older now than when they took his picture. Could be he's fatter, could be he's thinner. And the most important thing of all, you can't count on his mustache or his little goatee, because he might not have had them back then. And especially not his flattop hairdo, which wasn't even in style when most of these pictures were taken. So you have to try to forget all the hair, look past the hair and concentrate on the face—the bones, the forehead, the nose, the eyes, the mouth, the chin. They stay the same."

Nancy looked at the drawer. A formidable double row of pictures. Then she noticed that there were insert tags separating the pictures into groups. The tags read *Goatee, Mustache,*

Mustache and Goatee, Clean-shaven, Beard, Beard and Mustache, Glasses.

"If I'm not supposed to pay attention to hair, how come they're all arranged by hair?"

"Well, the hair might stay the same, you never know. Anyway, that's the way it's organized." He stood up. "I'm going to leave you alone, but I'll be right next door. If you find a picture that could be one of them, pull it out. You don't have to be positive. Anything possible, pull it out. And don't try to go too fast. Sometimes these picture cards stick together, and you don't want to miss one because it might be *the* one. Okay?"

"Okay."

Suddenly he put his hand on her shoulder. A hard heavy hand that made her feel glad he was on her side. "Some rape victims can't go through this," he said, looking down at her with great seriousness. "They tell us they're going to, but then after ten or fifteen minutes, they can't take it. It's too much for them. Too hard to look at the faces. They quit." He squeezed her shoulder. "I don't want you to quit. You're not going to quit."

"No," Nancy said, "I'm not."

"Good." He patted her shoulder. "Let's get 'em."

Left alone, she pulled the drawer toward her and looked at the first card. It was a three-by-five with two color pictures, a profile on the left and a full face on the right. It was a black man with a goatee wearing a dark blue T-shirt. He was older and heavier than either Bernie or The Other One, and his nose was too broad. The face staring into the camera was bland and expressionless. No resemblance. She wondered what crime he had done to what woman, and under what circumstances.

She flipped the card and looked at the next one. A mean and dangerous face glared back at her. She felt a jolt of terror. She shivered and looked away. *I don't want to do this.* Then she remembered her promise to Carlo and to herself and looked again. She would not want to meet this one, anywhere, ever. He had ragged corn-row hair, but she was not supposed to pay any attention to hair. His skin color was too light to be Bernie, and in profile the jawline was nothing like The Other One's. A real bad-looking man, but not one of her men.

She took a swallow of coffee. Next card . . .

She flipped through perhaps a hundred cards before one stopped her. A young, cheerful face with the right dark skin color and a flaring nose. Could it be Bernie? She closed her eyes to bring back the face she had seen in the dim light of the garage. Then she opened her eyes and looked again at the file picture. It didn't feel right. But did she really know what Bernie looked like? She had a moment of panic. How good was her memory? How good was that mental photograph she had taken? Suppose, after all, she could not remember him?

She closed her eyes again, this time for a full minute. Yes, she could still see Bernie's face, locked away. When she opened her eyes, she was certain this file picture could not be Bernie. But if she had that level of doubt about Bernie, how good was she likely to be about The Other One, whom she had seen only briefly under the streetlight?

In something approaching despair, she turned to the next card . . .

When the door opened, she was a third of the way through one side of the drawer.

"How's it going?" Vincent asked.

"Terrible. I'm not finding anything."

"Take a break. You want some more coffee? Are you hungry?"

"No, I had lunch before I came over." She pushed the drawer away. "I don't know. I'm not getting anywhere."

"Yeah, it's tough going. Lots of faces. Better take a break. There's a bathroom down the hall."

"No, I guess I'd rather keep going. Although— I don't know—it seems pointless."

"Well, it isn't." His voice sounded stern. "All right, do another twenty minutes or so, but then I'll make you stop. You don't want to lose your concentration."

When he left, she went back to the drawer. She wished she were looking for just one person instead of two, because then it would go much faster. The quick, easy ones to skip past were the faces that were too old, or that had scars or were too fat. But with almost all the other pictures she had to ask herself first, *Is that Bernie? Does the skin color match? Are the features right?* And when the answer was no, then she had to ask, *Could it be The Other One?*

The variety of hairstyles and clothes was mesmerizing. Vincent had told her these were not prison pictures but had been taken shortly after arrest. Although she had yet to see a flattop, she saw every other kind of hair: crew cuts short and long, corn rows, dreadlocks, shaggies, half-balds, pony-tails. Clothes were even more varied: jackets, T-shirts, old-fashioned white undershirts with shoulder straps, a bright blue net shirt, a red-and-white football jersey with a huge 55 numeral, gaudy sports shirts, a few naked torsos. There was even one man immaculately dressed in a business suit and tie.

But mostly it was faces, faces, faces . . .

Vincent came back and made her stop. He

did not care whether she had a cup of coffee, or went to the bathroom, or took a walk around the block, or went around the corner to Columbus Avenue for a slice of pizza, or even watched the basketball game, but she had to take a break.

"Okay," Nancy said. She pushed back her chair and stood up to stretch. "I guess I do need to stop for a while. But I'd really like to finish with this. I want to get it over with."

"You can't do it all today."

"Why not?" Nancy looked down at her spot in the drawer. "I've done a lot of pictures. And I'm getting the hang of it. I think maybe I could finish when I come back. Or most of it, anyway."

"Well," Vincent said, a little sheepishly, "there's another drawer."

"Another drawer! How many pictures do you have here?"

"Oh, maybe three thousand or so." Her face must have shown dismay, because he quickly added, "But you don't have to look at all of them, of course. You don't have to look at any whites. Or Hispanics. Or women."

"Thanks a bunch!"

"You'll have to do the parolees, but there aren't so many of those." When she looked puzzled, he said, "They're paroled, they get out of prison. You don't expect them to be cured, do you?"

"I don't know." She felt deeply discouraged by what still lay ahead. She should never have come.

"We had this case once. After the perp raped a woman in her apartment, he wanted to sit around and discuss politics with her. One detective said, 'Hey, that sounds just like so-and-so, he used to do that, talk politics every time. Only he's supposed to be in prison.' So we looked him up on the computer, and sure enough, he'd been paroled three months ago. We picked him up, and the woman ID-ed him right off. Back he went. So you got to do the parolees."

"Anything else?"

Vincent did not answer the question. "One thing at a time," he said.

How Was Your Weekend?

Breakfast at the Whittredge apartment had never been a social occasion. In fact, it was the most aloof hour of the day.

When Nancy and Basil were children in school, they were supposed to speak only to each other and in low voices while they ate their cereal and English muffins and drank their milk. That way they did not disturb their parents. Down at one end of the table their father was absorbed in the *Wall Street Journal*, and at the other end their mother was absorbed in the *New York Times*. Nancy used to marvel that her parents could eat and drink without ever taking their eyes from their respective papers.

Saturdays were more congenial because their father did not go to his office, the children did not have to hurry off to school, the *Wall Street Journal* did not publish and the *Times* was skimpy. There was actually conversation. But then, alas, came the Sunday *Times* which, like some enormous blob from outer space, squashed everything in its path.

Given this heritage, Nancy though it surprising that she had been attracted to the news business, although to the spoken word, not the printed word.

It was even more surprising, this Monday morning that the *Journal* and the *Times* lay unopened and ignored beside her parents' breakfast places. Here the three of them were, drinking coffee and looking at each other and even talking to each other.

"I think you ought to take some time off," her mother said. "This week or, at the very least, a day or two."

"But I feel all right. And I've got to do something. I can't just sit around feeling sorry for myself."

"Why not? Why shouldn't you?"

"Pat Ford said the sooner I can do normal things, the better I'll feel."

"That sounds right to me," her father said. "Going straight to work is probably the best thing."

"Oh, Whit, what do you know about it?"

"Just about as much as you do, I guess."

"You happen to be a man."

"No kidding? Is that supposed to disqualify me?"

"No, not entirely, but just the same—"

"Listen, please don't fight over me," Nancy said.

She could see solicitude sweep over both their faces.

"We're not fighting over you," her mother said. "We're just trying to help. If you really want to go to work, fine. But you're not going back to your apartment, are you?"

Her mother sounded alarmed at that idea, and it alarmed Nancy, too. She shook her head. "No, I can't face that. I couldn't walk around those streets. Just driving around with the detectives Saturday night, even though they had guns, I felt scared. I can't help it. I know they're still out there. I couldn't walk around thinking I might run into one of them. You know, maybe I'd just turn a corner and right there . . ." The thought of it stopped her in mid-sentence. "But I do need some of my own clothes."

"I could go down with you. Or Whit, you could take her, couldn't you?"

"Sure. Well, not during the day, but this evening."

Nancy said, "The detectives want me to do patrol again tonight."

"But darling, you said that was a waste of time."

"It was, but Carlo says maybe that's because it was a weekend night. Maybe on a weekday they'll come back and try the bank again."

"Put him off," her father said. "I'll help you get your clothes tonight, and you can do the patrol tomorrow night."

"He's not so easy to put off. Anyway, I've already thought about it. Jenny gets back from skiing, so I'll ask her to bring me up a suitcase. She won't mind. She knows where all my stuff is and what I'll need."

"I'd be glad to do it, and you'll be safe with me."

"Dad, thanks, but I'm not going to feel safe down there with anybody. Jenny won't mind."

"When does Tommy get back from the conference?" her father asked.

Nancy could tell her father thought Tommy's return was important. That Tommy would be a real comfort to her. Her father had no way of knowing how confused she felt about Tommy, about how to tell him and about what he would say.

"They're all flying back tonight."

"So you'll see him tomorrow?"

"Yes, I guess so."

"When you talk to Jenny," her mother said,

"as long as she's coming here anyway, will you ask her to bring back our Waterford glasses?"

Nancy's shift did not begin until eleven o'clock, but she went in an hour early. By now her colleagues must know what happened to her Friday night, and she hoped to get all that talk out of the way before starting work.

The only good thing about WZEY's office building was its midtown location. Handy for taxis, subways, even buses as a last resort, to get anywhere in the city. But the building itself was old, and the huge elevators, more like freight elevators, were creaky. She wished they could be in Rockefeller Center like WCBS, but Weezie's owners refused to pay that high rent. Instead, they had gutted the whole ninth floor of this dilapidated Broadway building and turned it into a modern, handsome station with all the latest equipment. After that investment everybody was sure they were stuck here forever.

Nancy braced herself before walking through the glass doors into the newsroom. Remember, she told herself, it wasn't your fault. And as Bellevue's "Emotional First Aid Sheet" reminded her, *The rape has not diminished your worth as a person.* No matter what anybody else thinks or says.

She walked through the door.

A dozen people sat on and around the central news deck, a raised platform that dominated the long, bright room. Phil Eckersley, the day editor, had the commanding seat in the center of the deck where he could look down at the broadcast booths and the editing booths. He was surrounded by service aides with headphones and by young NPAs, the news production assistants whose job was to do Phil's bidding and make life as easy for him as possible. Nancy and Ted Meadows had worked as NPAs together before they were made reporters.

Nancy decided she might as well face the music right at the top. She crossed the deck area to the editor's chair and said, "Good morning, Phil."

He looked up. "Oh, hi, Nancy." Then he went straight back to monitoring the on-air words coming out of the broadcast booth.

She could not believe it. Phil was avoiding having to deal with her. He was excellent at his job, but as a person he did not compare to Mike Barnes, who was the late-afternoon and evening editor. It was a trade-off: she preferred to work days and have her evenings free, but it meant she got more of Phil's shift and less of Mike's.

She said good morning to the others on the

deck but again got only a casual greeting. She was baffled. Had they all decided to pretend that nothing had happened? Impossible. The Weezie gang wasn't like that. Besides, they could not all be such good actors. Nobody's face revealed any knowledge of what had happened to her.

Then she realized what it was. They didn't know. They still didn't know. For three days, Mike Barnes had told no one. She remembered now that she had asked him not to tell, and he hadn't, but in some ways that made it more difficult. What was she supposed to do now?

As she walked around the back of the deck to pick up an assignment sheet and her equipment bag, she saw the writer Helen Cobb talking to Ted Meadows.

"Hi," she said. "Anything good happening today?"

"Not so you'd notice," Ted said. "Not even a decent plane crash."

This was an office joke because their most frantic day and night during the entire past year had been the big plane crash at La Guardia. Every reporter had worked on it, double shifts, and the station had called in every freelance to help out.

Then Ted asked what, under the circumstances, was a ludicrous question. "How was your weekend?"

How was she supposed to answer that? Well, Pat Ford had said go ahead and talk about it. All right, she thought, suddenly making up her mind, these are my friends. Here goes.

"Terrible. I got raped and robbed."

She saw shock and disbelief hit their faces.

Helen Cobb said, "Are you serious?"

Ted grabbed her arm. "Tell me you're kidding."

"I wish I could."

Helen stopped Julie Adams, another writer who was just walking past.

"Julie, you better listen to this. Nancy got raped."

Within a few minutes, Nancy was telling her story to ten people, including the station's news director, who rarely came out of his corner office, and the executive director's secretary, who was never supposed to leave her boss's phone untended.

As Nancy described the night and answered questions, some merely curious but most sympathetic, she realized Pat Ford was right: it really was better to talk about it than to conceal it.

When she told what happened in the garage, her audience was dead silent. No one interrupted as she tried to say, in acceptable language, what they had done to her. The women in particular looked horror-struck, but she could see the men were shaken, too.

At the end, there was a shocked silence. Then Ted Meadows said, in real anger, "Nancy, those two guys weren't blacks. Those were *niggers.*"

"Hey," Phil Eckersley called down from the news deck, "isn't anybody working around here?"

They all looked guilty and began to split up, but the news director, who outranked Phil, said, "Nancy's been raped and robbed."

"What?"

"Friday night."

"Jesus, Nancy, I'm sorry. That's terrible. Are you all right?"

"Yes. I mean, sort of."

"Why are you here? Why did you come in?"

"I'd rather be working."

At the assignment desk, she picked up the day's schedule and saw that this morning she had the high school principal, William Kirkus, who was under fire from his own school board for being too fierce a disciplinarian. She had never met Kirkus, but he was the kind of story she liked, a strong person in trouble for over-doing the right thing. In the afternoon she was supposed to follow up on her good story of last week about vicious bull terriers attacking people and other dogs. Today she was supposed to find out what the ASPCA thought about the controversy and about bull terriers in general.

A Class 3 story if there ever was one. Class 1 stories were the real news and had to run every twenty minutes, updated as often as necessary. Class 2 stories were supposed to run at least once and maybe twice an hour unless more important news broke. Class 3 stories might or might not run at all, depending.

She checked to see if Ted Meadows had been given any better stories, but he hadn't. As he said, it was a nothing day—at least so far. But one of the things she liked best about local news reporting was that you could never be sure. She never touched the regular standbys—sports and weather and traffic and the stock market and City Hall—but all the rest of New York City was a wide-open possibility every hour of every day. Anything could happen, and when it did, she might become part of it.

She took her beige canvas shoulder bag out of her locker and checked through it. That was another thing Mike Barnes had drilled into them: never take your equipment for granted, especially when you've been off for a couple of days. She went through the compartments to make sure everything was there and functioning.

The black Sony recorder in a leather case to protect it from damage. A clean tape cassette in the recorder. Backup batteries and cassettes. The microphone with its WZEY "mike flag," always to be held in such a way that the call letters would show up on camera if television was covering the same event—good free promotion for the station. The lightweight portable telephone, with batteries charged. The headset. The steno notebook and ballpoint pens. The address book with all her sources and contacts. Kleenex and Tampax. And the stack of quarters for pay phones.

Sometimes the portable battery phone developed technical troubles or even went dead. Sometimes the station told her that reception was poor and that she should use a pay phone instead. There was nothing worse than standing outside a phone booth with a good story and no quarters.

She picked up a new beeper and made sure that the batteries were okay. The beeper had only one signal, which meant *Call in immediately.*

Principal Kirkus was half an hour late for the interview in his office. Considering that school bells rang all day long to announce the exact time, educators were surprisingly tardy. But Kirkus was worth waiting for, a fierce, determined man with a lot on his mind and no inhibitions about saying it. Because he was outspoken not only about school discipline and interfering school boards but also about lazy parents and willful children, she taped more than she needed. This story could only run sixty seconds—ninety at most, if things were slow—but she had enough good quotes for several follow-ups through the day.

She called Phil Eckersley on her portable and told him what she had and how she thought it could best be used. He sent one of his assistants to an edit booth to take in her story. Since this story was not live but would be edited into various segments at the station, she gave them several alternate lead-in lines and transitions so that Kirkus's words would always make sense to the listener. Then she ran the principal's comments into the phone and closed with "Nancy Whittredge, WZEY."

A good story, especially if they gave it enough air time. She hoped Pat Ford would hear it and know she was back on the job.

At a deli near the high school, she bought a large styrofoam container of black coffee and took a cab to the ASPCA offices at East Ninety-second near the river. There was no lunch break during a shift. Everybody theoretically worked an eight-hour shift including one hour off for lunch, but through one of those curious union-management compromises, that hour came only at the end of the day's work.

The cab was still heading east when her station beeper went off. She dug out her phone and called the desk.

As soon as she spoke to Phil, she told the driver, "Turn right at the corner. I want to go to Third and Forty-eighth, as fast as you can."

"Make up your mind, lady."

No bull terrier reprise today. A speeding gypsy cab had swerved to avoid a truck, bounced over the curb onto the sidewalk, hit an undetermined number of pedestrians, and then smashed into the plate glass windows of two stores. Not a plane crash, to be sure, but no longer a nothing day.

Her taxi could only get within two blocks of the scene. She hopped out and ran, her ten-pound shoulder bag bouncing awkwardly. She used her press card to get through the police barrier. She was out of breath from running when she called the station to say she was here.

"All right. Ted's there and he has the sidewalk and the ambulance crews. You do the stores. Try to find somebody who saw the cab actually hit the windows. Bing's on his way, too, and when he gets there, he'll do the police. Call it in soonest. You have extension Forty-six."

"What about the cab driver?"

"Police custody, no interviews. Get going."

Ambulances. Police cars. Bodies. Stretchers. Medics. Cops. A tow truck. A fire engine, even though there was no fire. Television crews. And there on the sidewalk, with its crumpled hood jammed inside the shattered display window of a bookstore, was the brown gypsy cab that had caused all this. Jagged glass shards covered the sidewalk.

The key thing on a live disaster story was not to get too excited, not to make any technical goofs in recording and transmission. Too bad Ted got here first and won the sidewalk scene where there were bound to be more victims, dead or injured, than inside the stores. But there was enough here for everybody. She hauled out her mike and recorder and went to work.

For two hours WZEY drove all out on the story, airing a constant stream of reports from Nancy and Ted and Bing, accompanied by background information and complaints from City Hall about illegal gypsy cabs. Nancy worked both stores to the hilt, persuading people not to leave until she had a chance to tape them.

Her favorite was the plump, middle-aged lady who had been standing at the bookstore cash register, paying for the latest Danielle

Steele with her Visa card, when the cab crashed into the window ten feet in front of her. Eleanor Harris had been terrified at "this awful sound, like an explosion," and at "all that broken glass flying right past my nose." There was still terror in her voice when Nancy interviewed her. Phil Eckersley said it was very good, but Nancy knew it was better than that.

Only after Weezie had wrung everything possible out of the accident, only after the glass had been swept up, the ambulances departed, the cab towed away, the gaping storefronts barricaded, and the police barriers removed, did Phil Eckersley tell her that a detective from the Sex Crimes Squad had called her three times. "We didn't want to distract you," Phil explained.

She had actually managed to forget about it, but now she thought, with a great surge of hope, *Maybe Carlo caught them.* Why else would there be three calls? Her portable phone was signaling low battery after the day's heavy use, so she found a pay booth. Her hand was shaking with excitement as she dropped in the quarter.

"Is Detective Vincent there? It's Nancy Whittredge returning his call."

By the way he said hello, she knew he had not caught them. "You're a damn hard person to get hold of."

"I've been working."

"Listen, I got a better idea about tonight. Why don't we pick you up at your radio station instead of at your parents'? That way we get an earlier start, and we'll be closer to where we're going."

She was tired and hungry, as well as disappointed that he had no good news. "I'm not sure I'm going tonight."

"Yes you are. You might catch them."

"I thought *you* were supposed to catch them."

"Pick you up at six sharp."

"I won't have eaten."

"I'll bring you a candy bar."

It was the same beat-up Chevrolet but a different detective in the back seat, Zeke Matthews, the huge black man with the shaved head. He was as quiet as Billy Cooney was talkative. He looked as though he could pick up a full-grown rapist in each hand.

While Nancy ate her Milky Way on the drive down to Tribeca, Carlo filled her in on the news, such as it was. Two detectives had canvassed the neighborhood, door to door, but nobody had seen anyone answering to Nancy's descriptions of Bernie and The Other One. The bank's tellers and officials also came up blank on the descriptions.

The garage, the detectives learned through Con Edison's electricity account for that address, was owned by Schwarz Construction, a small firm consisting chiefly of one Frank Schwarz, who was trying to sell both his firm and the garage. He had never hired anyone answering the descriptions. He was surprised to learn that his garage had been used for any purpose except storing his dumpster. After a stern police warning, he promised to move his dumpster all the way inside the garage and lock the door.

"Con Edison," Carlo said, "they really cooperate. You ask them, they tell you. Not like the phone company. Used to be, we could call the phone company about any address in the city, and they'd give us the name and phone number. Now we have to get a court order before they tell us."

"Stacking the cards," Zeke volunteered from the back seat. "Anything we want from anybody these days, the cards are stacked."

"Why is that?" Nancy asked. "I thought everybody cooperated with the police."

"Got to be fair to all the nice criminals," Zeke said, then lapsed back into silence.

Vincent grunted. Then he said, "We might have something going at the lab. Your wallet."

Nancy remembered Officer Cruz picking her wallet out of the dumpster.

"Nothing doing on the wallet itself, you can't get any prints on corrugated leather, but there's some fingerprints on your credit cards. Probably yours, but who knows? Anyway the lab's giving the cards the super-glue treatment overnight, and they'll know more tomorrow."

"Glue?"

"Yeah. Well, not the glue itself, but the fumes from the glue. It brings out prints much better and clearer than dusting powder. It's some kind of chemical in the fumes."

"Cyanoacrylate," Zeke said.

"Yeah, I didn't major in chemistry."

Nancy was thinking back. "Bernie went through my wallet to get my bank card."

"Yeah, I told them that. So maybe the lab can develop the prints, and maybe they're not all yours, and maybe one of them is Bernie's, and maybe his prints are on file."

"All your maybes."

"Yeah. Anyway, we'll take your prints tonight when we go back to the station."

"I'm not going back to the station. I'm going home after this."

"No, you aren't. You have to keep looking at those pictures."

"Not tonight. I'm tired."

He thought that over and then made what was, for him, an enormous concession. "Tomorrow morning, then."

"I have to go to work."

"Not till eleven, you said."

"Carlo! For God's sake, I have a full-time job."

They were within two blocks of the bank cubicle, where they would begin tonight's patrol. He took his eyes off the road long enough to look at her.

"Nancy, being a rape victim is a full-time job. If you want to catch them."

Was It Exciting?

By phone she and Jenny went over the list of clothes she would need. Shoes and sneakers. Her parka. All sweaters, skirts and slacks. All underwear. Toilet articles and cosmetics and her blow-dryer. A couple of blouses. Her woolly yellow robe. The red-flowered knit dress, just in case. Earrings and bracelets. No need for gloves or scarves or slippers, she would go on borrowing those from her mother. Same with snow boots— Carol had an extra pair and there was no reason for Jenny to carry more than she had to.

"It's okay," Jenny said. "Sid's going to drive me up, so I can bring anything. That new gold dress in the closet, you want that, don't you?"

The dress. "No. No, leave that."

"You sure? I'll bring it up on the hanger. I won't even muss it."

It was too difficult to explain, even to Jenny,

how she felt about that dress. "No, I don't see any big parties ahead just now."

"Okay. Listen, are you all right?"

"I don't know. But at least I found out today that I can work."

"I can't wait to see you, sweetie."

"Me, too."

Nancy meant it. Although she occasionally ran into girls she had known way back in grade school, Jenny was by far her oldest true friend. Classmates and close friends straight through high school. They had worked together on the school paper and the yearbook, and they had played on the school's ghastly field hockey team, which had gone through two complete seasons without winning a single game. They spent so much time together that their parents became friends as well. Jenny called Nancy's parents Whit and Carol, and Nancy called Jenny's Sam and Ellie.

Even going to different colleges had not changed anything. They had made their own new friends, of course, but during holidays and vacations they still saw each other all the time. Even after two or three months of separation they never lost the closeness. It was always right there, waiting to be picked up. They could, and did, share confidences about everything, especially men.

When they found jobs after college—Jenny

didn't quite "find" hers, since it was in her father's electronics firm—they were able to do what they had always talked about: share an apartment. Whit found the apartment through his real estate friends, and the two mothers supplied most of the furniture and kitchenware, but it was still very much their own place.

When Jenny arrived with the two suitcases, she was alone. She dropped the suitcases, and they hugged each other.

"Let me see you," Jenny said. She held Nancy by the shoulders and studied her. "You look like yourself. Pretty much, anyway."

"I don't feel like myself. Where's Sid?"

"I sent him home so we could talk. Where are Whit and Carol?"

"Out to dinner."

"Good, then we really can talk. Let's have a big sloshy drink, and you can tell me about everything."

"I can't drink, Jenny. I'm on this medication, and they won't let me drink."

"Listen, don't let anybody push you around."

This sounded bizarre after what had been done to her Friday night. People kept tossing off casual comments that meant one thing to them but meant quite another to Nancy. It was as though there were two separate languages, hers and everybody else's.

"Come on," she said, "I'll get you a Scotch, and you can watch me unpack."

They took the Scotch and the suitcases into Nancy's bedroom.

Jenny said, "It's sure been a long time since we had a talk in the hencoop." That had been their high school word for each other's bedroom. Jenny flopped down on the bed, just like old times, and kicked off her shoes. "How are you really?"

Nancy lifted the bigger suitcase onto the bed, unfastened the catches and raised the lid. She did not know what to answer, how to answer, so she settled for saying what Jenny probably wanted to hear. "Pretty good. Considering. I'm sorry I made you bring up so much stuff."

"*Por nada.* Are the cops getting anywhere with those two pricks?"

"Not yet." Nancy began lifting out the folded clothes and laying them on the bed. Maybe wearing her own clothes instead of her mother's would help restore her sense of identity. "They've got me looking at all these pictures of sex criminals. It's scary, even though they're just pictures."

"Yeah, I suppose so. Aren't the cops themselves doing anything?"

"Oh, sure. But so far nothing's turned up. My detective, the one who has my case, he says we just have to keep trying."

"What was it like?"

Nancy looked up from her clothes. "What?"

"The rape. What was it like?"

"How do you mean?"

"Well, you know, every woman worries about getting raped. You can't help wondering what it would be like. I mean, was it at all exciting?"

Nancy looked at her. Jenny was propped up against the pillows. Her expression was one of genuine curiosity. Nancy did not know what to answer.

"Did you—well, did you come?"

"Jesus Christ."

"I mean, you said they did it to you a lot of times. I just wondered if you had an orgasm."

"You're not even trying to be funny, are you?"

"Don't get sore, sweetie. I was just asking."

First Basil, her own brother. Now Jenny, her oldest, closest friend.

No one knew what rape was like until it happened to you. It didn't matter how much you'd heard about it or read about it or thought about it. But the suggestion that Nancy might have found it sexually stimulating made her suddenly, explosively furious.

"Try it sometime! Just try it sometime!"

Get Back on the Bicycle

The granite boulder, jagged and huge, was falling on her out of the dark sky. It was falling straight toward her. It was going to crush her—smash her. Lying flat on the ground, she had only seconds to escape. She tried to roll out of the way, but she could not move. She was frozen. The boulder made a great roaring sound as it hurtled toward her. She opened her mouth to scream.

She woke up, shaking. She reached for the table lamp, almost knocking it over, turned it on and sat up in bed. She rubbed her hands hard against her cheeks. She took deep breaths.

How long will this go on?

She was in her own bedroom where she had slept for most of twenty years. Of course, it

173

did not look the same now. When she and
Jenny moved down to Tribeca, her mother
had redecorated it into a guest room. Nancy's
old flowered wallpaper had been scraped
away, and the walls were now painted soft
gold. The curtains were grown-up gray silk
instead of little-girl fluffy pink muslin. Her old
cork billboard, where she used to pin reminder notes to herself alongside pictures of
favorite rock stars and movie stars, was re-
placed by an abstract modern seascape. Her
mother could not bear to throw out Nancy's
stuffed animals—Babar and Celeste and the
squashy purple lion and the others—but they
were out of sight, stored on the top shelf of the
closet. Most of the furniture—the lamps,
chairs, bureau, bedside tables—was new.

She could not sleep after the boulder. She
got out of bed and put on her yellow robe over
her nightgown. Nancy almost never wore a
nightgown, but now it made her feel safer, a
slim sheath of protection for her body.

Her body.

She walked to the full-length mirror on the
closet door, one of the few things her mother
had not changed, and looked at herself. She
looked the same. Almost the same. A bit
hollow under the eyes, but almost the same.
An illusion, a lie of the mirror. She was not
the same at all, not the same person, not the

same woman. The woman—and long ago the young girl—who used to stand in front of this mirror to study herself had been totally different. Nothing bad had ever happened to her.

How old had Nancy been when she begged her mother for this big mirror? Somewhere in her early teens. Her argument to her mother had been that she needed to see the overall effect when she dressed for school or, more important, for a party. But this was subterfuge. What she really wanted to see was her whole new body. The breasts she had waited for, that took so long to appear. The new curves of her legs and hips, the soft little bush of hair that meant she was grown up.

The more her body filled out and developed, the more she liked and admired it—right here in this mirror. She remembered the first time she had gone to bed with a boy, she had come home and undressed and stood here looking at herself naked. She *must* look different. She felt different.

This woman tonight, standing here in the cuddly yellow robe, felt different, too. Horribly different. Destroyed. And yet it did not show in the mirror. Tonight she would not take off the robe and nightgown for a better look. She did not want to see her body, or touch it, or let anyone else touch it. She wondered if she would ever get over it.

She felt terribly alone in the night.

She pulled a chair into the closet and stood on it to reach the top shelf where the stuffed animals were stored. She took down Celeste, good Queen Celeste, Babar's wife. Celeste, once sparkling white, had turned so gray from constant handling that she had had to be dry-cleaned once a year. At the moment she was in her gray stage. And probably always would be from now on.

Nancy took Celeste to bed with her, as she used to do years ago. She finally fell asleep.

In the morning while they were having breakfast, the phone rang in the library. Her mother answered it, then came back to the breakfast table.

"It's Tommy," she said.

Nancy sat still for a moment. She had dreaded calling him. She had put it off on the grounds that he must be exhausted after getting in late from his conference.

"He already knows," Carol said. "He called you at home, and Jenny told him."

Her father looked up from the *Journal*. "Jenny shouldn't have done that. She should have left it to Nancy."

"Maybe it's easier for Nancy that Jenny told him."

Nancy wasn't so sure. She wasn't sure of anything. "How does he sound?"

"Just like himself. Very concerned about you, of course."

"What did he say?"

"Darling, I really think you should—"

"Carol, all Nancy asked was what did he say. What *did* he say?"

"I think that should be between Tommy and Nancy."

"But he spoke to you, didn't he? Is it a secret?"

Nancy left her parents bickering. In the library, she stared at the beige phone, lying there off the hook on the end table. She was afraid to pick it up. She guessed she had to.

"Hello," she said.

"Nancy! This is just awful. You should have called me in Bermuda. Jenny just told me. Are you all right? How did it happen? Are you all right?"

"I don't know how I am."

"How do you mean you don't know? Jenny said you weren't hurt."

What was the right answer to that? "No, I wasn't hurt, if that's what you mean. Nothing broken, anyway."

"Thank God for that. Listen, when can I see you? Suppose I come over right now before work?"

She hesitated. "I have to go to the police station."

"Now? This morning? What for?"

His voice sounded offended, when what she needed was comfort and warmth. She did not feel like explaining, and anyway it would have been difficult.

"We're trying to catch them," she finally said. It was the first time she had thought of the detectives and herself as *we*. As though they were a team. And in a way they were. She knew most of them now by their first names. "I have to help."

"But Jenny said you didn't know who they were. Just two goons off the street."

"Yes, but I saw them, so I've been looking at mug shots. Hundreds of them, but they aren't there. I finished all the pictures, and they aren't there."

He did not seem interested in that ordeal. "Nancy, I have to *see* you. I want to *hear* about all this."

Would she have to tell her story all over again? She was getting tired of telling it. Of course, this was Tommy, but how do you tell your lover this kind of story? She felt awkward about talking to him in private. How would he feel about her? She needed some safe, neutral place. "Why don't we meet at the bistro after work?"

"Well, if that's the soonest you can make it, sure. Six-thirty?"

"Fine. And Tommy?"

"Yes?"

She was surprised to find a sudden catch in her voice. "Tommy, don't have an office crisis tonight."

"Don't worry, I'll be there. And everything's going to be all right."

How do you know?

Carlo was waiting for her in the Sex Crimes bullpen. In a strange way, she was quite at home here. She said good morning to all the gang and accepted a cup of coffee.

She asked Carlo, "You hear anything about those fingerprints?"

He shook his head. "Too soon. We'll hear some time this morning if the glue turned up any prints of value. If it did, then they have to mark them up and then run them through the computer. To see if there's a match."

"Gee, maybe . . ."

"Yeah, maybe. But don't count on it. The prints could be anybody's."

"I won't. So what's this new step you mentioned?"

She recognized the sheepish look that came over his face. It meant he wanted to put her to work on something she wasn't going to like.

"Bring your coffee, and we'll go downstairs. It's easier to explain once we're there."

"Explain what?"

He didn't answer. He walked her down to the second floor and along a dingy corridor until they came to a gray door with a sign reading "C.A.T.C.H." Beneath it were the words "Computer Assisted Terminal Criminal Hunt." Carlo pushed through the door.

They were in a large square office with a gray linoleum floor and, in the center of the room, a cluster of light gray Formica tables. Around the walls stood row after row after row of dark green file cabinets holding drawer after drawer after drawer. Nancy knew right away what they were.

"More pictures! But you said I was finished."

"Yeah, well these are different. This here is Detective Olliphant. Ollie, this is the lady I told you about, Nancy Whittredge."

"Hello, Nancy. Come to see our pictures?" He waved proudly at the rows of file cabinets. Detective Olliphant was a butterball. With his stomach straining against his shirt and belt, he made even Carlo look relatively trim.

"This is a dirty trick," Nancy told Carlo.

"No, it isn't. What you've looked at in our place is sex criminals. Down here they got everybody."

"Just about," Ollie said. "Everybody arrested in Manhattan the last five, six years. Guess how many."

"I don't want to guess."

"Close to half a million, give or take. There's so many pictures we can't count them. We just measure them, so many to the inch."

"Carlo, I am not going to look at half a million pictures. Give or take. This isn't fair, and you know it."

"Have a seat, let's talk about it."

"I have to go to work."

He looked at his watch. "Not yet. Have a seat." He pulled out a chair for her and almost pushed her down in it.

"In the first place, you don't have to look at anything like all that many pictures. Down here it's organized, first by race, and then by age, and then by height. For Bernie, all you have to do is the drawers of blacks in their early twenties who are around five-feet-six. Nothing to it."

"Nothing to you. How many pictures is that?"

Carlo looked at Detective Olliphant, who said, "Oh, couple of drawers, probably. Couple of thousand, give or take. And Carlo said there were two perps, different age and height, so that would be a few more drawers."

Nancy stood up.

Carlo pushed her down again. He kept both hands on her shoulders. "Listen," he said, "there's something you got to understand about rape. If a guy's a regular rapist, a serial rapist, then that's what he sets out to do. He leaves home, he's got rape in mind. If he keeps on doing it, sooner or later we catch him and his picture winds up in our sex crimes file. Your guys weren't there, so probably they aren't regulars. Or maybe they never got caught at it. But a lot of rapes, a hell of a lot of rapes, it's just a crime of opportunity. The guy is out there doing a robbery or a burglary or auto theft, whatever his regular line of work, and some poor woman falls in his lap, and so he rapes her.''

He took his hands off her shoulders. "That's you. Your two guys were out for robbery, right? That's why they're watching the bank cubicle and why they got a shopping bag ready. Money and jewelry, right? That's what they were after. The rape was just a bonus for them. An afterthought.''

A bonus. An afterthought. "Well it sure didn't feel that way to me!''

Carlo nodded. His sharp little brown eyes were angry. "No, not to me either, by God. Robbery's one thing, but rape—'' He stopped himself. Then he said in a calmer voice, "What you got to realize, Nancy, if either of them was ever arrested for robbery or burglary or anything else, then they're here in this room. All you have to do is pick them out.''

"Suppose they were never arrested."

Carlo shrugged. "Then we try something else."

Nancy almost cried. She had been so sure she was through with the pictures. This was asking too much. She was sure the pictures were helping to make the nightmares.

"I don't want to do it."

"You have to."

"No, I don't."

"Listen, you want to catch them or not?"

"I want *you* to catch them."

"I got to have your help."

She made herself consider it. At least the way it was set up here in C.A.T.C.H., she could look for the faces one at a time. There would be a drawer where she was looking only for Bernie, shorter and younger, and then a different drawer where she would be looking only for The Other One, taller and older. Having to keep only one face in mind, it would be easier to concentrate. And she did want to catch them for what they did to her.

"All right," she said. "When I can get to it."

Carlo looked at his watch again. "I'll drive you down to work when it's time. You could start now, couldn't she, Ollie? Just for fifteen minutes or so. Just to get the hang of it."

Nancy's laugh was bitter. "Carlo, I already have the hang of it."

*   *   *

Often at the end of a shift, the reporters went straight home from wherever they happened to be in the city, taking their equipment bags with them. There was no need to go into the station, except to recharge equipment or pick up new batteries or tapes.

Nancy could have gone directly to the bistro to meet Tommy, but since she wanted to speak to Mike Barnes, she returned to the station. If you wanted to say anything personal to Mike, you had to go to the station, or else call him at home, which she would not have dared to do. When he was training a new reporter, they would talk back and forth with Mike giving instruction and answering every question. But during his shift as editor, all phone calls and transmissions must deal strictly with radio business.

He was sitting in the editor's chair in the middle of the news deck, his long legs stretched out on the table. He was taking a phone call from some reporter and at the same time monitoring what was going out over the air from the broadcast booth. He did not see her. She waited till he hung up before she walked up to him.

"Mike. Hi, it's me."

He gave her an even longer stare than usual, obviously checking her over. "Hello, Nancy." Another long pause. "It's good to see you."

Carefully noncommittal. Not asking any intrusive questions. And yet any number of people must have passed on the details about what had happened to her.

"I just wanted to thank you. For not saying anything about—about Friday night."

He nodded. "You asked me not to."

"I know. It was still a surprise to walk in here three days later and find that nobody knew anything about it. I appreciate it."

He nodded again. "It was your business if you wanted to say anything." He smiled slightly. "I gather you did."

"They told me at the hospital to go ahead and talk about it. It's supposed to be better to talk about it."

"And is it?"

"Yes, I think so."

"You look fine."

Not quite a question, but she chose to treat it as one. "I'm okay, thanks. Not exactly wonderful, but . . . And thanks for the advice. I did call my parents, and I did report it to the cops. They're working on it. We're trying to find the guys who did it."

He shook his head. "A terrible thing. I'm sorry."

"Well, anyway thanks."

He nodded. His phone rang again. He put his hand on the receiver, but before he lifted it he said, "You did a good job on that taxi crash. Nice work." Then he picked up the phone and said, "Barnes."

Good job. Nice work. He never volunteered praise unless he really meant it. She was very glad she had come in to talk to him. But she wondered if he had said the same to Ted Meadows and to Bing.

She left her equipment bag in the locker and walked across town to East Forty-fifth.

Tommy had discovered Bistro Paul through a friend at his cable channel. It was three blocks closer to his office than to hers but still a more-or-less midway meeting place. Sometimes they just had drinks at the wooden tables in the small bar area, but often they stayed on for dinner, moving into the dining room with its red-checked tablecloths, a lighted candle on each table, and Paul's rather fuzzy black-and-white photographs of Provence hanging on the walls. Because they were regulars, Paul always found them a table, provided they told him when they came in. Tommy usually ate the house specialty, cassoulet, which did nothing for his diet program.

She hoped he would be waiting for her but was not surprised to be first. She said hello to Jeanne, the lady bartender, and took the corner table. This early in the evening only one other couple was sitting in the bar section.

"Glass of red wine?" Jeanne asked her from behind the bar.

Wouldn't that be delicious, Nancy thought. "No thanks, not tonight. Just a Perrier with lime."

Jeanne's eyebrows rose slightly, but she said nothing. She poured Nancy's drink and handed it to her across the bar.

Whenever she was suddenly alone like this, she found herself going through all the *what ifs*. What if she had jumped into that man's car at the stoplight. What if she had not used the dark shortcut street to her apartment. What if she had not gone to the bank cubicle at all. Or what if she had gone to it half an hour earlier—or half an hour later. Maybe it would never have happened.

Nancy hoped Tommy was not going to be really late. She felt nervous. From her purse she took out the hospital's Emotional First-Aid Sheet that Pat Ford had given her. She considered it her bible. She read it several times a day and always the last thing before going to bed. She knew most of it by heart, but it still helped to read it over.

You survived the physical assault. You can survive the emotional assault as well . . .

Maybe you are still afraid. Maybe you still blame

yourself. Please remember—the rape was not your fault . . .

Talking about your feelings may not take them away, but it may help you to understand them and feel better . . .

It is O.K. to cry. It helps . . .

Find someone you can talk to—someone who can listen . . .

Something bad has happened to you, but that does not make you a bad person . . .

You were a victim. Now you are a survivor . . .

"Hi, honey. I'm not late, am I?"

His smile looked just the same. He bent over and hugged her hard, his cheek against hers. Then he sat down and studied her.

"You look wonderful," he said. "What's that you're drinking?"

"A Perrier. I'm not allowed any alcohol for ten days."

"Jesus, that doesn't seem fair." And then to Jeanne, "A vodka gibson on the rocks."

He took both her hands. His smile was natural, convincing. "Nancy, you're going to be okay. Everything's going to be okay. We're back together now, and it's all right."

She found his certainty too easy, but he was probably right. "I hope so."

"I'm sure of it." When Jeanne handed over his drink, he raised it to Nancy. "Cheers."

That was what he always said when they

shared a drink together, but now it did not seem appropriate.

"Jenny said you're staying with your parents. How long is that for?"

"I don't know. I'm scared to live down there. They could still be around—you know, just walking around the streets. I'd be looking over my shoulder all the time."

"I know. Jenny said she was nervous, too, down there all alone. She's thinking about moving in with Sid, at least till you come back."

"She is?" Nancy had talked to Jenny half a dozen times without learning that. Why hadn't she said anything? Maybe Jenny was trying not to put any pressure on her to come home.

Tommy put his arms on the table and leaned toward her. His dark eyebrows were raised, and his eyes were extra wide open, the way he always looked when he had something exciting to propose. Usually it was some wonderful idea, but now she had a small tingle of alarm. She was not ready for excitement.

"Listen," he said, "why don't you move in with me? Right now, tonight."

"Oh, Tommy, I couldn't."

"It's all right with Alex. I asked him."

"But it's not all right with me. I couldn't. I'm

too—I mean, I couldn't possibly. I'm still all confused. I'm just not ready to—"

He took her hands again. "Nancy, when you fall off the bicycle, you have to climb right back on. You'll see, we'll be fine, just like nothing happened."

She did not see at all. "But something *did* happen."

"I know, and it must have been awful, but the thing to do now—"

"*Bon soir, bon soir,*" Paul said, approaching their table. He was a large, comfortable man with a generous black mustache. His blue-and-buff striped apron hung from his shoulders to his ankles.

Nancy was grateful for the interruption.

"*Allo, allo,*" Tommy answered, smiling up at Paul.

"You will stay for dinner? Nice turbot tonight, flown in fresh." He kissed his fingertips. Paul had a tendency to overdo the French *patron* bit.

"Not tonight, Paul. Just the drinks."

"Oh, I'd like to," Nancy said quickly.

"Ah, Miss Whittredge makes the right judgment. I will save you a nice table."

When he had gone, Tommy said, "You don't like fish."

"I don't have to have the turbot."

"I think we should go somewhere where we can talk."

"But we talk here all the time."

He wanted to argue but then caught himself. She could see he was humoring the patient.

While Tommy had a second gibson, Nancy made him talk about his Bermuda sales conference. He humored her on that, too. He and his boss had had to give a half-hour talk with film clips on their programming plans, which had gone over reasonably well, but the rest of the morning work sessions consisted of dozing through sales presentations until it was time to play golf and tennis. Evenings were, as usual, devoted to poker, craps, four-handed gin and backgammon until quite late at night. As usual, Tommy had done well at poker—"well enough to pay for tonight's dinner." He thought sales conferences were an expensive, pleasant waste of time, with everybody drinking too much and then flying home exhausted. But all the salesmen liked it.

When they ordered dinner—cassoulet and Cotes du Rhone for Tommy, gigot with flageolets for Nancy—he had done enough humoring. "All right, I want to hear."

By now she had told the story often enough to know what to leave out. She tried to omit the worst parts, but Tommy kept asking for details. He would have made a good reporter.

But it was one thing to be interviewed by the cops or by hospital personnel and quite another to be interviewed by Tommy.

"So how many times altogether?"

She looked down at her plate. "I don't know. I didn't count."

"Poor old girl."

She could feel his sympathy, but she did not want to talk about this anymore. Instead, she told him about Carlo and the other detectives and about the picture files and the possibility of fingerprints on her credit cards.

He listened for a while, then stopped her. "You know what I think?" he said. "I think you should drop all that. It's only making it worse."

She half agreed with him. Half of her longed to drop it forever. But the other half wanted to get even. "Tommy, I'm trying to catch them. I'd really like to get them. So would the cops."

"Leave it to the cops. That's their job. What you ought to do is forget it."

"*Forget* it?"

He was embarrassed. "Not forget it, of course. I mean try to put it out of your mind. Get back to normal living."

"Well, that's what I'm doing. I'm back at work."

He shook his head. "That's not what I mean. You're up there living with your parents again, like a little girl."

He finished his glass of wine and filled it again. She wished he would not drink so much when she was not allowed to drink at all.

The waiter asked if they were finished. Tommy had eaten all his huge platter of cassoulet, but Nancy had barely touched her dinner. Much as she loved gigot and flageolets, she had almost no appetite since it happened. Having to tell Tommy about it took away what little interest she might have had. She must be losing weight—no drinks, almost no food.

The waiter cleared their plates and asked if they would like dessert and coffee. Just coffee, Nancy said.

Tommy's face turned very serious. "What about us?"

"What about us?"

"I think we should skip the coffee and go straight home to bed, that's what I think. Wipe all this out."

"Tommy, it isn't going to go away."

"No, not if you spend all your time thinking about it."

"Tommy, please. Please understand. I'm not ready for making love."

"You haven't tried."

"And I don't know when I will be."

They sat there staring at each other across the candlelit table.

Not This Year

In their duplex penthouse on Sixty-second and Park, the McNamaras were giving a fund-raising cocktail party for the homeless.

In the crush of well-wishers and contributors George Whittredge ran into his longtime friend Alf Perkins. Alf was also in real estate, and, as a leading black businessman, he was the city's consulting specialist on low-income housing.

"Hello, Whit, how are you? How's Carol?" They shook hands.

Whit did not want to tell Alf or anyone else about Carol. He was concerned about her. When she was not crying or worrying about Nancy, she was fighting with him over what was the best thing to do for Nancy.

"She's fine," Whit said. "She's around here somewhere. How's Barbara?"

"Same as ever. Too busy with Meals on

Wheels to come here tonight. Say, Whit, I've been meaning to call you. We didn't get your contribution."

For the last eleven years Whit had made his contribution to the Urban League through Alf, who was a member of the local board.

"No, I haven't sent it."

"You're as busy as Barbara, I suppose. Well, please don't forget."

"Alf, I'm not contributing this year."

"What's the matter, hard times? You don't look it."

"No, it's—Listen, Alf, my daughter Nancy has been raped."

"God, Whit, I'm sorry to hear that. I haven't heard a word about it. When did that happen?"

"A few days ago. By two blacks in a garage down in Tribeca. Raped and robbed."

"That's awful. Is she all right? How's Carol?"

Whit decided not to answer either question. "Yes, it's awful. Under the circumstances, Alf, I'm not contributing to black causes this year."

Alf's friendly smile lost none of its warmth, but his eyes narrowed. "What's that supposed to mean, old buddy? The Urban League isn't pushing rape this year. It's not one of our major programs."

"Just the same."

Alf studied him. Then he said, "What if they'd been white?"

"Who?"

"The two guys who raped your daughter. If they'd been white, would you stop contributing to white causes?"

"I can't explain it. It's how I feel."

Alf put his big hand on Whit's shoulder. "It's not how you're *supposed* to feel. I always thought we could count on you."

"Yes, I know. And you always could."

"You're not making any sense, Whit."

"Probably not. I'm sorry, but that's how I feel."

"It's because of crimes like that, bad punks like that, that you have to help the people who are trying to make things better. We have to fight things like that together."

"Tell me about it next year."

Next morning, knowing Alf was right and feeling guilty besides, Whit sent in his contribution. But it did not change the way he felt. Not this year.

We're Working
on It

As soon as Carl Vincent brought in the fingerprint report on the Whittredge case, Sergeant Bob Blaine read it word for word.

No valid prints were found in the garage itself. But among all the useless smudges and smears and overprints found in the contents of Nancy's wallet, the Latent Prints Division had classified six prints as being "of value." Four of these were only partials but had enough revealing characteristics to be distinctive. Two of the prints were full finger.

One of the full fingers and one of the partials turned out to be Nancy's own prints and were discarded. The other four were enlarged on the monitor screen one by one, and a latent print expert had marked every distinctive characteristic—the particular ridges, bifurcations, abrupt breaks—with a small red dot. These were transmitted to the central memory bank in Albany, where the computer was told to pick out all criminal prints on file containing the identical characteristics found on each of the four prints.

The final paragraph of the report said—in flat, technical language—that there were "no respondents." No prints with any of these unique sets of characteristics existed in the file.

Blaine tossed the report in his outbox. New York State had recently spent thirty-seven million dollars to create AFIS, the Automated Fingerprint Identification System. It was much quicker than the old manual system of flipping through fingerprint cards one by one, but when no matching prints were found by the computer, it didn't matter a damn how fast it was.

Blaine thought for a moment. Then he pulled out Carl Vincent's DD-5 sheets, the day-by-day chronological record of his investigation—all the phone calls, visits, witnesses, interviews, evidence. Blaine had read them before, but now he went over them again to see if he could find anything missing.

Nancy's Vitullo Kit evidence, collected that night at Bellevue, had not been processed, but this was normal. So many Vitullos came into the Police Lab every day from all over the city that they could not possibly all be processed. They were kept in cold storage, the evidence intact, until a defendant was arrested, or until the detective in charge had some special reason to request processing. There was certainly no such reason here, and God knows there were no defendants.

Blaine went to the door of his office to see who was in the bullpen. Zeke and Lucy and, of course, Carlo. Although it was strictly Vincent's assignment, everybody knew about everybody else's cases, and sometimes it was helpful to bat ideas around.

"You all got a few minutes?" he said. "Let's talk about Whittredge."

They followed him back into his office, bringing their coffee mugs. Zeke carried the necessary extra chair.

When they were all seated around his desk, Blaine said, "Tough break about the prints. Six good ones but not a single hit."

"Nancy's real disappointed," Carlo said. He was plainly disappointed himself. "I told her not to count on it, but she was hoping."

"It could still be one of the perps," Lucy said. She was always optimistic. She was a motherly looking detective, a whiz at dealing with terrified kids in child abuse cases. "Maybe his prints just aren't in the file. Maybe he's never been arrested. Or maybe he's got a record, but it's out of state."

"Maybe," Blaine agreed, "but that won't do us much good unless we find him. How're you coming, Carlo?"

Vincent grunted. "Not much."

"How's Nancy holding up?"

"She's working on the C.A.T.C.H. file. She's even picked out a couple of 'sort ofs.' Guys she says he 'sort of' looked like this."

"Anything close enough to follow up?"

Vincent shook his head. "Nowhere near. On the one-to-ten scale, she says they're maybe fives."

"Is she going to keep at it?"

Vincent hesitated. Then he said, "If I got anything to do with it. But you know how it is."

Blaine nodded. They all knew how it was. A woman would start out cooperating, really wanting to catch the rapist and then—sometimes early, sometimes late—she could not stand it any longer and would just walk away.

"Maybe it's time to do artist sketches," Lucy suggested. The specialty artists at police headquarters sometimes came up with a very good likeness of a perp, based on the victim's description.

"Last resort," Carlo said. "Only after she finishes the picture file." His voice sounded discouraged.

"Zeke?"

The huge, quiet detective seemed to fill any space he was in. "I keep wondering," he said, "how come the perps haven't tried her bank card again."

"The account's been canceled. The old code wouldn't work."

"Yeah, I know. But they don't know that."

"Carlo?"

"The bank's on alert. Anybody punches in Nancy's code word ORION, they call me right away. Manager claims it would show up immediately on their computer record. If it does, bank calls me."

Blaine looked back at Big Zeke.

Zeke shrugged his massive shoulders. "So why haven't they tried? How come they don't sneak back some night and give it a shot? I would. Nothing to lose."

"Maybe they're too smart," Vincent said. "Smart enough not to go back to the same place twice. We tried patrol down there but no luck, no sign of them. And the bank says no other cash machine incidents." He paused and slowly ran his hand over his hair, starting at the front and going all the way over the top and down to the back of his neck. "I keep thinking, they weren't just scared young punks. They didn't just grab her money and jewelry and beat it, the way you'd expect."

"Pros, you mean?"

"I don't know. I'm just saying."

"Maybe they move around," Lucy said. "Maybe they hit different bank cubicles. And if there's no rape, we wouldn't even hear about it."

"Good point," Blaine said. "Carlo, maybe it'd be a good idea to tell the D.A.'s office. Maybe call Joan Hennessy."

"Why?"

Blaine knew Vincent hated to let go any part of a case. "Suppose it does happen again, some place else like Lucy says, with or without a rape?"

"It's our case," Vincent said.

"It'll still be our case. But you know how the D.A. is. He doesn't like to be surprised. He hates surprises. Just suppose this happens again, and the press gets hold of it. Suddenly they'll be talking about a city-wide rape-and-robbery pattern all over TV and the newspapers. And we're sitting here saying, 'Oh yeah, we know all about that. We're working on it.'"

They all smiled, even Carl Vincent, because that sort of thing had happened before.

"And besides," Blaine reminded them, "there's the family. Nancy's father, what's his name?"

"George. They call him Whit."

"Right, George Whittredge. Big man in real

estate, big contributor to the Democratic party."

"Politics," Carlo said, with appropriate disgust.

"Yeah, politics. Maybe he even contributed to the D.A.'s last campaign, lot of businessmen do. Suppose Whittredge gets impatient we haven't caught them, and he gets on the phone to the D.A. and asks why haven't we caught those two bastards who raped his daughter. Why aren't we working harder on it? You think that's possible?"

Vincent thought it over. "I think," he said, "Whittredge is a man who likes action. I think he likes to get things done. Personally."

"So he makes this call to his friend the D.A., and the D.A. has to say, 'What daughter? What rape?' It's all news to him, a big surprise, and he's embarrassed. He's Mr. D.A. but he doesn't even know what the hell's going on in his own borough. So he hangs up the phone, very angry, and guess who he calls next?"

"Hoo!" Zeke said with a smile. "Tell him I'm not here."

"I think we better call Joan Hennessy," Blaine said. "That way our ass is covered. And then like Lucy says, Joan's office might know something we don't know. Something that might help us along."

"I doubt it," Vincent said.

"I doubt it, too, but I'm going to call her."

Defense attorneys liked to speculate about which would be worse: to face Joan Hennessy in court as a sex crimes prosecutor, the way they did now, or to face her in court as a judge, which someday she would surely become. It was a close call. Most lawyers decided they would prefer to face her as a judge. There was at least a chance that once she made judge, with the black robe and "Your honor" and all the perks and prestige, she might mellow and soften, as judges had been known to do. However, some defense lawyers predicted that Judge Hennessy would be even fiercer than Assistant District Attorney Hennessy, although they conceded this was difficult to imagine.

They would all just have to wait and see.

Hands thrust in the pockets of her wide open tweed jacket, long legs taking long steps, Joan Hennessy strode down the eighth floor corridor of Number One Hogan Place, hurrying toward her office. Judges never had to hurry. In fact, it would be unseemly for a judge to rush down the hall, robe billowing behind. A judge should be sedate, stately. That was not Joan Hennessy's style. She hurried because there was always urgent work to do

and because she liked walking fast. Young
A.D.A.s who worked in her department had
trouble keeping up. They would trot along
beside her, trying to squeeze in a question or
two before she got wherever she was going.

She had no intention of becoming a fusty
judge. She was having much too good a time
as a prosecutor, although she was too sensible
to tell anybody that. Oh, perhaps when she
was an old lady, her bright red hair turning
gray, her slim figure putting on weight, perhaps then it would be fun to waddle into her
own courtroom in a floor-length black silk
robe and hear the respectful bailiff call out,
"All rise!" Time enough then to become a
judge. Perhaps. But perhaps not.

She liked to win. Judges did not win. They
decided, or helped a jury decide, which of two
antagonists was going to win. No doubt there
was real satisfaction in this—good judges often told her so. And of course the pay was
much better—no judge had to tell her that. But
it would not be the same. *Joan Hennessy for the
People.* No judge ever got to stand up in court
and say those thrilling words. And they were
still thrilling, even though she had been an
A.D.A. for eleven years, ever since law school.

She whirled into her office without breaking
stride and, as she came through the door,
asked her assistant, "What's up?"

Moira had been trained, against all her sociable instincts, not to waste time saying good morning. She read off the list. The department was scheduled for four grand jury hearings today, only one of which, in Room five at eleven-thirty, was Joan's own case. The Astarte trial was postponed until tomorrow at request of the defense, pleading absence of a witness. The D.A.'s budget conference was still on for three o'clock and would take most of the afternoon. Viktor Tobias, the Legal Aid lawyer, had called to discuss his new client, one Juke Sims.

"Juke?"

Moira checked her notes. "That's what he said."

After all her years as an A.D.A., Joan Hennessy had learned to pay attention whenever a bell rang. The name of Viktor Tobias was just such a bell, a brilliant, bitter lawyer who had once been an A.D.A., then successful litigator in private practice, and now, for mysterious personal reasons, the best Legal Aid attorney in town. Anybody who had to deal with Tobias better pull up her socks.

She asked Moira, "How come Viktor Tobias knows about one of our cases before I do?"

Since this question was unanswerable, Moira did not answer it.

"Get me everything on this Juke Sims today. And an explanation, too!"

"Yes, ma'am."

"All right, what else?"

Moira went on with her list. Three A.D.A.s
wanted a word with Joan about their cases,
but only Thelma Bernstein, who had one of
today's grand jury hearings, was urgent. A
Time researcher working on a roundup story
about the way sex crimes were prosecuted in
five major cities wanted to interview Joan, but
she promised it could be handled by telephone. A *Newsday* reporter had called to find
out if there was anything new on the Smithers
rape-murder. Moira had told him no, but he
insisted on hearing it from Joan. And Sergeant
Blaine at MSCS had called with a problem, its
nature not specified beyond the fact that he
was sure Joan would want to hear about it.

A relatively quiet day, with the D.A.'s budget conference by far the most important
event. Joan Hennessy needed to add to her
staff, and the budget was, as usual these days,
so tight that everyone had been ordered to
squeeze. But she had done all her homework,
and she could prove that her fourteen A.D.A.s
were being swamped by the flood of child
abuse cases.

Her own grand jury appearance, like all
grand jury appearances, would be a piece of
cake for her, if not for her witness, but she
would have to help Thelma, a nervous new

A.D.A., with whatever her problem might be. Viktor Tobias would have to wait until she found out who this Juke Sims was and what he was charged with.

She would make time, as always, to return the press calls. Joan Hennessy approved of good press relations, which led to good publicity. But she was annoyed by the *Time* request. The magazine had never done a story on her and her department, even though it was the oldest and best in the country. She knew she made good copy, and everybody wanted to read about sex crimes. She had even dropped circuitous hints to *Time* that she would "probably" be available for rich, lengthy interviews, but the word had come back, also circuitously, that *Time* was not interested because *Newsweek* had already done her.

And now *Time* wanted to make her part of a five-city roundup, where she would get one quote and one statistic, maybe one whole paragraph if she was lucky. If the story ran at all.

She told Moira to make a date with the *Time* researcher here in the office. Once she got the researcher cornered, she might be able to convince her that the real story, the best story, was Joan Hennessy.

Fifteen minutes before the budget meeting,

she returned Blaine's call and heard, for the first time, what had been done to Nancy Whittredge. It was such an ugly, deliberately vicious crime that it made her even angrier than usual. And it was the kind of crime that might easily be repeated. She decided she would probably assign it to herself.

When she had time to look it up, she learned that George Whittredge had contributed, rather generously, to the D.A.'s last campaign. That clinched it: her case.

What's Best for Nancy

Whit thought his wife Carol was behaving like a real pain in the ass. And it was obvious she felt exactly the same way about him. This had nothing to do with love and friendship; after twenty-six years of marriage, they had no doubts about those. But ever since the night of Nancy's rape, they had been arguing about what was best for Nancy.

Whit thought it was good for Nancy to be back at work. Carol thought it was too much extra strain.

Whit thought Nancy should take advantage of the counseling offered by Bellevue. Carol thought it would only serve as a reminder of what happened.

Whit thought Nancy was right to be working closely with the police in an effort to identify the two men. Carol thought Nancy should leave that to the police and try to put the whole event behind her.

Whit thought they should leave it to Nancy to decide how much she wanted to be with Tommy. Carol thought Nancy should be encouraged to see more of Tommy, who was such a nice young man anyway.

The truth was, Whit admitted to himself but not to Carol, they were both guessing. Neither of them knew what was best for Nancy, what was the right thing to do. As Carol kept reminding him, even the police had told him the very night of the rape that he should have called them in immediately. If Whit had been wrong about that, as he was, he could be wrong about everything else.

And now this.

"I think it's time for you to do something," Carol said. "Use your influence."

"What influence?" Whit said defensively. These days, one of them was always on the defense, while the other was on the attack. They seemed to take turns.

They were sitting in the library with their after-dinner coffee. Nancy was off at the police station, looking at more pictures.

"You're always saying what an important man you are, so why don't you do something?"

"Carol, I am not only not *always* saying how important I am. I have *never* said it."

"No, but you think it."

Since this was approximately true, it made him angry. "What makes you think you know what I think?"

"We're married, aren't we?"

"Just precisely what is it you want me to do? Offer a reward?"

"Certainly not. We don't want a lot of publicity. And Nancy doesn't either. But how do we know the case is being handled the right way?"

"From what Nancy says, it sounds to me as though they're doing everything they can."

"What does Nancy know about an investigation? For that matter, what do *you* know?"

"For that matter, I'm going to have a Scotch and soda. You want anything?"

"No, thank you."

Very polite. Also very superior. She was indicating that while he might need to take refuge in a drink, she did not.

Whit fixed his drink from the library cabinet. This gave Carol time to regroup.

"Maybe they haven't given the case to the best detectives. Maybe they haven't put enough men on it. I want this thing to be over. Why don't you call the Police Commissioner and put some pressure on?"

Actually, that was not the worst idea in the world. "I barely know him," Whit said.

"Well then, what about the District Attorney? You certainly know him."

"Sure, but he's not running the investigation. He only comes in when there's somebody to prosecute."

"I'll bet if you talked to him, he'd talk to the Police Commissioner."

This was actually a very good idea. He wished he had thought of it himself. "That's not a bad idea," Whit said.

"Then why haven't you done it?"

"For God's sake, Carol, we just thought of it."

"Who is this 'we'? *I* thought of it."

"All right, all right. I'll call him in the morning."

"Don't forget."

"I won't forget."

"Good. Then I think I'll have a *very* light Scotch."

Peace offering. Accepted.

He got up to fix it.

Next morning from his office, Whit placed a call to the District Attorney. He did not expect to get through right away, and he didn't, but since he had contributed to the D.A.'s last two campaigns, he was sure his call would be returned. It was.

"Hello, Whit. How are you? How's Carol?"

Whit, who had a good memory himself, was

always amazed at politicians' memory for names. Of course, the D.A. might have asked her secretary about Carol's name before returning the call.

"Fine, thanks."

"Good. What can I do for you?"

"I don't know if you've heard about our daughter Nancy."

"Of course I have. A dreadful thing, really dreadful. You all have my sympathy. I understand your daughter is working closely with the police."

So the D.A. *had* heard about it. That was encouraging. "Yes. Yes, she is. I just wasn't sure that word had reached your office. You know how it is. I mean, there hasn't been anything in the papers."

"We keep in close touch with the police on important cases, so I know all about it. In fact, I was going to call you. I've assigned the head of our sex crime prosecution unit to Nancy's case. Joan Hennessy."

"Oh. Well, that's very good to hear."

"We're right on top of it, Whit. And the commissioner knows about my personal interest. I'll let you know first thing if there's any break."

They hung up.

Whit thought about what to report to Carol. It was *so* tempting to present himself in a wonderful light: he had called the D.A. as promised, filled him in, got him to put his best prosecutor on the case and persuaded him to talk to the Police Commissioner. These days, it would be nice to get some credit around the house for a change.

He shook his head. It had been Carol's idea, and she deserved to hear it just the way it happened. Maybe he would get a little credit anyway.

Go Ahead and Cry

Nancy had finished work for the day. She planned to spend an hour plowing through C.A.T.C.H. pictures and then avoid pressure from Tommy by joining Jenny and Sid for a late pasta. Tommy was acting hurt. She was still in the WZEY newsroom when the police radio report came in.

In the course of a burglary, Beverly Ryan, the television star of "Fast Lane," had been raped in her townhouse on East Seventieth Street. The assailant, a white male approximately five-feet-ten with crew-cut brown hair and wearing a light green wool jacket, had escaped.

When she heard it, Nancy ran up to Mike Barnes on the news deck. "Hey, Mike, I want that! Let me do it."

Mike was irritated. He made his own assignments, without any suggestions from the reporting staff. "Well, you can't have it," he snapped. Without another word to her, he told his assistant, "Beep Callohan for me."

Louise Callohan was Weezie's best reporter for any "woman's angle" story, as well as for many other kinds of stories. An old hand, very much the queen of the staff, she knew every cop and every celebrity in town. Nancy herself would have assigned Louise, but this story was different. This was a *rape*. As far as Nancy knew, that had never happened to Louise.

"Mike, please listen—"

He did not even glance at her. "Nancy, I'm busy."

Normally that gruff cutoff would have stopped any further discussion, but Mike did not understand what this meant to her. She picked up her shoulder bag. "I'm going anyway," she said.

"No, you're not."

The others on the deck were listening. No young reporter ever argued with Mike Barnes, much less defied him.

She took a deep breath. "I'm off duty, so I'm going. Maybe I can help."

"If you get in Callohan's way—"

She did not wait to hear what would happen if she interfered with Louise. She was out the door and hurrying to the elevator.

Beverly Ryan was an anomaly in nighttime

television drama. She played Melinda Mae, a smart-ass, blonde-wigged, scheming hussy, but she played her with such zest and humor that viewers, women included, loved her instead of hating her. Even Nancy, whose only serious television interests were news and old movies, liked Beverly Ryan.

Seventieth Street and its sidewalks were blocked off at Madison Avenue by blue wooden barricades with the legend, "Police Line—Do Not Cross." Nancy got out at the corner and showed her press pass to get through the barricade.

She had no problem picking out Beverly Ryan's townhouse. The four-story brownstone was ringed by police and lighted up by the first television news crew to reach the scene. Fancy wrought-iron grills covered the windows of the first two floors. A newspaper reporter was trying to persuade the cop at the foot of the front steps to let him at least go up and ring the doorbell. He was having no luck.

Lights blazed on every floor and at every window, as bright as a party. Nancy wondered which room Beverly Ryan was sitting in, telling her anguished story to the police and a doctor. No trip to Bellevue Emergency and the GYN room for Beverly Ryan. Everything and everybody would come to her. Perhaps, considering who she was, an assistant district attorney might already be on hand. But none of it—none of the attention and the privacy and convenience of being interviewed and treated at home—would make Beverly Ryan feel any better. Nancy wondered if she had been physically hurt. Hurt or not, she would want just to be left alone to cry.

Nancy was standing in the street looking up at the elegant building when her beeper went off. She hauled the portable phone from her shoulder bag and called the newsroom.

"You there yet?" Mike Barnes asked.

"Yes. Just this minute."

"We'll talk about this later," he said, briefly and ominously. "Meantime, get to work. Callohan's having dinner out in Connecticut somewhere. Pierce is on his way instead, but to start with, it's yours. You'll be live, and you'll be the lead. You're on in four-and-a-half minutes, so get everything you can fast. Give me three units—four if you have it. And some atmosphere."

Three units meant ninety seconds, a long story in radio news terms. And she could have two whole minutes if she had enough material. The station would already have broadcast the news and the police description of the rapist, but hers would be the first live story.

Using her best media smile, Nancy talked

quickly to several cops, collecting scraps. Yes,
Beverly Ryan's own physician was with her.
So was her press agent. So were detectives
from the local precinct. Nancy's friends from
the Sex Crimes Squad had not yet arrived but
were sure to get here soon. And yes, somebody—the cops didn't know who—had come
from the D.A.'s office. The rape had taken
place in the third floor master bedroom.

Nancy remembered the full-page picture in
People magazine: the king-size canopied bed
with Beverly Ryan lounging back, smiling and
sexy in her Melinda Mae blonde wig, on what
looked like twenty fluffy pillows. The cops
didn't know whether or not the rape took
place on the bed, so Nancy would have to
slide over that. The extent of Beverly Ryan's
injuries, if any, was not known. The cops had
no idea how the rapist-burglar got in, but
Nancy got one to speculate that it might have
been through a third or fourth floor window
that had no protective grill.

She stepped back into the street and looked
up at the bright windows. Her heart went out
to Beverly Ryan—popular, successful, rich,
but now feeling frightened and degraded.
Nancy wondered what she could contribute
beyond the sparse facts. There had to be some
advantage to knowing exactly what Beverly
Ryan was going through. Something that

would help listeners understand what this did to you.

Whatever Nancy said had to be right the first time, because there could be no editing when she reported live.

She checked her watch and called in. "Mike, it's Nancy."

"You ready? Hold for cue."

Mike would already have told the anchor, Bill Mason, that she would report live at the top of the next twenty-minute news segment. Bill or his writer would have prepared a brief introduction, setting the stage for her report. Now Bill punched her phone line into the broadcast so that she could hear her cue. She must be careful not to repeat any of his introductory words or phrases.

She could hear the Diet Pepsi commercial winding down. She was nervous.

She pulled her thoughts together. She felt tears for Beverly Ryan.

Then the anchor's voice was saying, "This evening actress Beverly Ryan, the very popular Melinda Mae of the television series "Fast Lane," was raped in her Manhattan home on East Seventieth Street. WZEY's Nancy Whittredge is there at the scene."

She was on.

"I am standing outside Beverly Ryan's elegant four-story townhouse. The street is barricaded and filled with police cars. Police officers are standing guard on the sidewalk. Every window of the house is lighted, as though for a party. But all the guests at this party have come to investigate Beverly Ryan's rape and, if possible, to comfort her.

"She is upstairs, receiving medical attention from her own doctor and police attention from detectives of the Nineteenth Precinct. They will soon be joined by experts from the Manhattan Sex Crimes Squad. Evidence is being collected. An assistant district attorney is taking down every detail that might be helpful in prosecuting the rapist, an unidentified white male, who is still at large. Police speculate that he may have entered Miss Ryan's home through one of the upper-story windows, which are not protected by grills. The rape occurred in the third-floor master bedroom, with its huge canopied bed covered by a great mound of fluffy pillows."

That covered the facts, but facts did not tell everything. Not when it was a rape. She still had time to add something more. She could feel tears in her eyes and in her voice.

"Beverly Ryan must know that, in addition to police and medical and legal support, she has the support and sympathy of all her fans. But none of that is any real consolation. Rape *hurts*. Rape hurts in your *heart*. You don't feel like answering a lot of questions. All you want to do is cry."

Nancy had to pause for a second before she was able to say, "Go ahead and cry, Beverly. Go ahead and cry. And if it's any help, just know that tonight many thousands of people are crying with you—and for you. This is Nancy Whittredge, live for WZEY."

At the station Mike Barnes shook his head. You give them all that training, you teach them everything you can, you try to prepare them for every eventuality, and then something like this happens. In one transmission, Nancy had just broken three rules. She had let herself be too emotional, she had editorialized during a news broadcast, and she had inserted herself into the story. No, make that four rules: she had also addressed Beverly Ryan personally. Four goddamn broken rules.

Except that it was *good.*

Barnes, who kept his own emotions under rigid professional control, had been moved by the throb in Nancy's voice and by the warm immediacy of her sympathy for Beverly Ryan. Bad journalism but first-rate copy. No other station, radio or TV, would have anything like it.

Art Fox, the assistant news director and Mike's superior, appeared beside Barnes's chair. "What the fuck was that?" Fox asked.

Barnes looked up at him. "How do you mean?"

"Why are you letting her report a rape? She's hysterical."

"That's funny. She didn't sound hysterical to me."

"How could you send her on a rape story? When it just happened to her." Fox's voice was loud enough for everybody in the newsroom to hear.

Barnes thought of saying that he tried to send Louise Callohan, but he had no intention of being defensive.

Fox's voice grew even louder. "All that shit about 'Go ahead and cry.' You should have known better. Get somebody else over there. Where's Louise?"

"Out of town. But as a matter of fact, Pierce should be there any minute now."

"Well, that's better," Fox said, slightly mollified.

Barnes thought over what he was going to say. He could see that everybody in the newsroom was paying close attention. "I very much doubt, Foxy, that Pierce can possibly do better. I thought Nancy was terrific."

Fox glared at him. "We disagree. Get her off the story as soon as you hear from Pierce."

"No, she stays on it. She and Pierce can work it together. And I'm going to rerun that last part of Nancy on the next segment."

"You certainly are not."

"I'm editing, Foxy."

"This is not a question of editing. This is station policy. You'll do as I say."

No sound in the newsroom. Nobody talking.

The phone rang. It was probably Pierce checking in.

"No," Barnes said, "I won't. If you don't like it, you can get yourself another editor."

The phone rang again.

Fox said, "I'm going to have to call Selwyn, Mike."

"Good. Because I'm busy." He picked up the phone and said, "Barnes."

It took Art Fox quite some time to reach Ed Selwyn, the executive editor, and to fill him in. By then Mike Barnes had run a live report from Pierce and tacked on a repeat of Nancy's emotional words about rape.

Art Fox could have kept his defeat private by phoning Mike Barnes from his office. Instead, he returned to the news deck and said, loudly enough for the staff to hear. "Selwyn listened to it. He agrees with you. Go ahead and do it your way."

Barnes knew what that public acknowledgment cost and appreciated it. "Thanks, Foxy."

"One thing. He says if you run it again, be sure we label it commentary."

"Fair enough. God knows it's that."

Barnes did run it three more times, along with straight reporting from Pierce and snippets from Nancy.

Station operators always screened outside phone calls to protect the working news staff. Useful news tips were passed on at once, but more often the calls came from listeners who wanted to argue with something they had just heard or to spout their private opinions, frequently bizarre. The operators recorded the calls as a measure of listener response, and once a week an analysis was sent to the executives. Only rarely did the volume and pattern of calls warrant immediate notification to the newsroom.

Art Fox made his third appearance of the evening on the news deck. This time he was able to make a joke of it. "It seems," he said to Mike Barnes, "that quite a few other folks like what Nancy said."

"Yeah?"

"Yeah. Mostly women, of course. Some of them actually tearful, according to the chief operator. Maybe," he said with a smile, "you should ask Nancy to do another commentary. Isn't this one getting a little stale?"

Next morning, shortly before noon, an outside phone call was put straight through to the executive editor's secretary and then straight through to Ed Selwyn himself.

"This is Robby Martin, Miss Ryan's press representative."

Oh-oh, Selwyn thought. "Yes, Mr. Martin?"

"Call me Robby. That was quite a job your girl did last night. Beverly—Miss Ryan—appreciates it. A lot."

Selwyn was stunned. "She was *listening*?"

"Are you kidding? With everything else that was going on? Shit, no. But I heard it. And of course we get everything said or written about Beverly from the monitoring service. Usually a couple of days later, you know, but something like this, it's got to be rush-rush-rush. Guess you're used to that in your business, huh? I played the tape for Bev this morning."

Selwyn tried to picture the scene but failed. He knew from experience that stars and their press agents were infatuated by any and all publicity, good or bad. But a rape victim listening to her press coverage the next morning? Perhaps over coffee? He shook his head. "She liked it, you say. You're very nice to call. I'll make sure Miss Whittredge hears about this."

"Yeah, well that's not why I called. Listen, Mr. Selwyn—you don't mind if I call you Eddie?"

He had never been called Eddie. "Uh-no."

"Well, Eddie, it's tough to know how to play this one. I mean, so far it's been easy to go right down the line." The press agent's voice took on a different note. *"Miss Ryan is in seclusion under her doctor's care. Fortunately, she did not sustain physical injury, but she is in no condition to make a statement at this time."* Back to normal voice. "You know? But we can't keep that up forever. Beverly's public property, and her fans need to hear from her. Her network's after me, wants to make sure whatever we do, we protect Melinda Mae and "Fast Lane." Not to mention fifty press calls, all urgent."

"I can imagine."

"No, you can't, not unless you've been in this spot."

"I suppose not."

"Bet your ass, no offense. So like I say, we both liked the way your girl handled it. Bev especially. Real sympathy, you know? Not just the scandal stuff. That's the way we want to play it. So Bev is willing to talk to her."

"To *Nancy?*"

"Yeah. I know you're local, but you must have some kind of national hookup arrangement, right?"

"Yes, with ABC. They can pick up from us."

"I could wish it was CBS, but what the

hell, it'll get the word out the right way. After that, we can figure how to handle all the rest of them. Now listen, Eddie, there's a couple of conditions. You there?"

"Yes, I'm here."

"I get to listen in. Your girl tapes it, and anything we don't like, she wipes it out then and there, okay? Before you air it."

"You want to censor it?"

"Come on, Eddie, don't use dirty words with me. What is this *censor* shit? We're doing you a big favor, right? So you do us a small one. That way Beverly's free to talk, say whatever's on her mind. If she slips up, language gets a little too salty, or she says something strikes a wrong note, we're protected. Okay?"

It occurred to Selwyn that the station would also benefit from having lots of conversation on tape that could then be edited into segments. At least three segments. He was more than willing to surrender a little freedom of the press.

"Okay."

"Good. Three o'clock then, Beverly's house. And for God's sake, don't let this get out ahead of time."

"But we have to promote it. We have to let the audience know it's coming."

"Yeah, you're right. Okay, but only one hour before broadcast. I don't want to spend the day explaining to everybody else how come it's you and not the big boys."

Nancy arrived ten minutes early. A cop was still on guard at the foot of the steps. Two women and a male photographer with three 35-mm cameras draped around his neck were also on guard, leaning against a car parked in front of the house. She did not recognize any of them. All three looked cold and profoundly bored.

When one of the women spotted Nancy's radio equipment bag, she said, "Join the stakeout, honey. There's nothing doing."

Nancy said an awkward hello. She was even more nervous than last night. She whispered to the cop, "I'm Nancy Whittredge. I'm expected."

He asked to see her ID, then waved her up the steps.

"Hey, what is this?" said an outraged voice behind her.

She rang the doorbell—two deep chimes. It was several moments before the door opened partway, held by a chain. Another cop inspected her ID before he unhooked the chain and let her in.

Selwyn had warned her about the press agent, Robby Martin, but she had not expected a maid, a secretary and a lawyer. They were all in the second-floor living room. So was Beverly Ryan, seated on an enormous white couch.

Without the blonde wig and the Melinda Mae grin, she looked vulnerable. Her real hair was soft brown, curly and cut short. She was wrapped in an orange silk housecoat. Nancy knew from the clips that she was in her middle thirties, but this afternoon she looked older. She had every right to. But to Nancy's surprise she got up from the couch to shake hands. She was several inches taller than Nancy and several inches more buxom.

"I want to thank you," she said in a voice that held none of Melinda Mae's brassiness. "I could tell you understood what it's like."

Nancy had not decided whether to say anything about her own experience, but this made it easy—almost necessary. "I was raped myself."

"I might have guessed. I'm so sorry."

"And I am really sorry for you, Miss Ryan."

She smiled. A tired, rather thin smile. "Since you called me Beverly on the air, please continue. Now tell me, how do you want to do this?"

"Right here is fine. But could we turn off the radio? And shut off the phone? And maybe take away the coffee cups so there's no clatter. The mike picks up everything."

"Don't I know. Susan? Angela?"

While Nancy was setting up her mike stand and recorder on the coffee table, the maid and the secretary took care of the soundproofing. The lawyer explained that he would also tape the interview. The press agent, a natty old fellow whom Selwyn had described as extremely voluble, said absolutely nothing after his initial hello. He sat still in an easy chair, his fingertips pressed together under his nose, and listened with total attention.

Although it was Nancy's first interview with a famous person, Beverly Ryan made it easy. Without any prompting she told how she had been in her bedroom, dressing to go out for dinner, when she heard a noise. "A thump, like something falling." Since her maid and secretary had left for the day, there should have been no one else in the house.

"I wasn't scared. I like being alone, it never bothers me. At least not before last night. I called out, 'Who's there?' There was no answer, but after a minute this—this man walked right into the bedroom."

She had never seen him before, had no idea who he was or what he was doing here. She described him, the same description she had given the police. She still wasn't frightened. She thought it must be a repairman—something in the house always needed fixing—and he seemed perfectly pleasant, not at all threatening. But she had almost no clothes on. She snatched up her robe and held it in front of her and said, "What are you doing here?"

He smiled at her and said, still perfectly pleasant, "Just looking around. I thought I might find something."

Beverly Ryan could not believe this now, today, but she still had no sense of alarm. She still thought it was some kind of mistake. She said, "I'm dressing. Please get out."

Then he reached in his pants pocket and pulled out a clasp knife and opened the blade. He held it out in front of him and waved it at her, back and forth, and then he walked toward her, still waving the knife and still smiling.

"And then he said, 'You don't need that robe, baby.' He reached out and yanked it away, right out of my hands. And then, of course, I knew."

Nancy had said almost nothing, but now in the long pause she asked, "Were you frightened then?"

A bitter little laugh. "Damn right I was. That knife. You know, you hear stories about what they do, even after you do what they want. I can't afford to have my face cut."

Another long pause.

"I don't want to talk about what he did.

Thank God, it was over very quickly. Then he went to my bureau and found my evening purse and stuffed it with the necklace and earrings I had put out to wear. He kept on smiling, but he was suddenly in a big hurry. Like he realized this wasn't just a burglary anymore. He didn't ask where was the rest of my jewelry. In fact, he didn't say anything. He just left and I could hear him running down the stairs. The police said he let himself out through the back door. I waited a few minutes to make sure he was gone. Then I called 911, and everybody came."

Nancy knew better than to ask her about medical evidence. Although Beverly would probably answer, the press agent would take it out, and even if he didn't, the station could not run it. Instead she asked, "Did he know who you were?"

"I don't know. He didn't say my name. I don't even know why he picked my house."

"How do you feel about him?"

A flash of deep, deep anger that would have looked great on camera. But it was in her voice, too. "I *hate* him. In my house. In my bedroom. In my own bed. In my body."

She began to cry.

Nancy kept silent, hoping the mike would pick up the sound.

After a while Beverly Ryan reached in her

pocket for a Kleenex. She sniffled and blew her nose. The mike would certainly get that.

"I'm sorry. I just—" She stopped.

Nancy said softly, "All you want to do is cry."

"That's right. Just what you said last night. All you want to do is cry."

Nancy stopped the tape. Then she thought of something else and pushed the record lever again. "Maybe this is an odd question, but what would Melinda Mae say about what happened to you?"

Nancy could see the change come over Beverly Ryan's face as she thought about her popular character. Nancy could almost see the blonde wig and the tight, low-cut dress.

The familiar brassy voice said, "Honeybunch, you can't trust them. You just can't trust a one of them. My advice to you is keep your door locked and keep your legs crossed."

Everybody in the room laughed, even the maid. Beverly looked pleased with herself.

Nancy shut off the tape. "Wonderful!"

The press agent said, "Yeah, wonderful. But you can't use that."

"Why not?" Beverly asked.

"It makes you sound like you didn't take it seriously."

"But it's Melinda Mae, not me. Everybody will recognize her."

He shook his head. "What we want is sympathy, not laughs."

"I agree," the lawyer said. "She has suffered great distress. We must stick to that. If her assailant is caught and brought to trial, we can't have his attorney show that she was able to make light of it the very next day."

"But—" Nancy said.

"Sorry, kid. It's out. You were real good, Bev. Exactly right. But there's one other line has to go. The part about you can't afford to have your face cut."

"But I can't!"

"I want that to stay in," the lawyer said. "It helps establish her fear of physical injury."

"Well, you can do that some other way. We don't want her fans and the press saying she lets herself get raped because she's thinking about her face."

"I agree," Nancy said. "All you're thinking about is your life."

She found the place on the tape, checked the numerical counter for the exact spot, and deleted the single sentence. Then she played it back to prove to them that the sentence was gone.

"But, Mr. Martin, I'd really like to keep Melinda Mae."

"Call me Robby. Sorry, take it out. What the hell, you got enough, right?"

Right. More than enough.

At the station everybody was waiting for her. Even Selwyn came out of his office to crowd into the editing booth. Nancy watched their faces as the tape was played and simultaneously copied so that nothing would be lost from the original during the editing process.

Sound quality was excellent. They could even hear Beverly begin to cry. For the first time, Nancy wondered if the actress had done it on purpose.

They were all silent: Selwyn, Mike Barnes, Foxy, the anchor Bill Mason and his writer who would have to prepare an introduction to the interview. Several others stood just outside the booth where they could hear what was almost a monologue from Beverly Ryan.

When it ended, everybody waited politely for Selwyn. He patted Nancy's shoulder, "Good girl," then said to Mike Barnes, "Top of the six o'clock segment. How many parts, Mike? Three?"

Mike thought about it. "Maybe four." Then he turned to Nancy. "Nancy, that is damn good."

Then she really knew. "It was all Beverly," she said, almost meaning it. "I didn't have to do hardly anything."

"You had to be there."

He was so obviously pleased with her that

she dared make a joke to him about work. "That's true. So thanks for assigning me last night."

Mike laughed. Everybody laughed because they all knew how he had tried to stop her from going.

"All right," Selwyn said, back to business, "we have a lot to do."

He told Foxy to notify ABC what they were about to get. Just as soon as it could be written, a short advance promo piece should run every ten minutes right up to six o'clock. Mike Barnes would supervise the editing of the interview, three parts or four parts, whichever worked best, but Selwyn wanted to hear it when it was done. And he wanted to read the introductions to each of the segments. A press release must be written but held until the interview started to air.

"Nancy," Mike said, "tape me a one-sentence description of her living room. And two sentences on what Beverly Ryan looked like, what she was wearing."

"I forgot."

"Obviously. So do it now, and we'll tip it in."

The promo piece did not mention her name. It only promised "an exclusive WZEY interview with Beverly Ryan, victim of a shocking rape last night." But her name was in the introduction to each of the four segments, as well as the press release. And of course each segment ended with her byline, "Nancy Whittredge, WZEY."

ABC picked up three of the four segments. WZEY managed to repeat the interview through most of the evening. Beverly Ryan and Robby Martin both phoned to congratulate her. Mike told her he would make sure Selwyn gave her a bonus and maybe even a raise. Ted Meadows told her, "I can't stand it. You're famous before I am." Her parents and friends told her how proud they were.

Her nicest compliment came from Pat Ford at Bellevue. "I just had to break the rules and call you. I heard you, last night and then again tonight. You were wonderful. All those things need to be said about rape. Out loud."

Nancy thanked her.

"Have the police caught those two men yet?"

"No," Nancy said, "not yet."

"Well," Pat Ford said, "sometimes they do."

C.A.T.C.H.

Nancy was flipping through still another drawer of C.A.T.C.H. pictures. This was a collection of black males, 5'10" to 6'1", ages 23 to 27. She had already finished all the drawers that might have contained Bernie. There had been a lot of them because Detective Olliphant had insisted she do both the 5'7" to 5'9" and the 5'4" to 5'6" drawers.

"Maybe you were just an inch off," Ollie said. "Or maybe he grew an inch or two after his picture was taken. Since you got your best look at him, let's make sure."

So she had made sure. How many drawers? How many hours? How many pictures? Better not think about it. She had looked at thousands. She was determined to finish, to get through the drawers to the end, just to be able to tell Carlo and herself that she had done her best. Then she could quit, leave it up to them,

241

as Tommy and her mother kept advising her to do.

She paused for a swig from her can of beer, now blessedly permissible. In fact, she had a slight hangover from last night's celebration of finally getting off the wagon.

Her fingers went back to work. She was concentrating on the left-hand color pictures, the profiles, the only way she had seen The Other One. *Flip, flip, flip,* making sure she did not miss any cards that were stuck together.

Two other people, a young man and an older woman, were flipping silently through their own drawers at the next table. The woman, Nancy knew, was hunting for the man who had robbed her on the street two nights ago. She had no idea what the man was hunting for.

Flip, flip, flip.

Three-quarters of the way through this stack of cards, she stopped. An odd knob of a chin had caught her eye. His chin looked sort of like that, didn't it?

Didn't it?

She studied the rest of the profile. The skin was the right color, lighter than Bernie's. A long, straight jaw led down to the funny little knob of a chin. That jaw certainly looked right.

She closed her eyes, trying to recapture that moment under the streetlight. She squeezed her eyes tight shut and kept them shut. Then she opened them.

The man had straight black hair that hung loose, not tied back the way she thought she remembered. The straight, vertical forehead looked kind of familiar. At least it didn't look wrong. And he had high, prominent cheek-bones. *Almost like an Indian*—the phrase suddenly sprang back into their mind. She had completely forgotten, but now she remembered thinking it at the time. *Almost like an Indian.* His cheeks did not seem quite as hollow as she remembered. But the nose—the nose was dead right, *a ski-jump nose.*

She took the picture card out of the drawer and held it with both hands. She studied the full face. In full face, the chin became less prominent, the long jaw and the vertical forehead were much less discernible, and the ski-jump nose seemed just a straight, ordinary nose. The eyes, slightly narrowed and smoldering, stared straight into her own. She had not once looked into those eyes, but she knew they were his. She shivered and laid the card flat on the table.

I've got you.

"Found something?" Ollie asked from his desk across the room.

She almost answered but then realized this prize did not belong to Ollie. She picked up the card and rose from her chair. "Excuse me," she said. "I'll be back in a minute."

She climbed upstairs to the Sex Crimes Squad.

Carlo was alone in the bullpen. When he saw her, he checked his watch and said, "You don't have to leave yet."

She walked over to his desk and slapped down the card. Carlo looked at it, then looked up at her.

"It's him. The Other One."

"On a scale of one-to-ten?"

"Eleven."

Carlo actually managed to jump to his feet. And then he hugged her. "Hey, Bob! Hey, Bob! Nancy found him!"

Sergeant Bob Blaine was out of his office in seconds, a giant smile on his face, to shake her hand. "Which one?"

"The older one," Carlo said.

"Well, goddamn it all to hell. To tell you the truth, I'd about given up."

"Me, too," Nancy said with a shaky laugh.

"How sure are you?"

She nodded.

"No mistake?"

She shook her head. "I don't think so."

"Well, well." Blaine picked up the card and stared at it. "Come on," he said, "let's see who we got."

Nancy and Carlo followed Blaine into his office where he sat down in front of the computer. Looking at the card, he typed in its NYSIS number, the New York State Identification System number assigned to every person arrested. He hit the Enter key, and they all watched the blank screen, waiting until the computer found him.

Just over two years ago James Garden, a first offender, had pleaded guilty to attempted robbery and, in return for his plea, got off with five years' probation. After six months of checking in regularly with his probation officer, he suddenly stopped, apparently bored with the process, like so many others. A warrant was duly issued against him for violating probation. But since there were some three hundred thousand warrants outstanding, this was a meaningless piece of paper. His last known address, before he vanished, was a housing project on Manhattan's Lower East Side.

"I'm on my way," Carlo said.

"Right," Blaine said, "only you can't go alone. Cooney will be back soon."

"I don't want to wait."

"Well, you have to wait. As you well know."

"I have to go to work," Nancy said. "You'll call me?"

"Don't worry. Soon as we get him, you'll have to do a lineup. You free tonight?"

"You mean I have to *see* him? Isn't the picture enough?"

"Afraid not," Blaine said. "And Joan Hennessy will want to talk to you, now that we have a positive ID."

"Who's Joan Hennessy?"

"She's the A.D.A. for sex crimes prosecution. I'll explain later. You go on to work."

"I thought it would be over."

"Huh," Carlo grunted. "Just starting."

James Garden no longer lived in the housing project. No forwarding address.

Detectives armed with copies of his picture went through the project, trying to find someone who remembered anything about him— whether he had a job, or where he might have moved to. But turnover at the project was high. People moved in and out all the time. Nobody cared where a former resident might have gone. Nobody seemed to remember his face or his name. Or if they did, they did not want to tell the police anything that might get them involved.

Carl Vincent had learned from long experience that sometimes the simplest approach works best. He looked up James Garden in the phone book, not just in Manhattan but also in

Queens, Brooklyn, the Bronx and Staten Island. Then he had them checked out one by one. No dice, none of them was right. Sometimes the simplest approach does not work best.

But plenty of other approaches were available, and Vincent took them.

Unlisted phone, which required a subpoena to the phone company. No dice.

Con Edison gas and electricity records. No dice.

Tax files, which also required a subpoena. No dice.

Welfare records. No dice.

Unemployment compensation records, another subpoena. No dice.

Car registration and driver's license, a computer search through the Department of Motor Vehicles. No dice.

Military service records and FBI records. No dice.

Gun permit. No dice, of course. Most guns were never registered.

Garden's probation officer could not remember anything about him, and his probation file revealed nothing new.

Now that there was a picture to show, detectives did a thorough canvas, going back to the bank and the garage neighborhood and the local stores, showing the picture over and over again. No dice.

Apparently James Garden did not exist. But as Vincent told Nancy, that could not be true. It was simply a question of finding the right button to push.

Nancy had to tell her story all over again to Joan Hennessy. What Nancy liked best about the red-haired prosecutor, sitting behind her folder-piled desk, was that the story made her so angry. Most listeners were shocked, but this one was angry. Joan Hennessy's light blue eyes narrowed as she listened. She took occasional notes with an old-fashioned fountain pen.

"Very good," she said at last, putting down her pen. "You'll make a splendid witness." She leaned forward, fixing Nancy with a determined stare. "I can count on you to press charges, right?"

"Well, he hasn't been caught."

"*If* he's caught—*when* he's caught—you will press charges?"

Nancy had not thought too much about the consequences of actually catching one of them. This whole process of going after a rapist was a renewable decision. She had to decide, over and over again, whether or not to go on with it. "I guess so. I guess I have to. Yes, I want to."

"Good. Not everybody does. Your friend Beverly Ryan, for instance."

Beverly Ryan's rapist had been caught almost immediately, turned in for the insurance company reward when he tried to sell her distinctive jewelry. But Beverly—or perhaps Robby Martin?—had decided that the publicity of giving detailed testimony at a rape trial was more than she wanted to endure. Beverly would not press charges.

"That's something that's been bothering me," Nancy said. "My mother and I have talked a lot about it. She's even more worried than I am. Suppose there *is* a trial, what can—I mean suppose I get on the stand and his lawyer starts asking me about—about—"

"Your sex life," Joan Hennessy finished for her. "He can't ask you one single question. Even if I was asleep, the judge wouldn't allow it."

"But I thought—"

"That's what everybody thinks. It's one of the four hundred reasons women don't come forward." She sounded thoroughly annoyed at the ignorance of rape victims. "The state law was changed way back in '78, but women still don't realize it. There are only two cases where you can be asked in court about your sexual history." She ticked them off on her long fingers. "One, if you had a prior relationship with the rapist, especially an intimate one. Two, if you've been convicted of prostitution in the last three years." She smiled. "I assume, Nancy, that you have neither of those problems?"

On her way home, Nancy dropped by the Sex Crimes Squad to learn about the team's progress. There wasn't any.

"We're still working on it," Carlo said.

Nancy felt gloomy. All that effort and then nothing. "Maybe he's left town," she said.

"Maybe, though I doubt it. He doesn't know he's got any reason to be worried." His heavy sigh made Nancy feel even gloomier. Carlo was not given to sighing. "But if he did leave town, if they both left, that would account for one thing that's been bugging us."

"What's that?"

"It was Zeke who thought of it. He said, how come they haven't come back to the bank and tried to get more money with your card?"

"The account's closed."

"Yeah, I know. But like Zeke said, why wouldn't they at least try? Nothing to lose. Which one of them has the card?"

"Does it matter?"

"I don't know. You never know what matters. Which one's got it? Let's go back over it."

"All right, but I have to think. Let's see. Well, first, Bernie's the one who took it out of my wallet. And then The Other One took it to the bank and tried to make it work. Twice. The second time he made me write down the code."

"Okay, and then the third time you offer to get the money for them, so you all go back to the bank together. Now what?"

"Well, he—

"Who?"

"The Other One—Garden. He used my card to open the cubicle door. Then we all went in, and he—"

"Who? Still Garden?"

"Yes. He put the card in the slot, and he was holding the piece of paper, and he started doing my code, only he was doing it wrong."

"And you punched it for him."

"Yes, but I had to start over again, or it wouldn't have worked. So I took the card and did it."

She stopped. She and Carlo looked at each other.

"So now you've got the card."

"Yes, I guess so. Well, I know so. I took it from him so I could make it work."

Carlo waited for her to go on.

"And then the money came out, and Bernie put all the bills in the shopping bag, and we left."

"That's it?"

"What do you mean, 'That's it?' That's

when I was sure they were going to kill me."

"Yeah, I know that. But where's the card now? Sounds to me like you've got it."

"I couldn't have. I've never seen it again. I'd know if I had."

"But if you've got it, *that's* why they didn't try to use it again. Because they didn't have it. So you must have it. You didn't give it back to them?"

"Not that I remember. I wasn't thinking about it, Carlo. All I was thinking about was being dead."

"Well, let's work on it. So they leave you in that dark alley, only first they give you back your dress. Hey, that's it! You put the card in your dress!"

"Carlo, there aren't any pockets in an evening dress. Maybe I had the card and lost it on the way home. Maybe when I was throwing up in the trash can."

"Maybe. Maybe not. Let's pretend you still have it. What did you do when you got home?"

"Well, I unlocked the apartment door, and then I locked it behind me."

"That's right. You couldn't remember how you got your purse back with the keys still in it. Then what?"

"I went to my bedroom and hung up the dress in the closet. I remember trying to

smooth out the wrinkles. I was still trying to
take care of it because it was so pretty. And
because it was all I'd saved."

"All right. Then what?"

"I wanted to brush my teeth, so— No.
That's not right. Before I went to the bathroom, I remember I took off my coat and
dropped it on the bed."

She stopped, frowning to herself.

"No, that's not quite right, either." She
thought for another long moment, and then
she said slowly, almost to herself, "First, I took
everything out of my pockets. My coat pockets
and my pants pockets. I emptied them. My
gloves and my scarf and everything, whatever
was in there. And I dumped it all in a pile on
my bureau."

"Where it still is."

"Where it still is."

Carlo stood up. "Jesus Christ, I'm too dumb
to be a detective. I thought because nothing
happened there—Come on, let's go."

She had not been back to her apartment
since the night of the rape. Carlo was slow
climbing up the steep flights of stairs to the
third floor. She remembered walking down
these stairs with her parents and the precinct
officers. A wretched memory.

A long time ago.

When she unlocked the front door and

opened it, she felt the wave of emptiness that fills a deserted apartment. With Jenny gone to live with Sid Carson, even the familiar furniture looked strange and forlorn.

When Carlo caught his breath, he said, "Where's your room?"

"This way."

Carlo's bulk seemed to fill her small bedroom. Together they looked down at the jumble on top of her bureau. Her wool gloves lay haphazardly on top of her rumpled green plaid scarf.

"Better let me do this," Carlo said.

His big hands delicately and carefully lifted first the gloves, one at a time, seeming barely to touch them. Then he picked up the scarf, his fingers holding it by the fringe.

"There it is," he said quietly, pointing to the shiny blue plastic card half hidden under a piece of Kleenex.

But Nancy's attention was riveted to a wrinkled oblong sheet of plain white paper. She stared at the five quivery block letters written on it by someone whose hand had been shaking with terror.

ORION.

"Yes, I see it."

"How did I get that?"

With his thumbs and forefingers, making sure to touch only the edges of the paper, he turned it over. They both bent down to look.

It was a paycheck stub from the Lanier Warehouse & Trucking Company on Hudson Street. It was made out to James Flowers.

"He changed his name," Carlo said. "But not much."

Lineup

"There it is," Vincent said.

"Yeah, I see it."

Billy Cooney, who was driving, pulled over in front of Lanier Warehouse & Trucking, an elderly brick building that occupied a third of the block. He parked in front of a fire hydrant, and they climbed out.

Both detectives were armed. Both carried notebooks. Billy Cooney had the handcuffs in his jacket pocket.

In a shabby, warehouse kind of way, the Lanier front office was strictly for business. No guest chairs or carpeting. A young man was seated behind a tall barrier counter. Vincent and Cooney took out their wallets, flipped them open and showed him their IDs.

"We'd like to see Mr. Lanier," Carlo said.

"There isn't any Lanier," the young man said. He was still staring at the IDs.

"Who's in charge then?"

"The manager. Mr. Jonas. You going to arrest him? What's he done?"

"No, we'd just like to see him. Please get him for us."

"I'm not supposed to leave the desk."

"We'll watch it for you," Cooney said. "And don't say anything about police."

"Yes, sir."

The young man went through a doorway. He returned a few minutes later with a stocky, middle-aged man wearing an open-neck plaid work shirt.

"I'm Jonas," he said suspiciously. "What you want?"

"We're police officers," Carlo said. "Detective Vincent and Detective Cooney."

Again they showed their IDs. Jonas took a pair of horn-rimmed glasses from his shirt pocket, put them on and studied the cards carefully, glancing up at their faces to make sure they were who their cards said they were.

"Okay," he said. "What's the trouble? We just got inspected last month."

"No trouble," Carlo said. "We'd like to talk to one of your employees, ask him a few questions." He pulled out a photocopy of the paycheck stub and showed it to Jonas. "Is this one of your pay stubs?"

Jonas studied it. "Yep, that's ours."

Carlo showed Jonas a copy of James Garden's picture. "This man works here, doesn't he?"

"Jimmy Flowers? Sure. In the loading department."

Cooney was jotting notes.

"What you want him for?" Jonas asked.

"Is he here today?"

"Sure. At least I saw him an hour or so ago. On the loading dock. Want me to get him?"

Now that he knew the detectives had no complaint against the business itself, Jonas was eager to cooperate.

"Yeah. Only we'd like to see him in private. Is there an office we can use?"

"You can use mine. Come on."

He lifted the wooden bar that guarded the entrance. Vincent walked through, followed by Cooney.

"And don't say anything to him about police," Carlo said. "Just bring him to us."

"Sure thing."

He led him to his small office and left them.

While he was gone, they did not speak, but Billy Cooney grinned at Carlo—a wild, happy grin. No matter how many times they did this, no matter how many arrests they had made, at this moment the adrenaline always came surging up.

After a few minutes Jonas returned through the doorway.

Right behind him came an athletic-looking black man. He wore olive-drab wool trousers and a black sweater, the sleeves pushed up to his elbows. His long black hair was tied back. Powerful shoulders. He walked with a casual arrogance, very sure of himself.

"These men want to talk to you," Jonas said.

"James Flowers?"

The man nodded. His eyes glanced from one to the other. He seemed only mildly curious.

"We're police officers."

For the third time they held out their IDs for inspection. Flowers did not even bother to look. His expression did not change. He waited for whatever was next.

"Thanks, Mr. Jonas," Billy said. He eased the disappointed manager out the door and closed it on him. He kept his back against the door and rested his hand on his gun butt, in case Flowers had any ideas.

"We're conducting an investigation," Vincent said. "Maybe you can guess what it's about."

There was always a chance, a hope, that at this moment a defendant would say something spontaneous, something useful and incriminating. Later at the station, before formal questioning began, he would have to be read his Miranda warnings, reminding him that he had the right to remain silent and to have a lawyer. But right here at the beginning, while he was surprised and still off guard, a defendant sometimes volunteered telltale information. Sometimes a lot of information.

James Garden, aka James Flowers, was not one of these. He put his hands in his pockets, still casual, and stared back at Vincent without saying a word. A very cool customer.

Vincent tried several other comments with the same result. Flowers continued to look at him with a silent, steady indifference that was not quite a sneer.

Finally Vincent had to admit this was hopeless. Maybe when they got him back on their own turf, handcuffed to a chair in a strange setting, it would be different, although Vincent was not so sure. He said, "I'm placing you under arrest and taking you to the station."

Billy Cooney got out the handcuffs. He pulled Flowers' hands out of his pockets and cuffed them behind his back. Then he frisked Flowers to make sure he had no weapon. Vincent, watching Flowers' face, saw no chance of expression. Very cool indeed. He looked at his watch. "Time of arrest is 2:13."

Billy Cooney checked his own watch. "It's 2:20. When are you going to break down and get a quartz watch?"

"It's my case," Carlo said, "so it's my watch. 2:13."

He opened the office door. Jonas was standing right outside. Carlo thanked him for his help. He and Billy Cooney each took a firm elbow grip on their prisoner and headed for the front door.

But just before they stepped out on the sidewalk, a thought occurred to Carlo. He turned back to Jonas and asked another question.

After notifying both Nancy and A.D.A. Joan Hennessy of the arrest and the plan for an evening lineup, Vincent and Cooney had a lot of work to do. Vincent had to conduct the interrogation and make all the necessary arrangements inside the station.

Billy Cooney and Big Zeke set off in an oversized police van for the armory at 168th Street and Fort Washington.

The old armory, now converted to a homeless men's shelter, was the prime source for lineup fillers. Sometimes, if a defendant was very young, the detectives went to high schools to find five people who looked more or less similar in height, age, color and general appearance. But for this case the armory was the obvious place. Not only was there a very large population to choose from, but the detectives never had to waste time explaining what they wanted. They came here so often that the homeless inmates knew exactly what they were here for. The city paid each lineup filler five dollars in cash, a bonanza to these penniless men.

The huge armory floor was lined, crammed, with row upon row of cots. As soon as Billy and Zeke walked through the main door, they were recognized.

"Hey, man, you want me! Me!"

"I'm just who you're looking for!"

"I'm the one! I'm the one!"

It took a while to explain, through the hubbub of eager volunteers, that this time the detectives were interested only in blacks and only in a certain age group. Although this eliminated a large number of contestants, Billy and Zeke spent well over an hour going down the lines, inspecting candidates one by one, and making their selections. One man offered to shave off his full beard then and there in order to qualify, but Cooney said they didn't have time for that.

When they had all their fillers, they piled them into the van and drove them back to the station.

There was still a lot to do.

Carlo and Joan Hennessy, who had chosen to be present, inspected the fillers. Carlo had gotten absolutely nothing from the interrogation, so the lineup, always crucial, took on added importance.

James Garden, still cuffed, was entitled to pick his own place in the lineup so there could be no charge of loading the arrangement. He chose number four.

The numbered cards were hung around the necks of Garden and the five fillers. They all took their chairs in the lineup row.

Billy Cooney, still armed, kept his eyes on Garden while Zeke photographed the lineup for the court record. The room was too small to shoot all six at once, so he had to shoot the first three from one angle, then the second three from the opposite angle.

Then he walked down the line with his notebook, taking each filler's name, current address and date of birth for the court record.

Billy and Zeke checked to make sure the two phones were working, the one inside the room that Billy would use, the other outside where Carlo would stand with Nancy when she looked through the one-way glass window.

"All set?"

"All set."

Carlo went over the checklist in his own mind. So much depended on this. Everything had to be just right. There must be no flaw in the procedure.

"Okay," he told Billy and Zeke, "keep them quiet. I'll prep Nancy."

When Carlo had called Nancy to tell her about the arrest and the plan for a lineup, he said something ominous.

"Better bring somebody with you."

Already alarmed by what she had to face, Nancy asked, "How do you mean?"

A pause before he answered. "Well, bring your mother or your father. Or your guy Tommy. Or your roommate, what's-her-name, Jenny. Somebody like that."

"What for?"

An even longer pause. "It's just that— Well, sometimes it can be kind of an ordeal. It's a good idea for you to have somebody close. We'll pick you up when it's time and drive you home after, but it helps to have somebody right there with you."

If Carlo admitted it was an ordeal, then it must be. But Nancy already felt that. Ever since she had heard about the possibility, the necessity, of a lineup, she had been frightened. It was one thing to look at inanimate pictures. It was quite another to have to look right at *him*, The Other One. That man. That angry man who tried to destroy her. All she wanted to do was forget him, if she ever possibly could. She did not want to see him again.

She could still back out. She had wanted to back out a hundred times. Once, when Carlo was making her go through all those C.A.T.C.H. drawers, she had picked up the phone to tell him she was not coming. Not coming today and maybe not coming ever again. Then she reminded herself what they had done to her and changed her mind. She kept the appointment. And finally picked him out of those thousands of pictures.

But now it was different. They had arrested him, and they had the evidence of his pay stub where she had written her code word ORION. For God's sake, she thought, that must be enough to convict him. But they always wanted more, no matter what it cost anybody else.

But suppose she didn't go tonight, and somehow, because of that, he got off.

She called the Metropolitan Museum where her mother was on docent duty and left an urgent message. Fifteen minutes later Carol called back.

"Mom, they arrested him. They're going to have that lineup tonight. Will you come with me? Carlo says I'll need somebody to hold my hand."

"Of course, darling. When is it?"

"They'll pick us up here at seven-thirty."

"Oh, dear, we have a dinner at the Swensons. Could they do it later, after dinner?"

"Mom, I really don't think so. I need you."

"Well, never mind, your father can make my excuses. Of course, I'll come with you. Are you all right?"

"No, I'm not. I'm scared. I'm going to have to look right at him."

"I still don't see why they have to put you through this."

Neither did Nancy. "I'm going to lie down for a while."

"All right. I'll be home in about an hour. Have a nice nap."

But a nap would have been impossible. Nancy went into her old bedroom and pulled the curtains shut. Then she lay down on her bed in the darkened room, closed her eyes, and tried to remember how he looked. Within a few minutes she was close to panic. She suddenly could not remember anything, not even the picture.

And yet she must do it. The team had explained to her that picking out his picture was very good but simply not enough. Billy Cooney told her a story, with his usual embellishments, about one rape victim who had made a positive ID from the picture file. Only then it turned out that the man she picked was still in prison and could not possibly have committed the crime. So the lineup was crucial, a key piece of evidence. She was terrified of failure.

By the time the police car picked them up at her parents' building, Nancy was too bewildered to do anything but clutch her mother's hand. All the way across town to the station she held tight. Her mother was the right choice. Carol did not say anything, did not make conversation with the driver the way she normally would. She was just there for Nancy.

Joan Hennessy and Carlo were waiting for them in Sergeant Blaine's office. As soon as they walked in, Carlo got up and closed the door.

Her mother told Joan Hennessy, "I'm Carol Whittredge, Nancy's mother," and they shook hands.

When Carlo got them seated, he said, "Joan and I want to talk to you for a couple of minutes."

Before Carlo could say anything more, Nancy asked what had been on her mind for hours. "Will he be able to see me?"

Carlo shook his head. "Not a chance."

"It's the first thing everybody asks," Joan Hennessy said. She was wearing a blue tweed suit Nancy had seen before. She was smoking a cigarette in a long holder. "The window is one-way glass. You can see him, but he can't see you."

"I'm not sure I can go through this."

Joan stamped out her cigarette, removed it from the holder and inserted another. "Yes, you can." She lighted her cigarette with a tiny gold lighter.

"I'll be right beside you," her mother said.

"Actually, Mrs. Whittredge, I'm afraid you can't be," Carlo said. He looked apologetic. "You can wait here, but Nancy has to do this by herself."

"But Carlo, you *told* me to bring somebody."

"Now, Nancy—" Carlo began, but Joan stepped in.

Joan said, "Nancy, I want you to listen to me." She leaned forward until her light blue eyes were only a foot from Nancy's face. She was kindly but intense. "I know you're nervous. That's perfectly natural. Having to look at him again is probably the most difficult thing you've had to do since the rape itself. Many women feel that way. But just put that out of your mind for a second and listen to me. You can't do anything about the rape. And we can't do anything about it, either. That happened to you, and there is nothing anyone can do to make it go away. But you *can* make sure he doesn't do it again to some other poor woman. You can help us lock him away for years."

She took a deep drag on her cigarette, and

Nancy realized Joan was nervous, too. Right now Nancy did not care about "some other poor woman."

Carlo didn't either. "Listen, Nancy, you and I been working together a long time. We know each other. I know there've been times you wanted to quit, and I don't blame you. It's damn hard work."

Her mother started to say something, but Carlo held up his beefy hand at her, almost in anger. Nancy had never seen her mother shut up so fast.

"The reason you didn't quit, and the reason I wouldn't let you quit, is we both want the same thing. To get even. Tonight, by God, we're going to nail it down. *You're* going to nail it down."

He stopped to look at her, to make sure she had taken it in. "Now I'm going to go through the procedure with you. It's very simple. I'll take you to a spot right outside the lineup room. The door will be closed, and there's a screen over the window. When I lift the screen, you'll see six men sitting in chairs in a row. They'll have numbered cards, one to six. You won't be able to see him, but Billy Cooney will be inside the room with the six men. He'll have his gun in plain sight, so they can't do anything.

"Nothing can happen. Remember, they can't

see you. They can't even hear you. There's nothing for you to be afraid of. All you have to do is look at the six men and tell me which one you recognize. Joan'll be there, too, to make sure everything is done right so it will stand up in court. There is absolutely nothing for you to be afraid of."

"Yes, there is." Nancy could hear her voice shake. "Him."

"He can't get at you." ·

"That's not what I mean."

Her mother said, "Really, Miss Hennessy, is all this necessary? Just look at her."

Joan gave her mother a tough stare. "Of course, it's necessary. Otherwise we wouldn't be doing it."

A knock on the door made Nancy jump. "Come in."

Big Zeke stuck his shaved head through the opening. "All set," he said. "Hello, Nancy. You ready?"

She was never going to be ready, but she stood up.

"You just wait here, Mrs. Whittredge," Joan said. "It won't take long, and then we'll be right back."

But her mother got up anyway to give Nancy a hug. "You can do it, darling. I know you can do it."

Carlo took Nancy's arm as they walked

through the office bullpen. His solid grip helped her get there. Joan Hennessy and Zeke followed behind.

When they stopped in front of an office wall, Carlo said, "Okay?"

"I can't do this." Her body began to tremble.

Carlo's grip on her arm tightened. "Nancy, you are not going to blow this now."

With his other hand he lifted the screen. He waited a few seconds and then said, "Do you recognize anybody?"

Nancy looked into the small room where, only a dozen feet away, six black men sat in a row facing her.

She glanced wildly at the six stolid faces. She had never seen any of them before.

"I can't. Carlo, I can't." She was shaking all over.

"You already did it with the pictures. Just do it again."

He put his arm around her waist to hold her steady, but she went on shaking. She thought she might be going to faint. She had to end this.

"I don't know," she whispered. Anything to get this over with. She took a blind guess: "Number Two."

"I couldn't hear that," Carlo said. "Just a minute." He picked up a telephone and said,

"Billy, bring them up to the window one at a time."

His arm around her waist squeezed so hard that it hurt. "Now you just shut up," he said. "Shut up and look. Really look."

Billy Cooney must have spoken to the man with number one on his chest. The man got up and walked right toward her. He stopped two feet from the window, so close she could not believe he couldn't see her.

"Turn him," Carlo said into his phone.

Billy apparently spoke to the man again. The man turned sideways so that his face was in profile. Nancy forced herself to take a quick look at him. Then the man returned to his seat.

When Number Two came up to the window and showed his profile, Nancy had a thought. She turned her own head sideways so that she could look at him out of the corner of her eye, the way she had seen him that night. *No.*

Number Three. *No.*

When Number Four walked up and turned, Nancy slumped in Carlo's arm. That long, straight jaw, that knob of a chin, that nose, that Indian look . . .

Click.

He returned to his seat.

"That's enough," Nancy said. "It's Number Four."

Carlo's tight grip relaxed, though he still held her.

"Louder," he said, "so Joan can hear you."

"I heard her."

"Number Four," Nancy repeated, her voice suddenly stronger.

"Are you sure?"

"Yes. Positive."

"When did you last see him?"

"The night of the rape. Under the street-light."

Carlo lowered the screen. He spoke into the phone. "Okay, Billy, she got him." Then he slammed down the phone and threw his big arms around her. "That's my girl!"

No one had to help Nancy back to Blaine's office. She practically bounced. Carlo kept patting her shoulder.

As they walked in together, Joan Hennessy told her mother, "She did it, Mrs. Whittredge."

Everybody was elated, congratulating her. Nancy knew she deserved it. Her sense of relief was extraordinary.

"Where's my team?" she asked. "Where's Billy? Where's Zeke?"

She saw Carlo and Joan exchange a quick glance.

"They're taking care of some things," Carlo said.

"God!" Nancy said. "I'm so glad that's over. I feel like celebrating."

"We'll have champagne as soon as we get home," Carol promised. "I must call your father at the Swensons' and tell him. He'll be so proud of you!" And then to Carlo, "Is it all right for us to go home now?"

"Well . . ."

"Mom, I have to wait for Billy and Zeke. Will they be long?"

That same quick glance between Joan and Carlo. Joan stuck another cigarette in her holder. Nancy realized something was going on, but she was too happy to care.

"Not long," Carlo said. "A few minutes."

"What do they do now?" Nancy asked. "With him, I mean."

"Later on they'll take him down to headquarters, to Central Booking," Joan said. "Then there's a big bunch of paper work. Tomorrow he'll be arraigned."

Nancy was so pleased with herself that she wanted to call up everybody she knew and tell them. She wondered what was keeping Billy and Big Zeke. If they didn't come soon, she would have to leave without talking to them. Already her mother was looking around for her coat.

The desk phone rang. Carlo picked it up, listened for a moment, and said, "Okay, I'll bring her over." He hung up and nodded to Joan.

"Now Nancy," Joan said, "I don't want you to be upset. You did great. But we are going to have to ask you to do the lineup again."

"Again! What for?" She definitely did not want see that face again. "Didn't I do it right?"

"It's just for the record," Joan said.

Joan must have heard her say Number Two when she was making a wild stab. Nancy felt a little embarrassed about that, letting the team down. She would not repeat that foolish mistake.

"I never heard of such a thing," her mother said. She stood up. "I'm not going to let you put Nancy through that again."

"It'll only take a minute."

"It's all right, Mom. I'm really all right now. Then can we go home?"

"Sure," Carlo said, "Come on, let's finish it up."

He took her to the same spot beside the window screen. "You okay?"

She nodded, although she had begun to feel nervous all over again. Not nearly so bad as the first time, however. Carlo did not have to support her.

He raised the screen. "Do you recognize anybody?"

To her amazement this lineup was totally different. She saw at once that these were six other men and that each one had a mustache and several had goatees. Not only that, but instead of numbered cards on their chests, they wore jaunty, bright yellow baseball caps. Each man's number was in the center of his cap.

Her eyes jumped to the chunky man at the end of the line. He had a small goatee and a rather pleasant grin.

"My God," she said, "there's Bernie!"

They were all seated around the bullpen. Smiles on every face, including her own. Carlo left the story to Billy Cooney, the squad's designated yarn-spinner.

"We're just walking out the warehouse door," Billy explained, "bringing Garden back here for questioning, when Carlo asks the manager, 'Say, by the way, do you have anybody working here named Bernie?' And the manager goes, 'Bernie? Sure, Bernie Webb. He's a good friend of Jimmy's. They pal around.'

"So Carlo and I look at each other, we're both still hanging on to Garden, and Carlo says to the manager, like it didn't really make much difference to us one way or the other, 'Could we talk to him for a minute?' So the manager goes and finds Bernie and brings him out, and we take one look, and Carlo hauls out his gun to cover them both and says, 'Billy, you better get another pair of cuffs from the car.'"

Everybody laughed, but Billy held up his hand to indicate that this part of the story was not quite finished.

"So the manager looks at us and then he looks at them, and then he goes, 'You're taking them *both*? How am I going to get my truck loaded?'"

Everybody laughed again.

"But why didn't you tell me?" Nancy asked. "Why didn't you tell me you caught them both?"

"We talked it over," Carlo said. "All of us, Joan, too. We figured you had enough to worry about with just one lineup to face. If you knew you had two, it might have been too much for you."

"I guess it could have been. I was kind of shaky."

"'Kind of shaky'!" Carlo said. "You'd have fallen down if I hadn't hung on to you."

Now that it was over, Nancy could join in the laughter.

"What was all that business with those yellow caps?"

"That was at my insistence," Joan Hennessy said. "I—"

But Billy Cooney was not about to let a mere chief sex crimes prosecutor tell his story in his own squad room. "That second lineup!" he broke in on Joan, talking straight to Nancy.

"Zeke and I are up in the armory picking out our fillers. The first ones, for Garden, that wasn't too hard—no harder than usual, anyway. But when we get around to fillers for Bernie, that was much tougher. You always made such a point about his flat-top haircut. Every time you described him, you mentioned it. So we're looking for guys somewhere around Bernie's build and age with mustaches and maybe goatees, only plus a flattop. Well, I tell you, Nancy, up there at the men's shelter, they don't exactly have the latest hairdos. Not too many visits to the barbershop, you know? We bust our asses—excuse me, Mrs. Whittredge—but we only find one flattop. So we have to settle for what we find, 'having used our best efforts,' like the instructions tell us, and we bring them back here.

"Joan takes one look and says, 'I don't see enough flattops.' And I say, 'Sorry, that's all we could find.' So Joan says, 'I am not going into court with a lineup picture that shows just two flattops out of six. This twerp's attorney would claim Nancy's ID is invalid because only one guy besides his client has that distinctive kind of hair. The judge would throw it out.'

"So Carlo says, kind of annoyed, 'What do you expect us to do?' And Joan says, 'Put the caps on them.'

"Well, Carlo and Zeke and me hit the roof. It's a key part of your description, and now Joan wants to cover it up, take it away from us. So we explain how we did our best and how important it is for you to see his hair, and Sergeant Blaine supports us, and we give Joan all the arguments. Damn good ones, too." Billy shrugged, smiled and held out his hands. "And so then we put the caps on them."

"I thought I was looking at some kind of crazy baseball team," Nancy said. "I didn't know what was going on."

"It doesn't matter," Carlo said. "You got him."

In the Amphitheater

Nancy sat in Joan Hennessy's paper-piled office, listening to her instructions. She was beginning to feel that as soon as you got through one thing, they dug up another for you. She wondered if all rape cases were like that.

"A grand jury," Joan promised, "is very straightforward. There's no judge and no defendant. There's no defense lawyer, and there are no defense witnesses."

"It sounds kind of one-sided," Nancy said.

Joan laughed. "One-sided is right. Unless the A.D.A. goofs up, a grand jury indicts practically every single case. It only takes a majority of the twenty-three jurors to indict, and there's no opposition—unless a couple of jurors take it into their heads to be skeptical and manage to persuade the others. In your case there won't be a problem."

"Good. I'm all for something easy." One of the things Nancy liked about Joan Hennessy was her hardheaded approach. She was direct and professional.

"I'll be right there with you. All you do is walk in, stand to be sworn in by the foreman, and then sit down and tell your story. Actually you don't even have to tell your story. I'll ask you direct questions about what happened, and you answer. You won't be there more than ten minutes."

"Great." Nancy knew Joan was doing her best to encourage her. She was ready to be encouraged. She had never testified before.

Joan's phone rang but she ignored it. "There are just a couple of things."

"You sound like Carlo. I knew there was going to be a catch."

"Not a catch, really. Just some things to be aware of. First, I want you to dress neatly and simply. A skirt and sweater, just like you have on now, is fine, but make sure it's not a tight sweater. Nothing gaudy or flashy, I want you to be ladylike. No jewelry. You wear something the least bit sexy, and the jurors might wonder if you provoked the attack. Some people always think a rape had to be the woman's fault. Sit up straight and remember

to keep your voice up so they can all hear you.
If they don't hear you, they sometimes get
confused. I'll stand in the back of the room on
the platform, and if you speak loudly enough
for me to hear, then they'll all hear you. You
keep your eyes on me, and it will be almost as
though you and I were having a private conversation. You have a good voice, so make
sure you use it."

"Okay. What's the hard part you're not
telling me?"

"Well, we want the maximum against these
two bastards, right?"

"Right. Sure."

"All right." Joan held up her hand and
ticked off the charges finger by finger. "Robbery in the First Degree as an armed felony,
both Garden and Webb. Rape in the First
Degree, both Garden and Webb. Sodomy in
the First Degree, one count against Garden,
two counts against Webb."

"Why two on Bernie?"

Joan's voice remained calm, methodical.
"Once in your anus, once in your mouth."

"But I thought sodomy had to be—"

Joan shook her head. "Under state law,
sodomy is not restricted to anal intercourse. It
is defined as any 'deviate sexual intercourse.'
In the law's eyes, that means anywhere other
than in the vagina."

"Oh."

"Right. Now we want an indictment on each and every one of these counts. In order to get that, you'll have to tell the jury exactly what they did to you." Joan's light blue eyes had a hard, level look. "And I mean exactly."

"Oh, shit."

"Right."

Many of the Weezies had served as regular jurors. The station executives were willing to write letters asking that an employee's jury summons be postponed because his work was too important, and they often wrote such letters for the business side. But Mike Barnes warned the news staff that if any reporter, writer or anchor tried to avoid jury duty, Mike would view that person very unfavorably. "Next to paying taxes," he said, "jury duty is the most valuable thing a citizen can do. And it's more interesting than paying taxes."

Actually, as they had learned, it was seldom interesting because men and women in the news business were routinely rejected. They might get as far as a panel, but then defense lawyers threw them out. Defense lawyers did not want jurors who were used to asking hard questions and weighing facts. Only when a defense lawyer had already exhausted his challenges might a reporter slip onto a jury.

Nancy had served once but, like most Weezies, had never sat on a case.

But a grand jury, Mike said, was different. With no one to challenge, anybody who was called got to serve. But when she asked around, Nancy learned that only two Weezies, Ted Meadows and Mary Ann Sims, had ever been on a grand jury.

Ted, as usual, considered himself the expert. "At first it's fun," he said, "because it's serious. You start right off hearing cases, sometimes five or six a day, and you have to decide whether or not they should go to trial. But it doesn't take long to realize that they're all pretty much the same. An assistant D.A. comes in and tells you you're going to hear about a robbery or whatever. Then he brings in the guy who was robbed and gets him to tell how the robber stole his wallet and what the robber looked like. Then they bring in the cop who made the arrest, and the cop says, yeah, he arrested the robber and recovered the man's wallet. Then everybody leaves the room and we vote. Sometimes we don't even have to discuss it, just raise your hands to vote yes. You do that three hours a day, and after a week or so, people start bringing their coffee or soda into the jury room and reading newspapers during testimony. Piece of cake. After a while it takes something really juicy to wake them up. Like a murder, or—"

Ted stopped, somewhat embarrassed. "Sorry. I guess you qualify."

Joan Hennessy stuck her head in the witness room, where Nancy was waiting with Carlo. "All right, Nancy, you're on."

Joan had already outlined the case to the grand jury, so they knew what they were about to hear.

"Remember to speak up," Joan said as she led her into the jury room, closing the door behind. Then she pointed down a flight of steps.

At the very bottom sat a gray-haired man poised over a stenotype machine. Next to him was an empty wooden chair. Nancy walked down the long flight to the chair and turned to face the jury.

It was like being in the pit of an amphitheater. The seats were ringed in a semicircle, the rows climbing steeply one above another to the top. Some twenty men and women were all staring down at her. Nobody was reading. Nobody was drinking coffee. They all stared intently, as though she were some kind of bizarre exhibit. It made her squirm.

At the very top, behind the rows of seats, a tall, middle-aged man with glasses stood up and said, "Please raise your right hand." Then he read from a card, "Do you solemnly swear that the evidence you are about to give will be the truth, the whole truth and nothing but the truth, so help you God?"

When she said, "I do," he sat down, and then Nancy took the wooden chair beside the stenotypist. She felt very lonely under all those eyes.

High in the back, off to one side of the jury foreman, Joan Hennessy asked Nancy to state her name, age and address. When she did so, the stenotypist told her in a harsh voice to spell Whittredge. She was so nervous that she actually stumbled over it, and he made her spell it again.

As they had rehearsed it, Joan led her through the mundane part: the date, the time of evening, the bank cubicle, the cash withdrawal, the departure from the bank, the walk down the dark side street in the direction of her apartment.

"And then what occurred?"

"I heard footsteps running up behind me."

"Please keep your voice up so that the jurors can hear you. And then?"

Nancy got through the gun and the robbery details, but when Joan had at last placed her inside the abandoned garage, kneeling on the floor with her clothes off, her voice faltered again. The ring of staring faces shook her. She hated to have to tell this to all these hungry-eyed strangers.

Suddenly Joan's voice turned hard and cutting. "Miss Whittredge, if you do not speak up loudly and clearly, the jurors cannot possibly hear your testimony."

Nancy flushed. She felt as though a friend had slapped her. She had been twisting her hands, but now she placed them firmly on the arms of the witness chair. *I have to do this right.* "I'm sorry," she said.

"Thank you. And then what occurred?"

"Then they raped me. Both of them."

"Yes. When you say they 'raped' you, what do you mean?"

She took a deep breath to strengthen her voice. "They inserted their penises, one after the other, in my anus."

She heard a woman juror gasp.

"Yes. Was that painful?"

"Very."

"You are certain that both of them did this?"

"Yes. After one did it for a while, he got off and then the other one did it."

"And then what?"

"Then they also went into my vagina."

"When you say they 'went into your vagina,' how do you mean?"

"With their penises."

"Both of them?"

Nancy nodded.

Joan said to the stenotypist, "The witness indicates by nodding that her answer is yes." Then to Nancy, "You are testifying that after both defendants inserted their penises in your anus, they then both inserted their penises in your vagina. Is that correct?"

"Yes."

"And why did you permit this?"

"They had the gun. I was afraid they would kill me."

"You were in fear of your life?"

"Definitely."

"Now how long did this go on?"

"I don't—".

"Approximately."

"Fifteen minutes, twenty minutes? I'm guessing. I was so scared it seemed like forever. They kept taking turns on me."

Her voice caught. The jury room was deathly still except for the tiny sound of the stenotype keys.

Joan let the silence hang for a long moment. Then she led Nancy through the defendants' attempt to get the rest of her money by using her bank code.

"And when the defendant whom you subsequently came to know as James Garden went back to the bank for the second time, did anything occur in the garage?"

"Yes, he—"

"The other defendant? The one you had heard addressed as Bernie?"

"Yes. He made me—"

"Did he say anything to you?"

"Yes."

"Can you recall what he said?"

"He said, 'How about a nice blow job?'"

This time there were not only gasps but movement. Several jurors shifted around in their seats. Joan waited for them to settle.

"And did you perform this act?"

"At first I said I couldn't, please don't make me, and then he threatened me with the gun."

"When you say 'threatened,' what do you mean?"

"He held it right in my face."

"And then you performed the act?"

"Yes."

"Under forcible compulsion, you took his penis into your mouth."

"Yes."

Joan was silent for a moment. Then she said, "I have no further questions for this witness."

Instantly a woman juror's hand shot up.

"A juror indicates that she would like to ask a question. Just a minute."

Joan had warned Nancy that when testimony ended, jurors frequently had additional questions, but that these must not be asked aloud until Joan could determine that they were proper and relevant. Frequently jurors' questions were only idle curiosity, but Joan said it was best to humor them if possible. An irritated juror whose question was rejected might get even by voting against indictment.

Joan walked to the woman's seat on the center aisle in the third row and bent down to listen. The woman, a perky, elderly lady with wire-rimmed glasses, said something in a low voice. Then Joan said something back to the woman, and they had more conversation. Nancy could not hear what they were saying.

Joan stood up and returned to her place in the back of the room. "Although the crime of armed robbery has already been established by the testimony of this witness, a juror would like to know, Miss Whittredge, if the defendants succeeded in getting any more money from your bank."

"They couldn't make my code work, so finally I had to go back and get the money for them."

Joan looked at the woman juror, who promptly raised her hand again. Joan went back to her and bent down. This time she did not bother to return to her place.

"Although the amount is not a factor in establishing the crime of armed robbery, a juror would like to know how much additional money you gave the defendants."

"Four hundred dollars. All there was in my account."

"Thank you. If there are no further questions—yes?"

A young man no older than Nancy had his hand up. Joan walked over to him.

"A juror asks how Miss Whittredge was able to identify the defendants. That will be established by the testimony of the next witness, a police officer. If there are no—yes, just a minute."

She went to the far side of the room where an older man had raised his hand. She listened to his question, then stood up, eyes flashing angrily.

"No, I'm sorry. There is no need to ask the witness that question. When I read you the law after all the testimony is completed, you will see that that information is unnecessary for you to reach your decision."

When there were no more questions, Joan said, "Thank you, Miss Whittredge. You are excused. The next witness I will call is Detective Vincent."

Nancy rose from her chair. She could feel the jurors' eyes follow her up the stairs and through the door Joan was holding for her.

Outside the jury room, Joan said, "Sorry I had to get a little rough with you. You did great."

"It was my fault. That room is so scary. What did that last man want to know?"

"When it's a sex crime, they can never get enough. He wanted to know if Bernie came in your mouth."

Back Home Again

When James Garden and Bernie Webb were indicted on all counts, Nancy decided it was time to move back to her own apartment. Her mother helped her pack, while trying to talk her out of it.

"I really wish, darling, that you'd stay here a little longer. Another week or two, just to get back on your feet. Your father thinks so, too. You know we love having you."

Nancy did not remind her mother that she had moved out in the first place to be on her own. With all her parents' help and concern these last weeks, she did not want to hurt anyone's feelings.

"I'm really okay, Mom. I have to pick up again."

She could see her mother, with a small pile of underwear in her hands, thinking over what to say.

293

"I know, but don't you think—well, wouldn't you feel safer here?"

"They're locked up. I won't have to worry about running into them on the street." She took the underwear out of her mother's hands and put it in the suitcase.

"I wish Jenny were going to be there with you."

"Me, too. Maybe she'll come back, once I'm back. If not, I'll just have to get another roommate."

She did not feel as airy about this as she sounded. If Jenny did not return from her experiment of living with Sid, finding a new roommate would be a real gamble. Everybody she knew had a horror story about someone who had looked great on the surface but turned out to leave glasses all over the living room or to think that frying pans could stay in the sink for three days before being washed.

"I wish you'd think about getting married."

This was too much. "Okay, so I'll think about it."

"Don't be annoyed, darling. I'm only worried about your welfare."

"Mom, I'm twenty-five. How about letting *me* worry about my welfare?"

After a moment Carol said, "Well, I'll let you finish packing."

So she wound up hurting her mother's feelings after all.

Somehow she was out of step even with the people she loved most. Like Basil. Her brother had called from college a couple of times, wondering how she was, sounding like old times. But it wasn't like old times for her, not after what he said when he first heard about the rape. Would it ever be the way it used to be between them?

But maybe now, with the two men locked up, she could start getting back to being herself, start putting it all behind her. Everything she had done with Carlo and the other detectives and Joan Hennessy, every picture she had looked at, served to perpetuate her memory of the rape.

Enough.

Her parents offered to drive her down to Tribeca, but she knew there would be less hassle if she went with Jenny and Sid and Tommy. Sid waited downstairs with his car while Jenny and Tommy, wearing sloppy weekend clothes, came up to help with the suitcases.

Her mother behaved perfectly, as she always did with company. Some parents were terrible with their children's friends, but not Carol. No tears. Smiles and pleasantries for Jenny and Tommy, how nice to see you both again. She did not even ask Jenny when she might be moving back. She did give Nancy a farewell hug, but neither too long nor too desperate.

So it was Nancy who made it a small occasion. "Mom, I couldn't have got through all this without you and Dad. A million thanks."

"For nothing, darling. That's what we're here for. Call us as soon as you're settled."

At the apartment in Tribeca, Nancy and Jenny led the way up the stairs. Tommy and Sid followed behind, lugging her suitcases. Jenny carried the tote bag with the welcome-home bottles of champagne.

When they unlocked the door and looked into their living room, Jenny said, "It sure could use a vacuum."

They could never figure out where all the dust came from. Even with the windows closed, the apartment needed dusting and vacuuming every few days. Now, unoccupied all this time, their living room wore a visible film on the floor and furniture. Jenny's theory was that a bottomless supply of ancient dust lay hidden in the old walls and came seeping out at night when no one was looking.

Nancy felt depressed that she would have to spend her first hours back home running the Eureka Mighty-Mite over every surface.

"First things first," Tommy said cheerfully. "I'll get the glasses." He dropped her suitcase in the dust and headed for the shelf above the stove.

Tommy had spent so much time here that he knew where everything was. Nancy could tell he was pleased to have her back in familiar surroundings instead of in her parents' apartment. Perhaps he thought everything would now return to normal. Nancy could barely remember what normal was like.

"It looks kind of dumpy," Jenny said, in the voice of someone who was not about to move back tomorrow morning.

Sid's apartment in a new high-rise building on upper Columbus Avenue was indeed cleaner and grander. But, furnished with austere modern metal chairs and a leather-and-chrome couch, it never felt like anyone's home. Nancy and Jenny used to agree on that, but maybe Jenny had made adjustments.

Tommy set four wine glasses on the coffee table. They made rings in the dust. He popped the cork of the first bottle and poured champagne, then handed out the glasses. Nancy could tell he was going to offer a toast.

"Well, here's to Nancy," he said, looking right at her with a fond sense of ownership. "Back home again, safe and successful."

"Hear, hear," from Sid.

They all drank. The champagne was almost cold.

"I better put those bottles in the fridge," Tommy said.

Nancy hated the word *fridge*.

When he came back, everybody sat down around the coffee table, same places as always. It looked like old times but didn't feel like it.

Sid, who never stopped being a lawyer, asked, "How does your case look, Nancy? From what Jenny says, it sounds like a shoo-in. You have a trial date yet?"

"Joan Hennessy hopes there won't be one."

"But sweetie," Jenny said, "they can't just let them go? After all you went through to catch them."

The question made Nancy realize how separated she and Jenny had become in a very short time. When they were roommates, they talked about everything that happened to either of them. Jenny would have known the same day Nancy knew.

"No, of course not. Joan's sure they'll plead guilty."

"Yes, that would be best," Sid said, nodding professionally. "It'll be over much quicker, and you won't have to sit there in court."

It was not sitting in court that Nancy longed to avoid. It was having to be a witness and be cross-examined.

"Why would they do that?" Jenny asked.

"They get shorter sentences if they plead."

"Is that what you want?" Tommy asked. "I thought you and that detective wanted them to get real long sentences. The longest possible." He got up to get more champagne.

"You have to be realistic," Sid called after him. "Nobody wants a trial."

"Well, if nobody wants a trial," Jenny said, "how come there's so many trials?"

"A trial," Sid explained, with lofty expertise, "is a last resort. It costs the state a lot of money and a lot of time, and you never know what might go wrong. All it takes is one quirky juror, or for the judge to make one funny ruling, and you can lose what looks like a perfect case. A million things could go wrong. Nobody wants to risk that. But fortunately for all us lawyers," he added with a smile, "enough cases do go to trial to keep us in business."

Nancy was irritated by Sid's comfortable superiority. Never in his life had Sid tried a criminal case, and he probably never would. His firm specialized in wills and trusts and estates. If Sid ever appeared in court at all, it was only to file papers or motions. But here he was, handing out his perceived bullshit.

"I better get unpacked," Nancy said.

"Hey, plenty of time for that. Let's finish this champagne." Tommy refilled the glasses.

Nancy sat through the champagne and the talk. What she wanted was to be left alone to unpack and start cleaning up. But this was her oldest, closest friend and her very enjoyable lover, who was also a friend. Even Sid was all right when not pontificating. And the three of them had come all the way down here to help her, bringing her favorite drink to cheer her on. So what felt so wrong?

She looked at them as the conversation bounced back and forth. Jenny with her shoes off and legs tucked up on the couch, chattering away with the bouncy vitality that made everyone forget she was not really pretty. Face too long, chin too long, and her long, brownish-blond hair had no particular shape to it. Obviously none of this bothered Sid, who sat beside her on the couch, beaming at her and holding her hand. Everybody liked Jenny and always had. Nancy most of all. Why didn't it feel the same?

And Tommy. Tommy, with his strong, block-shaped face and short, straight black hair and eyebrows and the merry eyes that kept coming back to her no matter who was talking. They had been lovers so long that they had pretty much run out of things to invent. Their bodies already knew everything that gave them pleasure. She could tell from his eyes that he could not wait to be alone with her. It was a feeling that, somewhere along the way, she had lost. And now did not share. But she could not go on turning him away.

What's wrong with me? As if I didn't know.

There was still a third left in the last bottle of champagne when Sid said, "Come on, Jenny, we have to be getting home."

Jenny made no protest. She slipped into her shoes and stood up. "Well, sweetie," she said to Nancy, "sorry to leave you, but I guess you'll be in good hands."

Sid stood up too. "You sure we can't give you a ride, Tomaso?"

"Are you kidding?"

Everybody laughed except Nancy.

When they had gone, Tommy closed and locked the front door and, in an almost continuous motion, put his arms around her and pulled her tight against him and gave her a long tongue-filled kiss. Nothing happened to her.

"Tommy, please. I'm tired."

"Good. I'll put you right to bed."

"No, I mean it. I'm too tired to feel anything."

"Feel this."

"I'm serious."

"Honey, you've been serious too long. You have to get over it. It's all over now. Come on, let's go to bed."

"Tommy—"

"I've been wanting you all this time. It'll make you all right again. We'll wipe it right out. I'm sorry, do your breasts still hurt?"

"No, they're not sore anymore. I just don't want to."

"That's good. They're so beautiful."

"It's just that I— Listen, I'm not myself. I don't feel like myself. Maybe later on. You have to give me a little time."

"I already have."

Maybe, after all, it would help her to get back to the person she used to be.

But it didn't. When she finally opened her legs for him and he slid into her, she felt no pleasure and no love.

There were different kinds of rape.

The next day Ed Selwyn summoned her to his office and told her about the bonus for her Beverly Ryan stories. He explained that he would have liked to give her a raise, too, but that it would throw the station's salary pattern out of whack. WZEY was rigorous about preserving salary patterns—or at least Ed Selwyn was.

Nancy did not care. The bonus was large enough to make her eyes pop. She could not wait to tell Ted Meadows. She pulled him off into a corner of the newsroom and lowered her voice.

"Guess what. Selwyn just gave me a bonus. For the Beverly Ryan stuff."

"Great. You deserve it." Then his eyes narrowed. "How much?"

"Guess."

"Five hundred?"

"Oh, come on. I did better than that."

"Seven-fifty?" When she did not answer, Ted looked alarmed. "Oh, no. Not a thousand?"

"No, not a thousand. Fifteen hundred."

"Holy shit!" he said, caught off guard. His expression was torn between awe and jealousy. But Ted was always quick on recovery. "There's that same old prejudice again," he said. "White folks get all the money, 'specially pretty girls, and us poor old black folks don't get nothing."

"Ha. Selwyn said he would have given me a raise, too, only he was afraid somebody might file an affirmative action complaint. Who do you suppose he meant?"

Ted pretended to look around the newsroom in search of a culprit. "I can't imagine."

"Seriously, isn't that great?"

"Yes it is. But that can't be Selwyn, he's too stingy. That's Mike Barnes. Mike talked him into it."

"I know. I've got to catch him this afternoon before he goes on duty."

"Tell him I'd like a bonus, too."

"What for?"

"Oh, I don't know. General charm and excellence."

They both laughed.

Ted said, "Congratulations, really. But don't think I'm not jealous."

"Like you always say, class will tell."

With a little jiggering of her assignment schedule, she managed to be in the newsroom when Mike Barnes walked through the swinging glass doors to take over his editing shift. His step was brisk and determined and, as usual, his slim, stern face was preoccupied. Nevertheless Nancy hurried up to him.

"Mike, Selwyn gave me my bonus. I just want to thank you."

He stopped, studied her, then smiled. He had a great smile, perhaps because it was rare.

"We all thought you deserved it," he said. "Selwyn, Foxy, Phil, everybody. Great job."

"Just the same. I know you had a lot to do with it."

Still smiling, he said, "Well, I wasn't arguing for the low end. I hope you were surprised."

"Surprised? I'm thrilled."

"Good." He nodded. Enough chitchat, time to get to work. "Why aren't you out on a story?"

"Oh," she said airily, "I just hit a gap between assignments."

He nodded again. He started away toward the news deck, then stopped. "I'm off tomorrow. How would you like to have a drink after you finish work? To celebrate."

As far back as Nancy could remember, Mike Barnes had never asked a reporter out for a drink. Sometimes they would all go out together at the end of a shift or after a big story was wrapped up, but not like this, not just one reporter singled out.

"I'd love to," she said. "I'll buy with my nice bonus."

"You certainly will not. The Gallery at six-thirty?"

"Where's that?"

"Place in my neighborhood. Second Avenue near the corner of Seventy-fourth."

"Fine. I'll be there."

He nodded again. "I expect you have some work to do."

"Well, as a matter of fact . . ."

"Yes, I thought so. See you tomorrow night then."

Nancy danced away. She decided she would not twit Ted Meadows about this particular triumph. It was not, after all, a professional triumph.

Totting Up

Joan Hennessy was conducting her totting-up conference. She had summoned only two other people.

"I wish they'd talked," Carl Vincent said. His bulk filled the wooden armchair facing Joan Hennessy's desk. He held his notebook and his folder of reports in his pudgy hands. "I always like it better when they talk. When they admit something."

"Well," Joan said, "they didn't." Her own case folder lay open on the desk before her. Many of her documents were duplicates of Vincent's.

Nancy Whittredge sat in the smaller chair beside Vincent. Joan thought Nancy looked more the way she must have looked before the rape. The first time Joan had talked to her, she was tense, nervous, still frightened. Even as late as the grand jury hearing, she was noticeably fragile. Now she seemed alert and interested, and Joan could see a new strength in her.

Strictly speaking, Joan did not need Nancy at this meeting, but she liked to have her rape victims understand everything that was going on. The more they understood, the better they cooperated.

"I never thought Garden would say anything," Vincent said. "Right from the minute Billy and I arrested him, he's a clam. But that Bernie, he looked like a born talker. I couldn't wait to get him back to the station, get him alone away from Garden, and start working on him. But after I read him his Miranda warnings, he just sat there. Wouldn't even give his name and address."

"Garden probably told him not to," Joan guessed. "You know, 'If the cops ever catch us, don't say anything, not one word. Wait for a lawyer'."

"If there's anything I hate," Vincent said, "it's a smart perp."

Joan Hennessy shrugged. On the whole she would much rather deal with a smart perp than with a smart defense lawyer. "Let's go over what we have," she said. "We have to give them the *Rosario* package."

Way back in the early sixties, she explained to Nancy, a man named Luis Rosario had been found guilty of murder. But the New York State Appeals Court overturned the conviction on the grounds that the defense had not been furnished a critical piece of documentation. Since then, the courts had extended the *Rosario* rule to the point where the defense was now entitled to almost every conceivable scrap of information—lineup photos, lab reports, police notebooks, video tapes, everything. Anything not turned over to the defense had become automatic grounds for reversal. *Rosario* was more damn trouble than *Miranda*.

"Okay," Vincent said. He opened his report folder. "On the down side, no confession, no admission of any kind. Also we can't find the gun. Also none of Nancy's jewelry has turned up anywhere, at least not so far. The way I see it, apparently Garden and Bernie—"

"I want to take them one at a time. Let's do Garden first."

This process was what her father, himself a very successful defense attorney, called "totting up." There always comes a moment in any case, her father said, when you should sit down and tot up—in an ice-cold, methodical way—exactly what you have and what you don't have. List every plus and every minus. Only then can you figure out the best way to jump. Joan had found her father's custom as useful for prosecution as for defense.

While Nancy listened, Joan and Vincent went through the evidence against James Garden, aka James Flowers. It was a hefty collection:

A positive identification by Nancy from the C.A.T.C.H. picture file, followed by a positive lineup identification. And Garden's real-life appearance matched the initial description Nancy had given the police at the time of the rape.

"That doesn't always happen," Joan told Nancy. "Defense lawyers just love to point out any discrepancy."

The paycheck stub, made out to James Flowers and identified by the management of Lanier Warehouse & Trucking, bore the jagged word ORION that Nancy had told police she wrote on the back. And the stub, subjected to super-glue fumes, had turned out to contain both Nancy's and Garden's prints.

Nancy's plastic bank card, found on the bureau in her apartment, also carried Garden's prints.

Nancy's Vitullo Kit, now processed, had clothing fibers that matched a pair of Garden's trousers. The serology lab had determined that saliva collected from Garden by court order showed the same telltale characteristics as the sperm samples collected from Nancy's body and clothes at Bellevue Hospital. The

wadded handkerchief picked up by Officer
Cruz at the garage also had a sperm sample
similar to Garden's saliva analysis.

"You mean," Nancy asked, "that saliva is
the *same* thing as sperm?"

Joan smiled at the expression on Nancy's
face. "No, of course not. But the bodily secretions—perspiration, saliva, and so on—carry
the same chemical information about blood
type that sperm does. Not always, but in most
cases. In fact, with four out of five people, you
get a match. They're called secreters."

However, short of expensive DNA genetic
fingerprinting, sperm samples were not con-
clusive proof of a perp's identity. Analysis
was only capable of showing that these samples *could* be Garden's. But it was important
that they ruled him in, instead of ruling him
out.

On top of all the physical evidence, Garden
had a prior conviction for attempted robbery,
and there was a warrant out against him for
violating his probation. This was not relevant
evidence in this case, to be sure. But any
judge—and any defense lawyer—would certainly have to consider Garden's record.

"And finally," Joan said, looking straight at
Nancy, "the victim has brought charges and is
prepared to testify. As you know, I'm sure it
won't come to that. With all this against him,
he's going to have to plead guilty."

She turned to Vincent. "I like it. You did a real nice job."

He shifted around in his chair. She thought he was embarrassed by her praise, but that was not it at all.

"If I'd gone to Nancy's apartment right away, like I should have, we'd have got him a hell of a lot quicker. Maybe if we'd caught him right off, right the next day, maybe he'd have talked."

Nancy put her hand on the detective's arm. "Hey, come on, Carlo. We got him, didn't we?"

Vincent was not mollified. "Dumb police work," he said.

Not the smartest, Joan thought, but as Nancy said, they got him, and in Joan's opinion no harm had been done. "All right," she said, "let's get on with Bernie Webb."

Unlike Garden, Bernie Webb had no prior arrests or convictions, so his picture and prints were not on file. Therefore no computer match had been possible on the first latent prints that had been recovered.

But Nancy had made an immediate positive identification when she saw Bernie in the lineup. And once Bernie had been fingerprinted, there was a smudged match on the bank card and two good matches on the other credit cards Bernie had sorted through in Nancy's wallet.

"Oh, he was there all right," Vincent said.

"Agreed," Joan said. "His prints put him in the garage. But there are no clothing fibers, except where he squeezed through the garage doorway."

"And no hair samples from Nancy's clothes or body," Vincent said.

"Does any of that matter?" Nancy asked.

"Not really," Joan said. "We can prove he's in the garage, and we can prove he's in your wallet, and you got him in the lineup. And he looks just like the man you described. But there is this other thing. He's a nonsecreter."

"What's that?"

"Remember what I said about Garden's saliva? Four out of five people reveal their blood type through their other bodily secretions. But twenty percent of the population is made up of nonsecreters. Their saliva and sweat don't tell us anything. Bernie happens to be one of those."

"But he raped me and he made me—he made me suck him."

"Right. And you could testify to that if you had to. It's just that it helps, especially in rape cases, to get all the backup scientific evidence we can lay our hands on. Juries are reluctant to convict on rape, so it helps to nail it down every way you can."

"Reluctant? How can they be reluctant?"

Joan nodded. "After all, there are usually no other witnesses to a rape, so it's the woman's word against the man's. It's her say against his say. Some jurors always think it must have been the woman's fault—if, in fact, it happened at all. So the more supporting evidence, the better."

"Why are you talking jurors all of a sudden? You said they'd plead guilty."

"Don't get upset, Nancy. They will. This is all just part of totting up what we have and what we don't have, that's all. We just have more on Garden than we have on Webb."

"Take it easy, Nancy," Vincent said. "Bernie's ice-cold on armed robbery."

"That's not enough. There was this rape, too."

"As a matter of fact," Joan said, "it's the same sentence for Robbery One and Rape One. They both rate eight-and-a-third to twenty-five years."

Nancy looked outraged. She was sitting up straight and her big brown eyes glinted. "But he *raped* me. And he made me *suck* him. Robbery's not enough."

"Don't worry about it," Vincent said. "Joan, what are you going to offer if they plead?"

"With everything we have, I'm going to ask for seven-to-twenty-one. And I'll get it."

"Good. See, Nancy? It's okay."

"I agree," Joan said. "I'm not worried about it, either. We're just adding up all the pluses and minuses. The case against Webb is almost as strong as the case against Garden."

She paused, wondering whether or not to bring up the next point. Nancy was already steamed up. However, Joan decided to stick to her rule that the victim should know as much as possible.

"Actually," she said, "I'm a bit more concerned about something else."

"What's that?"

"Bernie Webb's attorney. His Legal Aid defense lawyer assigned by the court. Webb drew Viktor Tobias."

"Viktor Tobias?" Vincent repeated. "Which one is he?"

She told him.

The first thing Viktor Tobias realized about his new client, Bernie Webb, was that he was young, poor, and black—par for the course. He was charged with rape, sodomy, and armed robbery—somewhat above par, although at least he had not killed anybody. On the other hand, Webb had a regular job and no previous criminal record. That was something to work with, and there was bound to be more. There always was.

Viktor Tobias took it for granted that all his

clients were guilty. Not just some of them, but all of them. And if they were not guilty precisely as charged in the indictment handed down by the grand jury, they were surely guilty of something. Otherwise the state would not bother to prosecute them.

All his clients were not only guilty but poor—too poor to afford their own lawyer, so the court picked a Legal Aid attorney out of the hat to defend them. Most of Tobias's clients were black or Hispanic, and most had some kind of criminal record. If they had not actually served time in prison, then they had usually been arrested once or twice—or five or six times. Bernie Webb did not have that particular problem.

The chance that one of his clients might actually be innocent of any crime was so remote that Viktor Tobias never gave it a thought. It didn't matter. He did not care one way or the other about guilt or innocence. That was none of his concern. What he did care about was helping his clients beat the system.

Viktor Tobias had observed the New York criminal justice system for thirty-seven of his sixty-one years. He considered it abominable. Sometimes he wondered why he had ever got mixed up in it. He might have become a chemist or a pianist or almost anything other

than a lawyer. But the law was what he had
chosen, so here he was.

In the 1930s, straight out of NYU law school
with highest honors, and in those days still a
believer in that noble word, *justice,* he served
three years as an assistant district attorney in
Manhattan. Those three years opened his eyes.
They cured him. From then on, the only time
he ever used the word *justice* was when he
was trying to persuade a judge or a jury. As
far as Viktor Tobias was concerned, there was
no such thing as justice. There was only the
system.

The curious thing about the system, he
discovered in his A.D.A. years, was that it was
only accidentally and unintentionally unfair,
not deliberately so. When he conducted hearings and arraignments, and later prosecuted
misdemeanors and felonies, he saw how
steeply the cards were stacked against the
poor, the uneducated, the unsophisticated. In
those days, the pool of potential criminals was
not so overwhelmingly black and Hispanic as
it was today. Back then, a lot of poor Irish and
Italians and even a few Greeks, like Tobias
himself, also wound up in court and, subsequently, in prison. For them, *justice* was swift.

Since Viktor Tobias turned out to have a
special taste and talent for the courthouse, he
collected more than his share of scalps as an

A.D.A. But when the well-to-do were hauled into court, as occasionally happened to everyone's astonishment, results were different. Well-paid, well-trained, well-dressed defense attorneys ran circles around the young A.D.A.s. A bewildering flurry of precedents, writs, objections, requests for continuance and motions for dismissal filled the courtroom air. The judges themselves became more respectful, more responsive, more lenient, when they knew the reputation of opposing counsel.

The discrepancy did not seem to bother Viktor Tobias's young colleagues in the District Attorney's office. Sincere, ambitious, proud of their high calling, which the D.A. always emphasized in his monthly staff meetings, they took each case as a challenge and did their very best with it.

Viktor Tobias quit in disgust.

He joined the litigation department of a large law firm, where the quality of the clientele was much improved, although, in his opinion, the quality of *justice* was no better. During his years with the firm, he learned many useful procedures, both in and out of the courtroom, not all of which could be classified as mere tricks, devices and gimmicks.

One of the most important things he learned, as he became more and more confident, was that confidence itself was a weapon. He was too short—barely five-feet-seven— and too skinny to be physically imposing. His early baldness ruled out the flowing mane sported by many of his colleagues, and he refused to bother with tailored suits and expensive ties. But he knew his cases and precedents and procedures down to the last inch. When he rose in court to tackle a judge or a jury or a witness, he commanded immediate respect and attention. The confidence was always evident in his hawklike expression, his sharp, slightly narrowed eyes, his dry, incisive voice.

In spite of being Greek, he became extremely successful in his blue-chip law firm. In fact, he realized it was only a matter of time before he became a senior partner, responsible for bringing in a major share of the firm's business. Since this future, and all the money that would accompany it, did not interest him, he quit again.

There was no point in trying to explain to his colleagues in the firm, or to the many lawyers he knew in other firms, or to all the judges and prosecutors he knew, why he gave it all up to become a Legal Aid defender. They would not have understood. And, although the Legal Aid Society was delighted to have him, its members did not understand, either.

They all thought he must be an idealist. This never failed to amuse him.

Viktor Tobias rather liked Bernie Webb, for a rapist. He had a certain naive charm.

He first saw Webb in the holding prison when he was brought into the dingy conference room where lawyers could talk with prisoners. They sat facing each other under the eyes of an indifferent guard. Webb was a chunky fellow in his early twenties. Big black mustache, tiny little black goatee, a stiff, flattop haircut. He wore an open-necked khaki shirt and looked very unhappy to be in this place.

It was the day after the Whittredge woman had picked him out of the lineup. Tobias would have preferred to be present at the lineup, although since Joan Hennessy had been there to see that everything was handled properly, it was unlikely that his presence would have yielded any advantage. Hennessy was good. Viktor Tobias could have wished, for his client's sake, that one of the other A.D.A.s in sex crimes had this case. For his own sake, he enjoyed doing battle against the best.

When Tobias introduced himself, the young man's first words were, "I didn't do anything."

This was such a common opening ploy that
Tobias ignored it. The truth, if there was any
such thing as truth, would come out later. "Is
that what you told the police? That you didn't
do anything?"

"I didn't tell them nothing."

Tobias wondered if that could possibly be
true. Webb did not look bright enough to keep
totally silent. "Nothing? You told them nothing?"

Webb shook his head. "Jimmy told me not
to."

That must be the accomplice. Two men had
been involved in this rape and robbery. The
other man was of no interest to Tobias unless
he had dumped on Bernie Webb. Often they
tried to blame everything on the other fellow.
Eventually Tobias would learn exactly what
had been said to the police, both by Webb and
by his accomplice, when he was given the
notes and tapes on the questioning.

"Did they read you your Miranda warnings?"

"What's that?" Webb asked suspiciously.

He was certainly an inexperienced criminal.
"Did they tell you you didn't have to say
anything and that you had the right to a
lawyer?"

"Oh, yeah. They said that. I didn't say
nothing, just like Jimmy told me."

If true, that was a good start.

"Now if I'm going to help you," Tobias said, "I need to know what really happened. Would you like to tell me?"

"Nothing. Nothing happened. I didn't do anything."

This was such a waste of time, but Tobias often had to go through the process, even with experienced criminals. "Look," he explained, speaking very slowly and using simple words, "I'm not a cop or a detective. I'm your lawyer. My job is to help you. Understand? The cops know a lot, because they arrested you and stuck you in here. They have to show me all the evidence they have against you. But I need to know much more than they know. If I'm going to help you, I need to know everything you know. Is that clear?"

Bernie Webb nodded. He thought about it for a while. Tobias gave him all the time he needed because he could see that his client's mind worked slowly.

Then Webb giggled. "Well," he said, "Jimmy had this idea about how we could get some easy money . . ."

As the story came out, Tobias scribbled an occasional note on his pad. He did not need notes to remember the details of the crime, but now and then he jotted down a phrase of Webb's, a phrase that later he might want to emphasize or to avoid, depending on how the case developed.

It was a rough case. The two men had spent a long time with the Whittredge woman, not just the few minutes needed to carry out a quick sidewalk robbery. That meant time for conversation, time for the woman to notice things. And it wasn't just simple, straightforward rape with a quick ejaculation. Not at all. It was repetitive rape. And even worse, there was all the sodomy. That was a very bad break. Everybody hated sodomy—judges, prosecutors, jurors.

On the other hand, according to Webb's account, the woman had been terrified, in fear of her life. That was bad in one sense, since fear of imminent death was very damaging. But it almost guaranteed that her memory would be shaky and confused about all sorts of things. Confusion was a powerful ally for the defense, if one knew how to exploit it. Tobias would have to find out what the accomplice's lawyer intended to do, and no doubt that would depend on how much evidence the cops had collected. From what Webb said, the accomplice had had the original idea, the accomplice had obtained the gun, and the accomplice had been the leader throughout.

A vague picture began to form in Viktor

Tobias's mind. His young client, innocent of any previous felony, with not even an arrest record, had come under the influence of an older, dominant figure, an experienced criminal. This nice young fellow Webb had been dragged into the affair, and, before he realized what was happening, it got completely out of hand. Perhaps Webb had actually tried to dissuade the other man?

This was only one possible framework. Tobias would have to wait until he received the *Rosario* material before deciding whether or not this framework was plausible. If not, there would be something else. There always was.

"All right, that will do for now," he told his client. He put his pen in his jacket pocket. The pad with his notes went into his briefcase. "I'll be in touch."

"You going to fix it?" Webb asked. His voice held a pathetic hope. "You going to get me out? I don't like this place."

"I don't like it either," Tobias said. "I'll do what I can."

Heavy Baggage

Nancy kept checking her watch as her cab crept uptown through the six o'clock traffic. She could not bear to be even a few minutes late for her drink with Mike Barnes, who set a high premium on promptness. "If you're late for an assignment," Mike used to tell her and Ted Meadows during their training program, "you can miss the whole story. So be on time." Of course, tonight was not an assignment, but Nancy was sure he would expect the customary promptness.

She had dithered about what to wear. Her first plan was to rush home and change from her working clothes to a dress, but she realized she would not have time to go all the way down to Tribeca and back uptown again. Then she thought of bringing a dress to the office and doing a quick change at the end of her shift. There would certainly be time for that.

324

But then she decided she must not make too much of this event. Mike had invited her for a drink right after work, so he would expect to see her in her usual uniform of sweater and slacks.

That was another of Mike's training admonitions that Ted used to imitate in Mike's gruff voice. "You're not dressing for a television camera, Meadows. So don't waste your time worrying about a color-coordinated tie and jacket. And you, Whittredge, you don't need a blow-dry hairdo and a different blouse every day. Wear clothes you can move around in fast." Then Ted would scowl ferociously. "But be sure you look presentable. Don't embarrass the station."

Nancy smiled to herself then checked her watch again. No way she was going to avoid being a few minutes late. She wondered what to talk about. What would Mike want to talk about? There was always Weezie, of course. She had the fare ready in her hand. The taxi finally turned east on Seventy-fourth but had to stop halfway down the block to wait for the next light.

"I'll get out here," she said. Sometimes she felt she spent her whole life jumping out of cabs before reaching her destination. She paid the driver, not waiting for change, and hopped out. She hurried down the block. If she ran, she would be not only flustered but out of breath—a poor entrance. She settled for an extremely brisk walk.

It was 6:34 when she passed under the pale yellow neon sign announcing "The Gallery" and climbed the stairs to a second-floor bar and restaurant. Maybe Mike would be late, too.

But of course he wasn't. As she came into the crowded, dimly lighted room, she saw his tall figure already standing up at a table. He waved his hand, and she hurried over. He had on his old brown tweed jacket and an open-necked shirt without a tie. She was glad she had decided to skip the dress.

"I'm really sorry," she said. "I'm a little late."

"You're not on assignment," he said, "so it's allowed." He held a chair for her and then took his own seat. Their table was right up against a glass wall overlooking Second Avenue.

"What a nice view," she said inanely. Second Avenue in the Seventies scarcely qualified as a view.

"I could see you practically running up the sidewalk," he said. "What would you like to drink?"

"What are you having?"

"Scotch on the rocks." He smiled a little.

"But I don't think that should influence you."

"That's fine for me, too." This was silly. She never ordered Scotch.

He held a finger up high so it could be seen in the dim light and waggled for a waitress. The waitresses wore red miniskirts and long-sleeved white shirts. "In case you care," he said, "this place serves champagne by the glass."

"Oh, that's what I want. How did you know?"

"I was at your birthday party, remember? Also, this is supposed to be a celebration."

A waitress came over. "Yes, Mike?"

Mike?

"Susie, my friend would like a glass of champagne."

"Right away."

"You come here often?"

"It's my club. I live just a couple of blocks away."

He seemed different, and she tried to figure out what it was. Same light blue eyes, same straight brown hair without a single wave in it, same slim face. But he looked less stern than usual, not so much the boss. His lips weren't pressed together in concentration, the way they were at the station. His mouth looked much more generous this way. She realized what it was: he was relaxed. Mike Barnes was relaxed! The knowledge made her feel less nervous.

When her champagne came, he lifted his glass and said, "Congratulations again. Damn good job. What are you going to do with your bonus?"

"It's so big I haven't decided. Buy some jewelry, for sure. Something to make me remember whenever I wear it."

He nodded. "How did it go today?"

So they were going to talk about Weezie. "Real quiet. No news to speak of."

He brushed that aside. "I know that." He smiled. "I listen to the radio, you know. I meant your meeting at the D.A.'s. Wasn't that supposed to be today?"

She knew she had not told him about her morning meeting with Joan Hennessy and Carlo to go over the evidence, but she had had to get permission to be an hour late coming to work. Even on his day off, Mike always knew whatever was happening to everybody at Weezie.

"Yes, it was. It went all right, I guess. No, it was better than that. They really have a lot of evidence on both men."

"You must feel very proud, Nancy. A lot of them never get caught at all."

He had guessed exactly how she felt. "I *do* feel proud. We all do, my whole team. The detectives I've been working with, the D.A.'s office, everybody. We did it. It's a good feeling."

"I'm glad. You have some good feelings coming to you. How do your parents feel about it?"

"Mom and Dad, they're mostly relieved I don't have to spend all my spare time with the police. Although they liked having me back in their apartment. Back in the cocoon. My mother especially."

"That's natural. And your friends?"

When she hesitated, Mike said, "I'm sorry. I guess I shouldn't have asked."

"No, that's all right. I can tell you. My friends" she paused, thinking of Jenny and Tommy and the gulfs that had opened—"they don't—I mean, I don't think they understand how much happened to me. They expect me to be just the same."

He nodded. "How could you be the same? But sometimes it's hard to put yourself in another person's place."

"Some people can. Ted, for instance. He treats the whole thing just right." She could afford to give old Ted a plug.

"Ted's a good man. How about some more champagne?"

"I'd love it. Did I tell you I wasn't allowed to drink for ten days? Because of medication?"

"I heard. It struck me as double jeopardy."

They both laughed. At the station he always seemed older than his mid-thirties, but tonight he seemed younger. He ordered another Scotch and another champagne. The Gallery was busy, people at almost every table in the long room, but their drinks came quickly.

"You must be an important customer."

"A long-standing one, anyway. I used to come here with my wife."

This was the first recorded instance of Mike mentioning his wife, from whom he had been divorced several years ago.

He gave Nancy a wry smile. "In our settlement my wife got the furniture, but I got the rights to this place. I think I came out ahead. The food's all right, too, if you don't order the veal." He hesitated. "Are you busy for dinner? Would you like to try it?"

"The veal?"

"No, the food."

"Of course. Since this is my lunch break."

They smiled over that strange union-management agreement that awarded an hour off for lunch at the end of a shift.

On Mike's recommendation they ordered The Gallery's garlic goulash with spaetzle and, since champagne could not stand up to the garlic, a bottle of the house red wine. Throughout dinner Weezie was never mentioned.

On the long subway ride home to Tribeca, Nancy thought this had been the nicest evening in some time. Perhaps since her birthday party.

The next evening—another drink with another man in another restaurant—was less pleasant.

Tommy Horgan was more baffled than angry. He sat back in his chair at the bar table in Bistro Paul. "I don't get this. You're not yourself."

"That's what I keep telling you. I'm not myself. Or maybe I'm more myself, but in a different way."

"That doesn't make any sense. I don't see what you're upset about."

"I'm not upset. I just think we need some time off from each other. Time apart."

"That won't solve anything. That never solves anything. What you need is to get back to normal."

"Tommy, all 'normal' means to you is going to bed."

That annoyed him. "It isn't all I mean. But anyway, what's wrong with bed? We both like it. No complaints so far, right?"

"I'm not ready for it."

"You've always been ready before."

"I can't help it. I have to tell you something.

I really didn't like making love the other night."

"Well, sure, it was the first time for you since—You can't expect everything to be terrific right away. Although personally—"

"Oh, Tommy, you don't get it."

"What don't I get? Is there somebody else?"

"No, there isn't. You should know better than that."

"Well then, for God's sake. What are you going to do? Give up sex? Just because two guys raped you one night? And by the way that doesn't matter to me one bit. Honest."

"But it does matter to me. Honest."

From behind the bar Jeanne asked, "You folks need another drink?"

"No thanks," Nancy said. "Not for me."

"Yes for me," Tommy said. "Nancy, you're going at this all wrong. All you think about or care about is your case. What you ought to do is try and forget it. Put it behind you."

"It's still going on. It isn't settled, and it won't be until they're locked away for keeps."

"Leave it to the cops. And the D.A. It's their job."

She shook her head. "It's my job, too."

"Does Jenny know about all this?"

"What?"

"Your wanting to split up."

"No, she doesn't."

"Try it on her. I bet she says you're being silly."

"Maybe. But I'm not being silly. It's how I feel."

Tommy leaned forward. He laced his fingers tightly together on top of the table. "Just what do you have in mind? How long is this vacation from each other supposed to last?"

"I don't know."

Jeanne reached over the bar to hand Tommy his drink.

"What do you mean, you don't know? A week? A month? A year?"

"Just what I said, I don't know."

He took a large swallow of his drink. "That's a shitty way to treat me."

"I'm sorry. I really am. If I knew, I'd tell you."

"Well, since you don't know anything, I'll tell you something I know. Don't expect me just to sit around with my thumb in my mouth."

"No, of course not."

He stared at her. "You mean you don't care what I do? Suppose I go screw somebody else?"

"I don't know. I haven't thought about it."

"Christ! You don't know anything."

Yes, I do, she thought. *Yes I do.*

*   *   *

She used to worry, when she came home
from college, about the quizzing from her
parents. They meant well and were genuinely
interested, but it was an ordeal. How were her
grades? How did she feel about her profes-
sors? Was she in good shape for exam period?
How was she getting along with her term
paper? How was her work at the college radio
station? Was she eating proper meals, not just
junk food? How was her social life? Any new
boyfriends? How did she spend her weekends? She wasn't drinking too much beer, was
she?

And this did not come out all at once, like an
exam. It would be a question here and then a
question there, plopped down in the middle of
some other conversation, so she had to be
slightly on guard all the time. Sometimes she
thought of saying, look, why don't we sit
down for an hour, close the doors, turn off the
music and get the whole thing over with, like
an interview? But such a suggestion would
have hurt their feelings, especially her mother's. And besides, she knew her parents did
not have a prepared list of questions. They just
asked whatever occurred to them at any given
moment.

She and her brother Basil talked it over and
decided that maybe the best solution would be

to launch into a full-scale confession, an all-out monologue, at the first sit-down family meal. *Let me tell you everything I'm doing! Everything!* Just snow them under with volunteered information. It would not eliminate further questions, of course, but it might clear away a lot of the underbrush.

Somehow it never quite happened that way—and it was not happening that way now.

She was home for Sunday dinner, roast lamb with garlic and rosemary. It was her first visit since moving back to her own apartment. Her father stood to slice the lamb, her mother checked to make sure the slices were just the right shade of pink. Her father forked the roast potatoes and then passed the plates to Carol for gravy, French-style string beans with slivered almonds, mint sauce (never mint jelly), and mango chutney. Nancy knew Carol had selected each dish for her, and she was hungry at the prospect of a complete home dinner, with all accountrements and a dessert course yet to come. She and Jenny never went to these lengths, not even for those very rare apartment dinners for Tommy and Sid. And now that Nancy was living alone, it was mostly pasta or salad or English muffins with canned corned beef hash. Nancy had learned good cooking from her mother, but cooking for one was no inspiration.

"This looks *glorioso*," she said as she picked up her knife and fork. Then she made her first mistake: "I'm starved."

"Aren't you getting enough to eat?" Carol asked.

"Oh, sure," Nancy said quickly. "Just nothing as wonderful as this." Since Carol still looked worried, she added, "I eat out quite a lot."

"Restaurant food," Whit said. He seemed to think no further comment was called for.

"And then I cook for myself when I'm at home."

"That can't be much fun."

"Oh, Dad, that's because you've never cooked. I enjoy it. I'm a whiz at pasta."

"Pasta?" Carol said. "Is that all you eat? That must be boring. And it can't be very healthy."

"Look at all the Italians, they seem healthy. Besides, it isn't boring. The stores carry everything these days. Linguine and fettuccine and tortelloni and tortellini and ravioli—even gnocchi. And then I make white clam sauce and red clam and marinara and pesto and primavera and—"

"Eat your nice lamb, dear, while it's hot."

So she had weathered that flurry.

Nancy was just finishing seconds on lamb when Whit said casually, "What do you hear from Jenny?"

"Not much, really."

Pause.

"Does she say anything about moving back?" Carol asked.

"I think she's going to stay with Sid. That's what she says, anyway. I've put the word out around the station that I'm in the market for another roommate."

"Good," Whit said. "I think you ought to have somebody down there with you."

"Yes, Whit, but not just anybody. Are you really sure, darling, that Jenny won't be coming back?"

"I can't guarantee it, Mom. I mean, anything could happen. She and Sid might have a fight and break up."

"That would be nice."

"Mom!"

"It would be nice for you if Jenny came back, that's all I meant."

The topic of Jenny subsided. Her father told a very funny story about his difficulties with a plumbing contractor. Over the years Nancy and Basil had concluded that plumbers made better stories than electricians or carpenters or even building inspectors.

Halfway through steaming hot brown Betty with vanilla ice cream Carol asked, "How is Tommy?"

"He's fine. Very busy as usual. I saw him just the night before last."

"That's nice. I hope you had a good time?"

Nancy took another spoonful. Carol made the world's best brown Betty, laced with extra cinnamon. Experience had taught Nancy that it was usually better to come right out with something than to have it pried out of her. But this one, given her mother's high expectations for Tommy, would not be easy.

"Actually," she said, in what she hoped was a fairly light tone, "we decided not to see quite so much of each other."

"Oh dear!"

"Hm."

"Why in the world would you do that?"

"Well . . . it's complicated."

Pause.

"But surely—"

"Carol, maybe Nancy doesn't feel like talking about it."

Her father certainly had that right, but she knew there could be no escape.

"Of course she does. She brought it up. What's the matter, darling? Is it anything serious?"

"I just feel kind of mixed up now. Since the rape. I need some time to myself."

"I don't think you should isolate yourself."

"Mom, I'm not isolated. I go to work every day. I still have things to do on my case. And I do go out in the evenings—sometimes. I don't just sit home and brood."

"I know, but living alone down there without Jenny. And now this business with Tommy. I think this is a time when you need your closest friends and your family."

"Well," she said brightly, "here I am with my family."

Carol was not put off. "Does Tommy agree with you about all this?"

"Not exactly. Can I get the coffee?"

"We'll have it in the library. In a minute. What does Tommy say?"

"He doesn't understand what I'm talking about."

"I'm not sure I do, either," Whit said.

"Well, Dad—"

"You don't want to lose him," Carol said.

"No, I don't. But right now I need my own space. I can't cope with a lot of heavy baggage."

"I'm sure Tommy would be *very* offended if he heard you call him that."

"I didn't mean him. Mom, I just can't go back to a love affair, that's all. As if nothing had happened. Not now, anyway. So we're not going to see each other for a while."

"A man like Tommy," her father said, "is not going to just hang around waiting for you."

"That's what he said."

"I mean, he's good-looking and—"

"I know what you mean, Dad."
"He's liable to go find somebody else."
"I know."
"Oh, dear!"

Nancy thought that was about enough. "That was a terrific dinner, Mom. Why don't I get the coffee, okay?"

Time to Play Poker

When he had studied all the *Rosario* material on the Whittredge case, Viktor Tobias conferred with James Garden's attorney, a competent enough fellow named Sam Rose.

"Yeah, I've read it," Rose said. "They got 'em."

"It does look rather bad."

"Bad? How bad is bad? No point wasting time on this one."

"You're going to take Hennessy's offer? Seven-to-twenty-one?"

Tobias waited for the answer. What he had in mind would be easier if Rose took the plea for his client.

"I've talked to my boy," Rose said, "and he understands the fix he's in. A goner all the way. He says, do the best I can for him."

Good, Tobias thought.

"Oh hell, I'll ask for five-to-fifteen, hoping

to get six-to-eighteen, but Joan sounds dug in. What are you going to do, Viktor?"

"Well, unlike you I have a first offender. And a few other odds and ends. I hope to do a little better."

"Yeah, well, good luck. You ask me, I think you're spinning your wheels. Like I always say, work on the ones where you got something to work with, and write off the ones where you don't."

Tobias felt just the opposite, but he said, "A good policy, Sam. Let me know, will you, if you manage to beat her down."

"I'd need a lead pipe. But yeah, I'll let you know. Sooner this one is over, the better."

Viktor Tobias was in no hurry to talk to Joan Hennessy. All the Legal Aid lawyers were overworked—too many clients, too much paper work, too many court appearances. Sometimes they were tempted to hurry things along, as Rose was doing.

But Tobias was convinced that delay was a powerful weapon for the accused. There was nothing like delay to hurt the prosecution's case. Witnesses might change their minds about testifying, or their memory of what happened might fade or get confused. Documents or evidence might get mislaid. The judge might become impatient because his calendar was piling up with unresolved cases, and he might press for a quick settlement, usually a bonus for the defense. The prosecution could grow impatient, too. A delay, a continuance or two, never hurt the accused.

When Rose reported back that he had had to accept seven-to-twenty-one for his client, Tobias half expected a call from Joan Hennessy. But apparently she was in no hurry, either. He admired her style.

A week later they ran into each other in a wide marble corridor of the Supreme Court Building. Half the business of the criminal justice system was conducted in the corridors outside the courtrooms. A tall, handsome woman, several inches taller than Tobias, with bright red hair. He considered her very attractive, very appealing, but he had never heard a word of gossip against her. Apparently she was faithful to her businessman husband, a fortunate fellow. In his younger days Tobias would certainly have tested that fidelity.

As usual, she was in a hurry, a fat manila folder clutched under her arm, but she stopped at the sight of him.

"Hello, Viktor. You and I have some business, but I forget what it is."

If she had really forgotten, she would not have stopped to talk. But he could not pretend to have forgotten, because he had to maintain his reputation for an infallible memory. It was a little edge, well worth preserving.

"The Whittredge case," he said. "Rape and robbery."

"Oh yes, that one. And sodomy too."

"I always overlook sodomy."

They both laughed.

"You got all the *Rosario*?"

"Yes thanks."

"Have you had time to read it?"

"Yes. Very interesting."

Her expression turned less casual. "Very solid, I'd say."

"I prefer 'interesting.'"

"Garden has already pled."

"Yes, I know."

She looked at her watch. "I'm afraid I'm due in court, Viktor. Call me when you're ready to talk it over."

"I'll do that."

But he didn't. Three days later, her secretary left a message at his office that Joan Hennessy would appreciate a call at his convenience. He did not wish to seem rude, which would be counterproductive, so he waited only twenty-four hours before returning her phone call.

She was strictly business. "On Whittredge. As you know, I'm offering you seven-to-twenty-one."

"Yes, I know. That seems rather steep."

"Not for this one."

"I see it differently."

Although she must have been disappointed, there was no change in her voice. "Very well. Then we should get together. What's good for you?"

They consulted their desk calendars, trying out different times on each other. Tobias did not try to irritate Hennessy by being unavailable, as he might have done with a more junior A.D.A. She was too cool, too experienced to be rattled by that kind of treatment. Besides, he wanted her to expect a routine discussion, just a little back-and-forth poker playing. He agreed to a date the day after tomorrow. She promised to find an unused jury room so they would not be disturbed by phones.

He was punctual. She was not.

He waited for her in the small, shabby jury room. The long wooden table was surrounded by a dozen plain, sturdy chairs. Along one side wall was the coat closet with its tangle of bent wire hangers. Doors to the men's and ladies' toilets were at one end. The tall, grimy windows looked out on the bleak masses of other court buildings.

In the old days there would have been ashtrays on the table, crammed with butts from the latest session of jury deliberation. Nowadays there were so many virulent nonsmokers on every jury that the ashtrays had disappeared, and smokers were banished to the outside hall when the urge overcame them. Tobias sometimes wondered if this change in smoking habits hastened or delayed a jury's decision, or perhaps even altered it in some subtle fashion. As with every other aspect of the system, it would depend on the individual jury.

Even after all his years in litigation Tobias was still fascinated by juries. They were so gloriously unpredictable. With a jury of "twelve good men and true," some of whom were not good and some of whom were not true, and half of whom were women, anything could happen. Unless he was armed with some legal technicality that would virtually compel a judge to rule in his favor, Tobias far preferred to face a jury rather than a solitary judge. With a jury there was always a chance, even in what appeared to be a hopeless case. All it took was one or two resolutely pig-headed men or women. During the *voir dire* of jury selection, he was always hoping to detect that gleam of stubbornness—and, of course, hoping that the prosecution would not detect it. All part of the game.

Joan Hennessy walked in and closed the door behind her. Time to play poker.

"Sorry to be late," she said. She placed her folder on the table, and they took chairs opposite each other. "No papers?" she asked.

"I just thought we'd talk. If we need to check anything, I'm sure you have it."

"Fine. Now, Viktor, you might as well know something from the start. I consider this a particularly vicious crime, and I am prosecuting it accordingly. This lovely young woman from a fine family was brutally raped and sodomized and her life threatened by these two thugs. You've seen the *Rosario*. The evidence is overwhelming. There is no question—no question whatsoever—that I would get the full eight-and-a-third-to-twenty-five in court. And you know as well as I do, if that happened, after a crime of this severity, no parole board would even consider releasing them the first or second time they come up for consideration. So they would be looking at more like ten or twelve years, even with good behavior. Maybe longer. So seven-to-twenty-one is the best I can do for you."

"Joan, there's *always* a question what you would get in court."

"Nonsense. Not this time. It would be a ridiculous waste of the state's time and money to try this one."

"It's not my time. It's not my money."

"No, but it's your client. I would see to it that he got the absolute maximum. You have my assurance on that."

"You've seen Bernie Webb."

"Of course. After his arrest and at arraignment."

"Well, I doubt he was at his best on those occasions. Although I think it's sensible to acknowledge that he made no admission of any kind. Not a word. That, by the way, is thanks to the good advice of his friend Mr. Garden."

"I thought that was probably it."

"Yes, poor Bernie is too naive to have arrived at the wise decision to keep his trap shut. Unlike you I have had extended conversation with Bernie. He's really quite likable, quite charming. That is, when he isn't committing rape and sodomy."

"I don't see your point, Viktor. Am I supposed to be sympathetic?"

"Certainly not. I'm not particularly sympathetic myself. I'm only saying that he makes a nice impression. He has a steady job. Believe it or not, he also has a mother, whom he occasionally visits. Nice family man. A little stupid perhaps, and definitely naive, but on the whole rather likable. He probably didn't realize he was doing anything very wrong."

Joan snorted.

Tobias smiled at her. "I'm merely suggesting how others might view him. A juror, for instance, sitting right here in this room. Bernie does not look or act like a thug, to use your epithet. He is quite unlike Mr. Garden, who is clearly a vicious and brutal criminal."

"Oh. I see where you're headed."

"Yes. May I elaborate?"

"Sure. That's why we're here."

"Yes. Well then." He put his fingertips together under his chin and stared at her across the table. "Here is how I see it, Joan. It's perfectly obvious that poor young Bernie was completely dominated by his older, street-smart friend Garden. Bernie looked up to him, followed him around. Anybody at that ware-house where they worked could testify to that. It was Garden who had the idea, as Bernie puts it, to 'get some easy money.' It was Garden who obtained the gun. It was Garden who threatened the Whittredge woman with the gun—if indeed that happened at all. Since no gun has been recovered, one cannot help but wonder if it ever existed. When they are frightened, young women have been known to get hysterical and start imagining things. In any event, it was Garden who ran the show from start to finish. Bernie just went along. He had no idea that things might get serious. In fact, it is quite possible that when he saw the turn things were taking, he tried to dissuade Garden."

"You don't seriously expect me to swallow that."

"Certainly not. This is pure hypothesis. I am describing how it might look to someone with, let us say, less experience than yourself. After all, Garden has already accepted a very stiff plea, so he must have realized it was entirely his fault."

"And when they got to the garage, Viktor, what did Garden do? Did he force Bernie at gunpoint to unzip his pants? Did he force Bernie to have intercourse with Nancy Whittredge?"

"I'll come back to that, if I may. For the moment I am dealing with the robbery."

"You do admit there was a robbery."

"Oh yes indeed, not much question about that. The computer printout of withdrawals from the bank account appears to establish that."

"*And* Bernie's print on Miss Whittredge's bank card. *And* his prints on other credit cards in her wallet."

"The print on the bank card is a smudged partial, surely open to reasonable challenge. Besides, I suspect Bernie may just have been going through her wallet looking for more easy money. Under Garden's orders, of course. Doesn't that make sense?"

"You are something."

"Thank you."

"Tell me the part where Garden makes Bernie fuck her. Anally, vaginally and orally."

"He didn't."

"I'm delighted to hear it. In my considerable experience I have yet to hear of one man forcing another to commit rape and sodomy."

"In my much longer experience, I haven't either. But you misunderstood me, Joan. Garden didn't force Bernie to commit rape and sodomy. Bernie simply did not do it."

He was pleased to see that he had at last broken through her professional composure. He kept his own face expressionless as he watched her struggle to recover.

"That," she said finally, "is the funniest thing I've heard all month."

"I'm glad it amuses you. That means you must not have read your own serology report."

"Of course I read it." Not quite a snap, but almost.

"Hard luck, I'd say."

Joan Hennessy shrugged. "Since one out of every five people is a nonsecreter, we have to expect that now and then."

Beautifully done, Tobias thought. He really admired it. Just the proper degree of professional acceptance. Just one of those awkward facts that a good prosecutor must learn to live with. But of course the fact that Bernie Webb was a nonsecreter was not what he was referring to, although Joan Hennessy might devoutly hope so. She might hope that Tobias, not a specialist in sex crimes and serology, would overlook the intricacies of the damage contained in the report.

"I am referring," he said, "to the results of the electrophoresis and the isoelectric focusing." These tests were further breakdowns of the information contained in sperm samples.

Even though she must have been hoping, her face did not change. "What about it?"

It was time to hit her with the extent of his knowledge. "I can't quote you the exact technical wording, although it must be there in your folder. But as I understand it, electrophoresis says that all the sperm samples collected—all of them—are PGM 1. Not terribly surprising, since fifty-five percent of blacks are PGM 1. But then isoelectric focusing says that *all* the sperm samples collected are subtype 1+. Now we're talking less than forty percent of the PGM 1 population."

"Thirty-seven point six."

"Just so. You know much more about this area than I do. What it comes down to, however, is that in spite of all the extensive sexual activity that supposedly took place in Miss Whittredge's various orifices, you have only one classification of sperm to show for it. PGM 1, sub-type 1+." He spread his hands on the table, palms up, and gave Joan Hennessy his most benign smile. "All Mr. Garden's sperm, of course. Bernie Webb did not participate in this heinous assault. In fact, if I'm not mistaken, he probably tried to talk Mr. Garden out of it."

"That is preposterous. I can always go to DNA genetic fingerprinting."

"Ah yes." Tobias nodded several times. "I was quite certain that when I gave you my layman's analysis of the serology report, we would get around to DNA."

"Then you know that DNA fingerprinting would clearly and absolutely distinguish two different specimens of sperm, Garden's and Webb's."

"Very expensive. A good many samples to analyze, and each one would have to be fingerprinted three times for the three people involved. Very expensive indeed."

"If I request it, the D.A. will let me do it. All I have to do is ask for it."

"No doubt, since you're the boss. And how many other departments and people would have to sign off on it? A dozen?"

"Less. Maybe ten."

"Well, if you want to go through all that. But I doubt that it would make your colleagues very happy. Here we are with this strict budget problem, and here is Hennessy calling for this very costly procedure."

"I wouldn't hesitate."

She could easily be bluffing, but he could not tell.

"Be that as it may," he said. He leaned forward across the jury table. "I'm going to tell you a secret, Joan. I have this little ambition. At this stage in my career I don't have too many of them left. Not too many things I haven't already done. But one of them is to fight DNA fingerprinting in front of a jury. With my own expert witnesses. It's a very complex procedure, and there's already been just enough doubt and confusion. I'm sure you read the interview with the DNA expert who said *he* would not want to be judged on genetic fingerprinting unless he had performed the test himself. In theory it's reliable, but in practice . . . ? I would certainly call that gentleman for the defense. And you must be familiar with the recent Connecticut case where there was plenty of physical evidence and eyewitness testimony, but the 'infallible' DNA test didn't match. The jury convicted anyway. And then there's the Central Park jogger, where you had so much mixed-up sperm that DNA couldn't match anything. Oh yes, there's a great deal here to play with, and I'd love to have a crack at it. My name might even go down in the lawbooks."

He sat back in his chair.

Joan Hennessy did not say anything for several moments. "Just what are you after, Viktor?"

"The interests of my client, of course. I agree with you, Joan. This case should not have to go to trial. After all, Bernie does appear to have been present at a robbery. Although as you can tell, I am prepared to go the trial route. If necessary."

"So?"

"I think, just to save you and the state all this trouble and expense and time and uncertainty, I could be persuaded to settle for the B felony minimum. Two-to-six years. You would have to reduce the charge, of course."

"Viktor, that would be *obscene* in a crime of this violence. I would not even consider it."

"Your decision, naturally. And then I will have to make mine."

"Yes. You know, in all your fun and games, you have left out the single most significant factor in this entire case. My witness. Nancy Whittredge."

Tobias slapped his forehead in feigned astonishment. "Good heavens, how could I have forgotten?" He laughed. Then he turned serious. "Listen, Joan, I've been around. This is

not the first rape case I ever heard of. The
prosecution *always* claims the victim is prepared to testify. Half the time she isn't. Who
wants to go through all that? Or she plans to
testify and then changes her mind. The prosecution also claims, *always*, that the victim is
going to be a wonderful witness. And then
when the time comes, she isn't." He shook his
head, showing her a little irritation. "So don't
threaten me, Joan, with your witness. I've
been around."

She was silent for such a long time, staring
straight at him, that he wondered if he should
say anything more. No, he decided, he had
placed his bet. It was up to her to call or
fold.

At last she spoke. "Would you like to meet
her?"

He had not expected her to raise. "The
woman?"

She nodded.

"Under what conditions?"

"In my office. Off the record. Nothing you
can use in court."

"With you present?"

"Of course."

"And I can question her?"

"Certainly."

"Without any interruption from you?"

"I won't say a word."

It was much, much more than he had hoped for. Joan Hennessy was putting her witness in his hands with none of the restraints that would have been imposed in open court.

"That's an interesting proposal. I accept."

A Calculated Risk

"Two-to-six years! For what he did to me? And I could have been killed. I could be dead."

"Nancy, two-to-six is just his bargaining position. I don't take it seriously. When you plea bargain, both sides do a lot of bluffing."

"But that—that's—"

"The word I used was obscene. It's an obscene offer, and I'm not going to accept it. Tobias knows that."

"But then what's all this talk about a trial? You promised me we'd never go to trial. Is he bluffing about that, too?"

There was a time of silence. Nancy was gripping the phone so hard that her hand ached. She shifted to her other hand.

"I don't know," Joan said at last. "He has an interesting theory. Really quite ingenious. Unfortunately, the forensic evidence has a few holes that help him. And, of course, he can always demand a trial. That's his right."

"But you promised."

"I know, but that was before Tobias got into it. Before I heard what he had to say."

"When would it be?"

"The meeting?"

"No, a trial."

"Oh, several months, at least. Both sides have to have time to prepare, and the court would have to set a trial date that fits into the calendar. And then Tobias could probably get that date postponed a couple of times for one reason or another. They usually do. I'd press for trial, of course, but it could be quite a while."

Nancy felt a deep sadness. "I thought it was over," she said. Maybe it was never going to be over."

"I know. So did I."

"A friend told me, a lawyer, that something can always go wrong in a trial."

"Well, yes, that's theoretically true. A jury can always— Look, I don't want to mislead you, Nancy. Tobias is very tough. We were just unlucky to draw him."

"I don't want to meet him."

"I'll be right there with you."

"I hate it. I'm afraid of him."

"There's nothing to be afraid of. It'll be a private, off-the-record conversation."

"Joan, I have to tell you. You shouldn't have said I'd do it. Not without asking me."

"I had no choice." Joan Hennessy's voice was suddenly harder now. "Believe me, Nancy, I had to make my decision right there—right there at the table. It was a calculated risk. I wanted to show him we were so strong that I could afford to let him talk to you. Prove to him you're willing to testify. I couldn't say maybe, or let me consult you, or let me think about it. I *want* him to meet you. You have to convince him. Tobias has to know that if he insists on a trial, his client can get a very long sentence. That's our leverage."

"If we win."

"Of course. If we win."

Nancy thought for a moment. Then she said, "Bernie wasn't as mean as The Other One. Garden."

"Nancy!"

"Okay, okay. I'll think about it."

"I don't want you to think about it. Just do it. If we back off now, after my offer, Tobias is going to be sure something is wrong. It will make him that much harder to deal with."

"I don't have to deal with him."

"No, that's my job. All you have to do is talk with him."

"I'll think about it."

"Nancy—"

"I'll think about it."

An emergency family conference in the Whittredge library.

"Oh, darling, not a *trial*?"

"I know. That's what Joan's trying to avoid. That's why she wants me to talk to him."

"Jesus," her father said, "that's just what we need. A trial means real publicity, Nancy. That's newspapers and everything, the whole works. We certainly don't want that, no matter what."

"I wasn't thinking about publicity so much. I just don't want to go through it."

"And you don't have to," Carol said. "I've said all along, you've done your part. More than your part. Leave the rest to them."

"I think so, too," Whit said. "It's time for you to drop it."

Nancy thought it was probably the first time her parents had agreed on anything since all this happened. "Well," she said, "there's no trial if I don't want to testify."

"And you don't," her father said. "We can eliminate that as an option. But let me make sure I understand something. If you do nothing, don't meet with this lawyer, Bernie still goes to prison?"

"Yes, supposedly. But not for very long."

"And the other guy's already in for seven

years or more? That's not such a bad result,
Nancy. A lot of times they never get caught at
all. I say take it."

"Joan says if I don't talk to Mr. Tobias, he'll
think something is fishy. Maybe then he won't
agree to anything."

"But he already agreed, didn't he?"

"Joan says he could change his mind."

"God," Whit said, "this thing is really
screwed up."

"Darling, you have to let go. You have to
put it behind you. That's what Tommy kept
telling you."

"Mom, Tommy doesn't have a vote anymore."

"Once all this is over, darling, I'm sure
you'll get back together."

Nancy wondered. What would it be like to
have it over?

Whit looked at Carol. "I suppose," he said,
"Nancy could have this meeting with the
lawyer. That wouldn't commit her to anything."

"I don't think she should have to go
through another ordeal. It's been one ordeal
after another. This has to stop somewhere."

Her father nodded. "You're right. I agree."

Another conference, called at Nancy's request, in the office of the Manhattan Sex

Crimes Squad. Her team. Carlo and Billy Cooney and Sergeant Bob Blaine.

When she told them, Carlo was the first to respond. "Son of a bitch," he said.

Then he and Billy looked at Blaine, waiting for him to speak first.

"Lawyers," the sergeant said. He sighed. "Fucking lawyers. Sometimes they make you feel that every perp should be 'shot while trying to escape.' Either of you guys know this Tobias?"

Carlo shook his head. Billy Cooney said, "I never ran up against him. He's been around a long time though. Supposed to be good."

They were all drinking coffee in Bob Blaine's office.

"What I want to know," Nancy said, "is what should I do? I mean, I can't believe this. Here we catch them, and suddenly there's all this talk about some tiny little prison sentence, or else it's a trial."

"It's a tough one," Blaine said.

Now that Blaine had spoken, however inconclusively, Billy Cooney felt free to jump in. "I think you got to meet with him, Nancy. Hennessy made the offer, so you got to give it a shot. You don't want to make her look bad. What the hell, he can't hurt you."

"It's not my fault if she looks bad. Carlo?"

Carl Vincent thought about it. His beefy face

was without expression. "Sometimes," he said slowly, "it just doesn't work out." His voice sounded not just disappointed but resigned, as though he had been here before.

"Isn't there anything more we can do?" Nancy asked. "Any more evidence we can get?" *Come on, team.*

"Well—" Billy began.

"No," Carlo said. "We got all we're going to get."

"My parents think I should drop it."

They all looked at each other.

"Anyway," Carlo said finally, "we nailed Garden."

"Jenny, it's me."

"Hi, sweetie. What's up?"

Nancy told her.

"You mean you're *still* messing around with that? Forget it. Listen, I've got to run. Let's get together real soon, huh?"

"I don't see what you're so nervous about," Ted Meadows said. "You've had to tell a lot of people what happened to you. What's one more?"

"All the other times it was friends. Or people trying to help me."

It was a long list. Her parents. The precinct cops, Cruz and Brine. Pat Ford and the nurse

at Bellevue. Her brother Basil. Jenny. Tommy.
Carlo and Billy, especially Carlo, going over it
with him again and again, trying to come up
with some forgotten detail that might make a
difference. Parts of it to Zeke and Lucy and the
other detectives in Sex Crimes. Joan Hennessy.
All the gang at Weezie. Even a little of it to
Beverly Ryan. Was there anybody she hadn't
told?

"But it's still the same story," Ted said.

She had asked him please to have a drink
with her at the end of their shift. They were in
a booth at Marlo's Bar, the Weezie hangout
just around the corner from the station. Nancy
with a glass of white wine, Ted with a schoo-
ner of draft beer.

"Yes, but he's the enemy. He'll be trying to
trick me. Or confuse me, make me look stupid.
Or try to get me to admit it was my fault. I
don't know what. It's not the same at all."

Ted looked as though he was about to make
some kind of joking remark, but he sup-
pressed it. "I think it could be interesting.
Kind of a contest."

"I don't need a contest. Christ, Ted, I'm so
sick of it. Really sick of it. I keep wishing it
was over, but it never is."

"Yeah, I can imagine."

"I don't want to do it. Honest to God, I've
had enough."

"Well, like they say, it's your call."

"That's kind of funny. It hasn't been my call since the minute I walked out of that bank cubicle. It's always been somebody else's call. Now it's Joan Hennessy's turn."

"No," Ted said very definitely. "No, you got that dead wrong, Nancy. It's *not* her turn. This one's up to you. But you know what I'd do? Anything I wasn't sure about, something that really mattered? I'd talk to Mike."

Professionally, Mike Barnes treated her as though they had never had that celebratory drink and dinner together. In the newsroom, or whenever she reported to him over the phone, he was all business, crisp and efficient, no words wasted. If he had occasion to praise her work or to criticize it, it was exactly the same as before. No special treatment, no special favors, no acknowledgment. Business as usual.

But when he was not at his editor's desk, it was different. She could tell from his smile, from the tone of his voice, from the way he looked at her, that he had enjoyed the evening, too. Maybe not as much as she had, but enough so that she was not afraid to ask him.

On her day off he agreed to meet her in the Exxon Garden, the tiny block-wide park behind the Exxon Building. The Rockefeller Center location and the wooden benches screened by shrubbery had proved extremely attractive to drug dealers, especially during lunch hour. But plainclothes police had closed in and made so many arrests that the dealers moved somewhere else. During the ten minutes she had to wait, no one offered Nancy anything, not even marijuana.

She had made up her mind not to be late for this second meeting with Mike Barnes. It was a cold, breezy day, just sunny enough for her to leave her parka open, but not warm enough to persuade the Exxon people to turn on their wall-size waterfall. The tall, bare trees scattered through the little park were not persuaded either. No leaves in sight. Only the evergreens in the planter boxes looked cheerful.

She saw him walking through the park toward her, tall and bareheaded. He was one of the few journalists she knew who did not look slightly absurd in a trench coat.

"Well, Nancy," he said, sitting down on the bench beside her. "Not a very nice day. What's the problem?"

"I'm sorry to drag you down here early, but Ted said I should ask your advice."

"You need Ted's recommendation for that?" He grinned at her. He was as relaxed as the night at The Gallery.

She told him where things stood. She was used to reporting to Mike. She had the facts organized for him. He was a good listener, his eyes fixed on hers, not interrupting with questions. She told him what everyone thought: Joan Hennessy, the detectives, her parents, her friends.

When she finally stopped, he said, "How come you need so many votes? Don't you know what you want?"

"It's all mixed up. I'm all mixed up. I just know I thought it was over, only now it isn't. That's what I want, I guess. For it to be over."

He nodded. "Yes, of course." His eyes roamed around the park, deserted now in mid-afternoon except for the two of them sitting together on the bench. His eyes came back to hers. "The thing is," he said in a hard voice, "it will never be over. I think you should realize that. It will never really be over. It happened. It's part of you. It's going to stay part of you."

He stopped and looked around the park again. Then his voice was kinder as he said, "You know, Nancy, I've listened to you and watched you since the night it happened. I was the first person you called, remember?" He gave her a small smile. "So I could send somebody else to cover that charity ball, remember? Very professional, I must say. Although I doubt that many women in those circumstances would have made that their first phone call."

She laughed. "Training, I guess. You taught us, always let the station know. I didn't know what I was doing."

"Maybe. Anyway, ever since then you've been working on it. Trying to catch them. And then you did catch them, you and the detectives. That night at The Gallery, you told me something that really struck me. You said you felt proud. Not just you yourself, but what you called your 'team.' You said you all felt proud. I thought to myself, here's this young woman who has gone through just about the worst experience a woman can possibly endure, and what she feels is *proud*. I was very moved."

"You were? It didn't show."

"Well," he said drily, "perhaps not. Things don't always show. But I was."

Nancy did not think of Mike Barnes as being moved by anything.

"And then I think about your story on Beverly Ryan and then that interview with her the next day. A damn good piece of work, of course, but it was more than that. It obviously moved a lot of listeners, made them realize what it must be like."

She thought he was in the middle of a thought, but he stopped right there.

"So what are you saying, Mike?"

"All I'm saying is that you have quite an investment in this. I can't advise you what to do, because I don't know. And even if I thought I knew, I probably wouldn't tell you. Advising other people is not rewarding. Hell, Nancy, I don't know if you should meet with that lawyer. I don't know if you should go through with a trial, if it comes to that. It sounds as though it might. A difficult decision."

So he wasn't going to help her. She felt disappointed.

He looked at his watch. "I'm afraid I have to get to work."

She stood up at once. So did he.

Then he put his hand on her shoulder. She could feel the firm grip through the fluffy down of her parka.

"Nancy, you should do whatever will make you keep on feeling proud. Whatever that is. Not just now, but afterward. Don't lose that."

I Remember

Joan Hennessy arranged her ashtray, cigarettes, gold lighter and cigarette holder in the center of her desk. When she met with Viktor Tobias in the vacant jury room, she had deliberately not smoked, partly in deference to jury sensibilities but mostly because she did not want to distract herself in any way while bargaining. This morning all she had to do was listen.

She made sure Moira had a full coffeepot on the hot plate, clean mugs, sugar cubes, fresh cream and spoons. Although she drank her own coffee black, she insisted on serving visitors properly. Every A.D.A. office at One Hogan Place kept coffee available all day long—for victims, witnesses, cops—but it was cardboard cups, paper packets of sugar, powdered cream and those horrible plastic stirring straws that went limp in hot coffee. Joan

371

Hennessy wanted people to see she had standards, even if many of her visitors were too distraught to notice. She turned off her phone buzzer and told Moira to hold all calls except from the D.A. himself and to postpone even him unless he demanded to be put through. She straightened the floppy silk bow at her throat.

All set.

Viktor Tobias was first to arrive, stepping quickly through the door that Moira held open for him. No briefcase, no folder of papers. And no smile of greeting.

He wore a black suit too big in the shoulders for his slight figure. Since his suits never seemed to fit very well, Joan assumed he was indifferent to clothes, but he was always clean. No spots on his striped blue tie or his pale blue shirt. His sparse gray hair was brushed back at the sides, with no attempt to conceal the large bald area in the middle of his head.

"Good morning," he said briskly. He sat down in one of the two wooden armchairs facing her and looked at his watch. "She hasn't changed her mind, has she?"

"Of course not. Would you like some coffee?"

He shook his head.

"I'd like some please," she said to Moira, who was still standing in the doorway.

When Moira brought Joan's brown china mug and placed it on her desk, Nancy walked in right behind her.

"Good morning, Nancy."

Viktor Tobias stood up halfway to say, "Good morning, Miss Whittredge." They did not shake hands.

"Coffee, Nancy?"

"Yes please. Black."

So much for the display of coffee-serving amenities.

Moira brought Nancy a mug and then left the office, closing the door.

Joan could see Tobias measuring Nancy, the quick, narrow-eyed appraisal of a witness. Nancy wore dark slacks and a brown sweater that almost matched her eyes. She had tiny pearl-dot earrings and a thin, gold-chain necklace. She looked nervous, but she held her shoulders back, and she did not slump in her chair. Joan hoped Nancy was not too tense to remember all the advice she had given her.

"Let me review why we're here," Joan said, "and what Mr. Tobias and I have agreed on." This speech was not necessary, since Nancy already knew, but it would give her time to settle down. "Mr. Tobias is Bernie Webb's attorney. I've told him that you are prepared to testify in court, if that should be necessary. I also told him that you have a clear and complete memory of the event and of the participants. I have invited him here to question you so that he can satisfy himself on these points. I have placed no restrictions on anything Mr. Tobias wants to explore, but this conversation is off the record. Nothing we say here can be used in court by either side. Since this is Mr. Tobias's meeting, I will keep quiet. Is that our understanding, Viktor?"

He nodded. "Precisely."

He made a deliberate show of turning his chair away from the desk so that he faced Nancy directly, just a few feet away. Joan saw Nancy flinch back in her seat. Tobias saw it too, of course. He stared at her in cold silence. Piercing eyes. Strong, pointed nose. Joan had seen that look in court before: Viktor Tobias for the defense, so everybody better watch out. His hands rested on the arms of his chair. Nancy's hands were twisted tightly in her lap.

It seemed quite a long time before he spoke.

"Miss Whittredge," he said finally. "are you familiar with the term *fellatio*?"

Nancy nodded.

"You are familiar with it? We really can't converse if you don't speak. You are familiar with the term?"

"Yes." Small voice.

Speak up, Nancy.

"It's cocksucking, right?"

"Objec—!" Joan began automatically, but caught herself. Tobias was trying to shock Nancy into immediate disarray.

He swung his head to face Joan and held up his hand. "No interruptions, if you please."

He turned back to Nancy. "Well?"

"Yes."

"And I assume you've done this before?"

Nancy looked startled. "Joan said—Miss Hennessy said you're not allowed to ask any questions about my sex life."

Good for you.

"In court, no. But as you can see, we are not in court. We are merely exploring. You've done this before? Do you enjoy it?"

Nancy hesitated. She shot a glance at Joan, seeking help. When Joan kept silent, Nancy got angry. "I think that's none of your business."

Tobias nodded, as though to say that was just what he expected. "Well, Miss Whittredge, let's get to something that is very much my business. It's your contention, I understand, that my client 'forced' you to perform *fellatio*."

"That's right. He did."

"Miss Whittredge, I am an older man, but my memory of younger days remains vivid. In my experience, it is very difficult to 'force' a woman to perform *fellatio* if she doesn't want to. No matter how nicely the man asks, if she doesn't want to, she doesn't. In fact, it is virtually impossible to persuade her otherwise."

"He stuck the gun in my face." Nancy now had her anger under control. "He said if I didn't do it, they'd kill me."

"Ah yes, the gun. There's a great deal of talk about this gun, but somehow, despite what I am sure was exemplary diligence on the part of the police, it has never turned up. No gun has been discovered anywhere." He paused to underline his implication that there had never been a gun. "What kind of gun was it?"

"I don't know. I don't know anything about guns."

Good. Joan had told Nancy to admit anything she did not know or could not remember. Admit your ignorance at once, don't let him drag it out of you.

"A pistol? A revolver?" He gave her a twisted little smile. "Perhaps an assault rifle?"

"A handgun. I don't know what kind."

"If this mythical gun did accidentally turn up, would you recognize it?"

Nancy shook her head. "I don't think so." Then she corrected herself. "In fact, I know I wouldn't. I was much too frightened. All I could see was that barrel, right in my face. I just know they had a gun, and they kept threatening to shoot me."

"How big was it? A twenty-two? A forty-five? Something in between?"

"I don't know."

"Was it loaded?"

"I don't know. They acted like it was. I sure thought it was."

Joan had taught Nancy that the law does not require a gun to be loaded, only that the victim believes it to be loaded. Tobias was getting nowhere with the gun. He evidently thought so, too, because he changed the subject.

"Now you say it was dark in this garage."

"Yes, but not completely dark. There was a light in the back."

"A very dim lightbulb, according to you. How dim?"

"Enough to see by."

"The police report describing the scene says it was twenty-five watts. That is a very small bulb way in the back of a big garage, wouldn't you say? They don't make light bulbs much dimmer than that."

"Just the same, I could see. Especially when Bernie and I were sitting right under it."

Tobias ignored that comment. "According to your story, while you were being raped, you were in the front part of the garage where it was dark. You couldn't see anything. Is that correct?"

"Yes, that's right." At the memory a wounded look came into Nancy's eyes. "They made me get down on my hands and knees. I couldn't see anything."

Tobias's voice held no trace of sympathy. "So you could not see which of them assaulted you."

"No."

"You had no idea which one?"

"It was both of them."

"You're on your hands and knees in the dark, you can't see, you don't know who was doing what to you, and yet you still claim it was 'both of them.' Frankly, Miss Whittredge, a jury would have to view that claim with the most extreme skepticism."

"It was both of them. They kept taking turns on me. One would get off, and then the other would get on. And they both did it to me in both places. Several times."

"How could you tell? How can you be sure?"

"They kept talking to each other. Encouraging each other to take turns. They were cheering each other on."

Joan scribbled a note. Nancy had never used that word *cheering* before. She liked it. If there was a trial, she wanted to make sure Nancy used it again.

"Oh? What did they say?"

"I can't tell you. I was concentrating on just trying to get through it. To live through it, just to come out alive. That's what I kept saying to myself while they were raping me: *just come out alive.*"

With no transition, Tobias abruptly shifted. "When they first accosted you on the street, who had the gun?"

"The Other One. Garden."

"You're sure?"

"Yes. He stuck it in my back and said, 'Don't make me use this.' Bernie held the shopping bag."

"Oh? 'Bernie held the shopping bag'? You mean he introduced himself to you right there on the sidewalk?"

Nancy wasn't rattled. "No, he never said his own name the whole time. But I learned it later. Garden called him 'Bernie' three or four different times."

"He called him 'Bernie.' To give him orders?"

Nancy had to think about that. Joan liked the way she concentrated, searching her memory. Anyone could see she was working hard to recapture the exact truth. Tobias had to see it too.

"Yes, that's right. He said, Bernie do this, and Bernie do that."

"So Garden was giving the orders. Garden was clearly the boss?"

"Oh, definitely."

"He was the dominant figure?"

Tobias was nailing that down hard. Joan stuck a cigarette in her holder and lighted it.

"Yes," Nancy said. "The only time Bernie did anything on his own was when we were alone in the garage. When he made me—when he made me do *fellatio*."

Tobias had to hate that answer but of course did not show it. "Now according to you, Garden took your jewelry as well as your money?"

"Yes. My two bracelets and a necklace and my mother's sweetheart ring. And my watch. The watch wasn't worth anything, it was just a Mickey Mouse watch."

"But none of those items has been recovered. So it's just your word that they took them?"

"Yes."

"Well, whatever may or may not have been taken from you, that was Garden?"

"Yes. Bernie held the shopping bag."

"But Garden held the gun? And told you to put them in the bag?"

"Yes."

"And also a dress, I believe?"

"Yes, a new dress, but I got that back."

"Just so. And who gave you back the dress?"

"Bernie."

"That was very nice of him."

"He wasn't being nice. When I asked for it, he said, 'Who wants it?'"

"Now it was Garden who went back to the bank with your bank card to get the rest of the money?"

"Yes."

"He went alone?"

"Yes."

"Three of four times? And always alone?"

"No, two times. He couldn't make my code work. The second time he made me write it down. ORION."

"ORION. Why that particular code word?"

"Well, it had to be a five-letter code. When I was little, my father taught me to recognize the constellations. Orion was the first one I learned, so I used it."

"Yes. In Greek mythology Orion was a great hunter. A mighty hunter. Is that how you see yourself, Miss Whittredge? Are you a hunter? You like to catch things? You like to destroy things?"

"No. I just like the stars."

"So he made you write it down for him. Garden did."

"Yes, sir."

"Going after the rest of your money was all Garden's doing?"

"Until the end. Then the three of us went back to the bank together."

"And it was still Garden who tried again to use your bank card?"

"Yes, but he was still doing it wrong, so I had to show him how."

"Garden."

"Yes. But Bernie was standing right there in the cubicle beside us. When the money came out of the slot, he laughed and said to Garden, 'You blew it.' Then he took the money and put it in the shopping bag."

"Garden took the money."

"No, sir. It was Bernie."

"You claim you were terrified."

"Yes, I was."

"And yet you say you remember exactly what Bernie said and what he did."

"I do remember."

"I suggest to you, Miss Whittredge, that you are simply making up a great deal of this. You were terrified. You were hysterical. That is nothing to be ashamed of. It's very common for women in this situation to become hysterical. What Garden did to you upset you so much that you didn't really know what was happening."

Nancy stared at him. It was plain that what Viktor Tobias had just said offended her in some profound way. "No, sir," she said in a quiet voice, "that is not true. That is not true. I don't remember everything, because I was so scared they were going to kill me. I'm only telling you what I do remember. I'm a reporter, and part of my job is to remember what I see and hear and then tell exactly what happened."

Joan had not discussed that point with her. Nancy was suddenly off on her own now, volunteering. With a witness this was always dangerous. Very bad things could happen when a witness was on the loose.

"And in spite of being afraid they were going to kill you, with this unidentifiable gun that no one seems able to find, you still claim to recall everything that was said?"

"No sir, not everything. I told you I can't remember what they said to each other while they were raping me." Nancy paused. Then she took a deep breath. "But I remember what Bernie said to me when we were alone in the garage. You want to know what he said, Mr. Tobias? He said, 'How about a nice blow job?'"

Tobias said nothing.

"And," Nancy said, her large brown eyes filling with anger, "I remember something else. I remember the way he smelled when he made me do it. It was the worst thing I ever smelled. I remember that."

Tobias said nothing.

If they had been in court, Joan would have been applauding to herself. She could imagine the twelve jurors leaning forward, straining to catch every word, sharing Nancy's anger and disgust. Holding their breath, waiting for what would come next. There was no way in the world a jury would not believe this witness. Not just believe her, but know that it was all true. True beyond any conceivable doubt, reasonable or otherwise.

"It made me sick," Nancy said. "Physically sick. When they finally let me go, I had to throw up on the way home. Right on the street, in a trash basket. I remember that, too."

There was a long silence during which Viktor Tobias continued to study Nancy. Then he turned to Joan. His gaze was perfectly steady. He was, after all, a professional.

In a flat, even voice he said, "How about five-to-fifteen?"

Winners. But Joan knew she must not gloat, not even reveal any sense of triumph. There would be other days, other cases, other witnesses, when she had to face Viktor Tobias again.

She shook her head. "Seven-to-twenty-one. I told you, Viktor. It's the best I can do."

He considered it for only a moment. His eyes did not change or flicker. Then he got to his feet. No emotion, no expression on his sharp, narrow face.

"Done."

The Real Me

She woke up in her apartment thinking: *this is the last day.* And the wonderful thing is that I don't have to do a single thing about it. I don't even have to be there in court.

First Joan Hennessy, and then Carlo, had asked her if she wanted to attend the sentencing.

"You won't have to say a word," Joan explained. "Their lawyers and I will do all the talking to the judge—it's a routine procedure. Everything's settled, so it's only a formality. You can sit in the back of the court."

No thanks.

"Nothing to be afraid of," Carlo said. "I'll sit right beside you."

No thanks.

She was not afraid. She just did not want to see them again. All she wanted now was to get on with her life.

She threw back the covers, shivering, and slipped into her woolly yellow robe. Her apartment was always cold in the mornings before the heat came clanking up in the old radiators. She put a pot of water on the stove for instant coffee and took the English muffins and the almost-empty carton of orange juice from the refrigerator. She split a muffin, buttered it and stuck it in the toaster oven.

She poured the last glass of orange juice and took a swallow. It had the sour, slightly fizzy taste of just-turning-bad. Borderline. Still barely drinkable, if necessary. Deciding it wasn't necessary, she poured it down the sink.

She really must do something about finding a new roommate. It was not just loneliness or needing someone to split the rent. She did not enjoy shopping or cooking or cleaning for one. She did not like cartons of orange juice that turned bad before one person could finish them. She had to find a roommate, although many women refused to live all the way down in Tribeca, picturesque or not.

Last night was better than most. She did not have a nightmare, although she did wake up twice, suddenly afraid to be alone in the dark. Maybe she should keep a light on, the way little kids did. She was entitled to a few adjustments. She had given up the local bank branch and switched her account to midtown near the Weezie office. She would never use a cash cubicle again, not even in broad daylight with people around. She no longer used the shortcut street to her apartment. Maybe she would get over that. Maybe not. Wait and see. As Pat Ford said, it was up to her.

This was the first day since it happened when she was truly free to be herself.

At the radio station, while she was checking the assignment sheet, Ted Meadows said, "Hey, what are you doing here? Isn't today the big day?"

"You mean the sentencing?"

"Sure, isn't it today? How come you're not in court?"

"Weezie can't spare me."

Ted laughed and flapped the assignment sheet at her. "This doesn't read like it. We could both take the day off."

"I don't feel like going."

"I don't get it. You spend all this time chasing them down, and then you don't want to finish it?"

"I don't have to. I already finished it."

"Suppose something goes wrong. Suppose the judge wants to ask you a question."

"I guess he'll be out of luck. Anyway, Joan Hennessy says nothing can go wrong. It's all arranged. She's going to call me when it's over."

"Myself, I'd want to be there."

Nancy shook her head. "Not me, Ted. I'm happy to let it pass."

Just the same she left word with Phil Eckersley, the day editor, to be sure to have somebody beep her when Joan Hennessy called.

She spent a frustrating three hours interviewing the managing agents of big co-op apartment buildings. They were all protesting, in virtually identical words, what one called an "unjust, unfair and totally irresponsible" apportionment of the city's real estate taxes. All her life Nancy had been hearing about city real estate from her father, but tax apportionment bored her to death—and so did her interviews. She doubted that any of it would ever get on the air. But Ed Selwyn, the executive editor, was president of his own co-op building. Since he had suggested the story, maybe it would run in spite of its lack of merit.

The beep came in mid-afternoon. Call Joan Hennessy's office right away. She found a phone booth and dialed the familiar number.

"Nancy? It's all done. No surprises." Joan's voice was jubilant.

"That's good."

"What's the matter? You don't sound very pleased."

"Yes, I am. Of course, I am. Congratulations, Joan."

"The other way around. You ought to feel on top of the world. I know I do. Hang on a second. Carlo wants to talk to you."

A pause while the phone changed hands at the other end. Nancy realized that, for the last time, she must not let them down. Then she heard the gruff voice, triumphant at last.

"We got 'em, Nancy. We got 'em."

"That's great, Carlo. You did a terrific job. Everybody did. The whole team."

"That's right. Sometimes it works. Listen, Nancy. I'm no good at this, but we're proud of you. All of us. I'm real proud of you. You're a pro."

After all the weeks and all the hours, it was the first time he had ever praised her like that. She was touched, and her voice caught. "Thanks, Carlo. That means a lot to me. Tell Billy thanks, too. All the gang."

"You bet. Take care of yourself."

They said goodby.

She realized that what she had shared with them was over. That intense common purpose. Carlo, Billy Cooney, Bob Blaine, Zeke, Joan Hennessy, most of all herself. It was over. She could call them up sometime and say hello, and they'd be glad to hear from her, ask her how she was doing. Maybe someday when she was in the neighborhood, she could even drop in at the Sex Crimes office for a cup of coffee. Everybody would be nice and friendly, she knew they would be, especially Carlo. But the urgency, the drive, the team commitment would be gone. Better just to leave it at goodby.

Goodby to what seemed like a whole lifetime. Now that it really was over, she could not be sure what her feelings were. She knew she felt older. And also stronger. She had always known she was good at her work and that people liked her, but she had never known she was strong. Maybe she hadn't been strong. Maybe she had just grown that way. Anyway, a different woman.

She looked at her watch. She had promised Mike Barnes to let him know right away what happened, but by now he would be on his way to the station. Once he was on duty, she could not call to tell him personal news. Instead, she left a message at the station saying everything had gone as expected. She should call her parents, too, but that could wait till the end of her shift.

She had one more dreary interview to do with one more managing agent, Douglas Elliman. She already knew what he would say.

At four-fifteen her beeper went off again. Thank God, she thought, a new assignment. Maybe she could skip Douglas Elliman. On her portable phone she dialed the news desk.

"Barnes."

"It's Nancy, Mike. What's up?"

"Nancy! I just got your message. What a great day for you!" His voice held none of its usual brisk efficiency. "Congratulations."

She took the receiver away from her ear and looked at it in amazement. This was Mike Barnes? During business hours?

"Mike?"

"I said congratulations. You must be very proud."

She could see him at the editor's desk, his long legs stretched out, his feet resting on the tabletop, jacket off, shirt open at the collar, cuffs flipped back. She knew he would still be monitoring every word coming out of the anchor booth.

"Yes. Yes, I am. Thanks very much. You have a story for me?"

"I—Just a minute."

The phone went silent. He had put his hand over it to deal with some studio matter. Then his voice came back.

"What are you doing Thursday night? Are you busy?"

Mike Barnes? During his shift? Asking about a date on his night off?

"No. No, I'm not busy."

"Good. Let's you and I have dinner. A big victory dinner. La Cote Basque."

One of her most favorite restaurants. As beautiful as it was expensive. Usually she got to go there only with her parents. La Cote Basque was not just a date. It was an *event*. A serious event.

"I'd love to."

"Good." His voice snapped back to business. "How's your tax story?"

"It's—it's not much. They're all saying the same thing."

"Right. Call it in anyway. We'll see."

He cut her off.

Taking a long shower before getting dressed for the evening at La Cote Basque, she wondered how she and Mike would ever work all this out.

He worked five days a week from four to eleven. She worked five days a week from eleven to six. Even their weekends were different, Saturday and Sunday for her, Thursday and Friday for him. How much time together could be carved out of that schedule? She wondered if he was working on that problem, too. She smiled to herself. That thought might be premature, although she did not think so.

Maybe she would have to switch to the afternoon-evening shift, although she preferred the day shift. Or maybe he and Phil

Eckersley could switch shifts. Pretty unlikely.
Or maybe Mike would finally be named news
director, as everybody hoped. Even if that
happened, she knew she and Mike could keep
it professional. In fact, he would bend over
backward to avoid the slightest taint of favoritism. So would she.

But how would the other station executives
feel about it? And the other reporters and the
writers and anchors? Ted would just kid the
pants off her, claiming she had an unfair
advantage that was not available to him, but
what about the others? Maybe the executives
would insist that she find another job? In these
enlightened days of women's rights, surely
they wouldn't dare. But there were bound to
be problems. What a delightful dilemma! Although, to be sure, just a bit premature.

She turned off the shower and dried herself.
She could look at her body now in the long
mirror on the bathroom door. Not like those
nightmare nights in her old bedroom where
she was afraid to look at her own body. She
still had the nightmares—maybe she would
always have them—but she was no longer
afraid. It was a most satisfactory body, in spite
of all the violations committed on it and in it.
The bruises on her breasts were long, long
gone. As for the other bruises, the ones in her
heart, she would learn to live with them.
Perhaps they, too, would fade.

Still naked, she put on dusting powder and perfume and makeup. As always, she wished she had two more inches of height, but nothing could be done about that. Then bikini pants and her prettiest lacy bra that covered barely half of her breasts. As her mother always said, if a woman looks pretty inside, she will feel pretty outside. She brushed her hair hard until it was fluffy and stood out around her face. Maybe she should change her hairstyle. She hadn't changed it since college, when she cut it short for the first time.

She went to her bedroom closet to take down the light-gray knit dress that she had decided was her best bet for La Cote Basque. Quiet but distinguished, and it clung to her body with just the right amount of soft flattery. But was it too quiet? She did not feel quiet tonight.

Her hands went to the back of the closet and found the lacy gold-and-white dress that she had known she would never be able to wear. She held it high to admire it.

Still on its hanger, she carried it to the long mirror on the bathroom door. She held it up against her, just the way she had that morning in Saks. Still wonderful.

Why not? she thought. That was all so long ago.

She took it off the hanger and slipped it over

her head, careful not to smudge her makeup. Careful not to crush the gauzy gold cuffs as she wriggled her arms into the long sleeves. She settled the dress on her shoulders, then fluffed out the matching gauzy gold fringe around the low-cut neckline.

She stood back to look at herself. It was still absolutely beautiful.

Yes, she decided. Yes, that's the real me— whatever that turns out to be.